Shadows Gothic and Grotesque

Shadows Gothic and Grotesque

Black Spirits and White

Ralph Adams Cram

&

Tales of the Supernatural

James Platt

Coachwhip Publications

Landisville, Pennsylvania

Contents

Black Spirits and White

Ralph Adams Cram

No. 252 Rue M. le Prince

When in May, 1886, I found myself at last in Paris, I naturally determined to throw myself on the charity of an old chum of mine, Eugene Marie d'Ardeche, who had forsaken Boston a year or more ago on receiving word of the death of an aunt who had left him such property as she possessed. I fancy this windfall surprised him not a little, for the relations between the aunt and nephew had never been cordial, judging from Eugene's remarks touching the lady, who was, it seems, a more or less wicked and witch-like old person, with a penchant for black magic, at least such was the common report.

Why she should leave all her property to d'Ardeche, no one could tell, unless it was that she felt his rather hobbledehoy tendencies towards Buddhism and occultism might some day lead him to her own unhallowed height of questionable illumination. To be sure d'Ardeche reviled her as a bad old woman, being himself in that state of enthusiastic exaltation which sometimes accompanies a boyish fancy for occultism; but in spite of his distant and repellent attitude, Mlle. Blaye de Tartas made him her sole heir, to the violent wrath of a questionable old party known to infamy as the Sar Torrevieja, the "King of the Sorcerers." This malevolent old portent, whose gray and crafty face was often seen in the Rue M. le Prince during the life of Mlle. de Tartas had, it seems, fully expected to enjoy her small wealth after her death; and when it appeared that she had left him only the contents of the gloomy old house in the Quartier Latin, giving the house itself and all else of which she died possessed to her nephew in America, the Sar proceeded to remove everything from the place, and then to curse it elaborately and comprehensively, together with all those who should ever dwell therein.

Whereupon he disappeared.

This final episode was the last word I received from Eugene, but I knew the number of the house, 252 Rue M. le Prince. So, after a day or two given to a first cursory survey of Paris, I started across the Seine to find Eugene and compel him to do the honors of the city.

Every one who knows the Latin Quarter knows the Rue M. le Prince, running up the hill towards the Garden of the Luxembourg. It is full of queer houses and odd corners,—or was in '86,—and certainly No. 252 was, when I found it, quite as queer as any. It was nothing but a doorway, a black arch of old stone between and under two new houses painted yellow. The effect of this bit of seventeenth-century masonry, with its dirty old doors, and rusty broken lantern sticking gaunt and grim out over the narrow sidewalk, was, in its frame of fresh plaster, sinister in the extreme.

I wondered if I had made a mistake in the number; it was quite evident that no one lived behind those cobwebs. I went into the doorway of one of the new hôtels and interviewed the concierge.

No, M. d'Ardeche did not live there, though to be sure he owned the mansion; he himself resided in Meudon, in the country house of the late Mlle. de Tartas. Would Monsieur like the number and the street?

Monsieur would like them extremely, so I took the card that the concierge wrote for me, and forthwith started for the river, in order that I might take a steamboat for Meudon. By one of those coincidences which happen so often, being quite inexplicable, I had not gone twenty paces down the street before I ran directly into the arms of Eugene d'Ardeche. In three minutes we were sitting in the queer little garden of the Chien Bleu, drinking vermouth and absinthe, and talking it all over.

"You do not live in your aunt's house?" I said at last, interrogatively.

"No, but if this sort of thing keeps on I shall have to. I like Meudon much better, and the house is perfect, all furnished, and nothing in it newer than the last century. You must come out with me to-night and see it. I have got a jolly room fixed up for my Buddha. But there is something wrong with this house opposite. I can't keep a tenant in it,—not four days. I have had three, all within six months, but the stories have gone around and a man would as soon think of hiring the Cour des Comptes to live in as No. 252. It is notorious. The fact is, it is haunted the worst way."

I laughed and ordered more vermouth.

"That is all right. It is haunted all the same, or enough to keep it empty, and the funny part is that no one knows *how* it is haunted. Nothing is ever seen, nothing heard. As far as I can find out, people just have the horrors there, and have them so bad they have to go to the hospital afterwards. I have one ex-tenant in the Bicêtre now. So the house stands empty, and as it covers considerable ground and is taxed for a lot, I don't know what to do about it. I think I'll either give it to that child of sin, Torrevieja, or else go and live in it myself. I shouldn't mind the ghosts, I am sure."

"Did you ever stay there?"

"No, but I have always intended to, and in fact I came up here to-day to see a couple of rake-hell fellows I know, Fargeau and Duchesne, doctors in the Clinical Hospital beyond here, up by the Parc Mont Souris. They promised that they would spend the night with me some time in my aunt's house,—which is called around here, you must know, 'la Bouche d'Enfer,'—and I thought perhaps they would make it this week, if they can get off duty. Come up with me while I see them, and then we can go across the river to Véfour's and have some luncheon, you can get your things at the Chatham, and we will go out to Meudon, where of course you will spend the night with me."

The plan suited me perfectly, so we went up to the hospital, found Fargeau, who declared that he and Duchesne were ready for anything, the nearer the real "bouche d'enfer" the better; that the following Thursday they would both be off duty for the night, and that on that day they would join in an attempt to outwit the devil and clear up the mystery of No. 252.

"Does M. l'Américain go with us?" asked Fargeau.

"Why of course," I replied, "I intend to go, and you must not refuse me, d'Ardeche; I decline to be put off. Here is a chance for you to do the honors of your city in a manner which is faultless. Show me a real live ghost, and I will forgive Paris for having lost the Jardin Mabille."

So it was settled.

Later we went down to Meudon and ate dinner in the terrace room of the villa, which was all that d'Ardeche had said, and more, so utterly was its atmosphere that of the seventeenth century. At dinner Eugene told me more about his late aunt, and the queer goings on in the old house.

Mlle. Blaye lived, it seems, all alone, except for one female servant of her own age; a severe, taciturn creature, with massive Breton features and a Breton tongue, whenever she vouchsafed to use it. No one ever was seen to enter the door of No. 252 except Jeanne the servant and the Sar Torrevieja, the latter coming constantly from none knew whither, and always entering, *never leaving*. Indeed, the neighbors, who for eleven years had watched the old sorcerer sidle crab-wise up to the bell almost every day, declared vociferously that *never* had he been seen to leave the house. Once, when they decided to keep absolute guard, the watcher, none other than Maître Garceau of the Chien Bleu, after keeping his eyes fixed on the door from ten o'clock one morning when the Sar arrived until four in the afternoon, during which time the door was unopened (he knew this, for had he not gummed a ten-centime stamp over the joint and was not the stamp unbroken) nearly fell down when the sinister figure of Torrevieja slid wickedly by him with a dry "Pardon, Monsieur!" and disappeared again through the black doorway.

This was curious, for No. 252 was entirely surrounded by houses, its only windows opening on a courtyard into which no eye could look from the hôtels of the Rue M. le Prince and the Rue de l'Ecole, and the mystery was one of the choice possessions of the Latin Quarter.

Once a year the austerity of the place was broken, and the denizens of the whole quarter stood open-mouthed watching many carriages drive up to No. 252, many of them private, not a few with crests on the door panels, from all of them descending veiled female figures and men with coat collars turned up. Then followed curious sounds of music from within, and those whose houses joined the blank walls of No. 252 became for the moment popular, for by placing the ear against the wall strange music could distinctly be heard, and the sound of monotonous chanting voices now and then. By dawn the last guest would have departed, and for another year the hôtel of Mlle. de Tartas was ominously silent.

Eugene declared that he believed it was a celebration of "Walpurgisnacht," and certainly appearances favored such a fancy.

"A queer thing about the whole affair is," he said, "the fact that every one in the street swears that about a month ago, while I was out in Concarneau for a visit, the music and voices were heard again, just as when my revered aunt was in the flesh. The house was perfectly empty, as I tell you, so it is quite possible that the good people were enjoying an hallucination."

I must acknowledge that these stories did not reassure me; in fact, as Thursday came near, I began to regret a little my determination to spend the night in the house. I was too vain to back down, however, and the perfect coolness of the two doctors, who ran down Tuesday to Meudon to make a few arrangements, caused me to swear that I would die of fright before I would flinch. I suppose I believed more or less in ghosts, I am sure now that I am older I believe in them, there are in fact few things I can *not* believe. Two or three inexplicable things had happened to me, and, although this was before my adventure with Rendel in Pæstum, I had a strong predisposition to believe some things that I could not explain, wherein I was out of sympathy with the age.

Well, to come to the memorable night of the twelfth of June, we had made our preparations, and after depositing a big bag inside the doors of No. 252, went across to the Chien Bleu, where

Fargeau and Duchesne turned up promptly, and we sat down to the best dinner Père Garceau could create.

I remember I hardly felt that the conversation was in good taste. It began with various stories of Indian fakirs and Oriental jugglery, matters in which Eugene was curiously well read, swerved to the horrors of the great Sepoy mutiny, and thus to reminiscences of the dissecting-room. By this time we had drunk more or less, and Duchesne launched into a photographic and Zolaesque account of the only time (as he said) when he was possessed of the panic of fear; namely, one night many years ago, when he was locked by accident into the dissecting-room of the Loucine, together with several cadavers of a rather unpleasant nature. I ventured to protest mildly against the choice of subjects, the result being a perfect carnival of horrors, so that when we finally drank our last *crème de cacao* and started for "la Bouche d'Enfer," my nerves were in a somewhat rocky condition.

It was just ten o'clock when we came into the street. A hot dead wind drifted in great puffs through the city, and ragged masses of vapor swept the purple sky; an unsavory night altogether, one of those nights of hopeless lassitude when one feels, if one is at home, like doing nothing but drink mint juleps and smoke cigarettes.

Eugene opened the creaking door, and tried to light one of the lanterns; but the gusty wind blew out every match, and we finally had to close the outer doors before we could get a light. At last we had all the lanterns going, and I began to look around curiously. We were in a long, vaulted passage, partly carriageway, partly footpath, perfectly bare but for the street refuse which had drifted in with eddying winds. Beyond lay the courtyard, a curious place rendered more curious still by the fitful moonlight and the flashing of four dark lanterns. The place had evidently been once a most noble palace. Opposite rose the oldest portion, a three-story wall of the time of Francis I., with a great wisteria vine covering half. The wings on either side were more modern, seventeenth century, and ugly, while towards the street was nothing but a flat unbroken wall.

The great bare court, littered with bits of paper blown in by the wind, fragments of packing cases, and straw, mysterious with flashing lights and flaunting shadows, while low masses of torn vapor

drifted overhead, hiding, then revealing the stars, and all in absolute silence, not even the sounds of the streets entering this prison-
like place, was weird and uncanny in the extreme. I must confess
that already I began to feel a slight disposition towards the horrors, but with that curious inconsequence which so often happens
in the case of those who are deliberately growing scared, I could
think of nothing more reassuring than those delicious verses of
Lewis Carroll's:—

"Just the place for a Snark! I have said it twice,
   That alone should encourage the crew.
   Just the place for a Snark! I have said it thrice,
   What I tell you three times is true,"—

which kept repeating themselves over and over in my brain with
feverish insistence.

Even the medical students had stopped their chaffing, and were
studying the surroundings gravely.

"There is one thing certain," said Fargeau, "*anything* might
have happened here without the slightest chance of discovery. Did
ever you see such a perfect place for lawlessness?"

"And *anything* might happen here now, with the same certainty
of impunity," continued Duchesne, lighting his pipe, the snap of
the match making us all start. "D'Ardeche, your lamented relative
was certainly well fixed; she had full scope here for her traditional
experiments in demonology."

"Curse me if I don't believe that those same traditions were
more or less founded on fact," said Eugene. "I never saw this court
under these conditions before, but I could believe anything now.
What's that!"

"Nothing but a door slamming," said Duchesne, loudly.

"Well, I wish doors wouldn't slam in houses that have been
empty eleven months."

"It is irritating," and Duchesne slipped his arm through mine;
"but we must take things as they come. Remember we have to deal
not only with the spectral lumber left here by your scarlet aunt,

but as well with the supererogatory curse of that hell-cat Torrevieja. Come on! let's get inside before the hour arrives for the sheeted dead to squeak and gibber in these lonely halls. Light your pipes, your tobacco is a sure protection against 'your whoreson dead bodies'; light up and move on."

We opened the hall door and entered a vaulted stone vestibule, full of dust, and cobwebby.

"There is nothing on this floor," said Eugene, "except servants' rooms and offices, and I don't believe there is anything wrong with them. I never heard that there was, any way. Let's go up stairs."

So far as we could see, the house was apparently perfectly un-interesting inside, all eighteenth-century work, the façade of the main building being, with the vestibule, the only portion of the Francis I. work.

"The place was burned during the Terror," said Eugene, "for my great-uncle, from whom Mlle. de Tartas inherited it, was a good and true Royalist; he went to Spain after the Revolution, and did not come back until the accession of Charles X., when he restored the house, and then died, enormously old. This explains why it is all so new."

The old Spanish sorcerer to whom Mlle. de Tartas had left her personal property had done his work thoroughly. The house was absolutely empty, even the wardrobes and bookcases built in had been carried away; we went through room after room, finding all absolutely dismantled, only the windows and doors with their casings, the parquet floors, and the florid Renaissance mantels remaining.

"I feel better," remarked Fargeau. "The house may be haunted, but it don't look it, certainly; it is the most respectable place imag-inable."

"Just you wait," replied Eugene. "These are only the state apart-ments, which my aunt seldom used, except, perhaps, on her annual 'Walpurgisnacht.' Come up stairs and I will show you a better *mise en scène.*"

On this floor, the rooms fronting the court, the sleeping-rooms, were quite small,—("They are the bad rooms all the same," said

Eugene,)—four of them, all just as ordinary in appearance as those below. A corridor ran behind them connecting with the wing corridor, and from this opened a door, unlike any of the other doors in that it was covered with green baize, somewhat moth-eaten. Eugene selected a key from the bunch he carried, unlocked the door, and with some difficulty forced it to swing inward; it was as heavy as the door of a safe.

"We are now," he said, "on the very threshold of hell itself; these rooms in here were my scarlet aunt's unholy of unholies. I never let them with the rest of the house, but keep them as a curiosity. I only wish Torrevieja had kept out; as it was, he looted them, as he did the rest of the house, and nothing is left but the walls and ceiling and floor. They are something, however, and may suggest what the former condition must have been. Tremble and enter."

The first apartment was a kind of anteroom, a cube of perhaps twenty feet each way, without windows, and with no doors except that by which we entered and another to the right. Walls, floor, and ceiling were covered with a black lacquer, brilliantly polished, that flashed the light of our lanterns in a thousand intricate reflections. It was like the inside of an enormous Japanese box, and about as empty. From this we passed to another room, and here we nearly dropped our lanterns. The room was circular, thirty feet or so in diameter, covered by a hemispherical dome; walls and ceiling were dark blue, spotted with gold stars; and reaching from floor to floor across the dome stretched a colossal figure in red lacquer of a nude woman kneeling, her legs reaching out along the floor on either side, her head touching the lintel of the door through which we had entered, her arms forming its sides, with the fore arms extended and stretching along the walls until they met the long feet. The most astounding, misshapen, absolutely terrifying thing, I think, I ever saw. From the navel hung a great white object, like the traditional roe's egg of the Arabian Nights. The floor was of red lacquer, and in it was inlaid a pentagram the size of the room, made of wide strips of brass. In the centre of this pentagram was a circular disk of black stone, slightly saucer-shaped, with a small outlet in the middle.

The effect of the room was simply crushing, with this gigantic red figure crouched over it all, the staring eyes fixed on one, no matter what his position. None of us spoke, so oppressive was the whole thing.

The third room was like the first in dimensions, but instead of being black it was entirely sheathed with plates of brass, walls, ceiling, and floor,—tarnished now, and turning green, but still brilliant under the lantern light. In the middle stood an oblong altar of porphyry, its longer dimensions on the axis of the suite of rooms, and at one end, opposite the range of doors, a pedestal of black basalt.

This was all. Three rooms, stranger than these, even in their emptiness, it would be hard to imagine. In Egypt, in India, they would not be entirely out of place, but here in Paris, in a commonplace *hôtel*, in the Rue M. le Prince, they were incredible.

We retraced our steps, Eugene closed the iron door with its baize covering, and we went into one of the front chambers and sat down, looking at each other.

"Nice party, your aunt," said Fargeau. "Nice old party, with amiable tastes; I am glad we are not to spend the night in *those* rooms."

"What do you suppose she did there?" inquired Duchesne. "I know more or less about black art, but that series of rooms is too much for me."

"My impression is," said d'Ardeche, "that the brazen room was a kind of sanctuary containing some image or other on the basalt base, while the stone in front was really an altar,—what the nature of the sacrifice might be I don't even guess. The round room may have been used for invocations and incantations. The pentagram looks like it. Any way it is all just about as queer and *fin de siècle* as I can well imagine. Look here, it is nearly twelve, let's dispose of ourselves, if we are going to hunt this thing down."

The four chambers on this floor of the old house were those said to be haunted, the wings being quite innocent, and, so far as we knew, the floors below. It was arranged that we should each occupy a room, leaving the doors open with the lights burning, and

at the slightest cry or knock we were all to rush at once to the room
from which the warning sound might come. There was no commu-
nication between the rooms to be sure, but, as the doors all opened
into the corridor, every sound was plainly audible.

The last room fell to me, and I looked it over carefully.

It seemed innocent enough, a commonplace, square, rather
lofty Parisian sleeping-room, finished in wood painted white, with
a small marble mantel, a dusty floor of inlaid maple and cherry,
walls hung with an ordinary French paper, apparently quite new,
and two deeply embrasured windows looking out on the court.

I opened the swinging sash with some trouble, and sat down in
the window seat with my lantern beside me trained on the only
door, which gave on the corridor.

The wind had gone down, and it was very still without,—still
and hot. The masses of luminous vapor were gathering thickly overhead, no longer urged by the gusty wind. The great masses of rank
wisteria leaves, with here and there a second blossoming of purple
flowers, hung dead over the window in the sluggish air. Across the
roofs I could hear the sound of a belated *fiacre* in the streets below. I filled my pipe again and waited.

For a time the voices of the men in the other rooms were a companionship, and at first I shouted to them now and then, but my
voice echoed rather unpleasantly through the long corridors, and
had a suggestive way of reverberating around the left wing beside
me, and coming out at a broken window at its extremity like the
voice of another man. I soon gave up my attempts at conversation,
and devoted myself to the task of keeping awake.

It was not easy; why did I eat that lettuce salad at Père Garceau's? I should have known better. It was making me irresistibly
sleepy, and wakefulness was absolutely necessary. It was certainly
gratifying to know that I could sleep, that my courage was by me
to that extent, but in the interests of science I must keep awake.
But almost never, it seemed, had sleep looked so desirable. Half a
hundred times, nearly, I would doze for an instant, only to awake
with a start, and find my pipe gone out. Nor did the exertion of
relighting it pull me together. I struck my match mechanically, and

with the first puff dropped off again. It was most vexing. I got up and walked around the room. It was most annoying. My cramped position had almost put both my legs to sleep. I could hardly stand. I felt numb, as though with cold. There was no longer any sound from the other rooms, nor from without. I sank down in my window seat. How dark it was growing! I turned up the lantern. That pipe again, how obstinately it kept going out! and my last match was gone. The lantern, too, was *that* going out? I lifted my hand to turn it up again. It felt like lead, and fell beside me.

Then I awoke,—absolutely. I remembered the story of "The Haunters and the Haunted." *This* was the Horror. I tried to rise, to cry out. My body was like lead, my tongue was paralyzed. I could hardly move my eyes. And the light was going out. There was no question about that. Darker and darker yet; little by little the pattern of the paper was swallowed up in the advancing night. A prickling numbness gathered in every nerve, my right arm slipped without feeling from my lap to my side, and I could not raise it,—it swung helpless. A thin, keen humming began in my head, like the cicadas on a hillside in September. The darkness was coming fast.

Yes, this was it. Something was subjecting me, body and mind, to slow paralysis. Physically I was already dead. If I could only hold my mind, my consciousness, I might still be safe, but could I? Could I resist the mad horror of this silence, the deepening dark, the creeping numbness? I knew that, like the man in the ghost story, my only safety lay here.

It had come at last. My body was dead, I could no longer move my eyes. They were fixed in that last look on the place where the door had been, now only a deepening of the dark.

Utter night: the last flicker of the lantern was gone. I sat and waited; my mind was still keen, but how long would it last? There was a limit even to the endurance of the utter panic of fear.

Then the end began. In the velvet blackness came two white eyes, milky, opalescent, small, far away,—awful eyes, like a dead dream. More beautiful than I can describe, the flakes of white flame moving from the perimeter inward, disappearing in the centre, like a never ending flow of opal water into a circular tunnel. I could not have moved my eyes had I possessed the power: they devoured the fearful, beautiful things that grew slowly, slowly larger, fixed on me, advancing, growing more beautiful, the white flakes of light sweeping more swiftly into the blazing vortices, the awful fascination deepening in its insane intensity as the white, vibrating eyes grew nearer, larger.

Like a hideous and implacable engine of death the eyes of the unknown Horror swelled and expanded until they were close before me, enormous, terrible, and I felt a slow, cold, wet breath propelled with mechanical regularity against my face, enveloping me in its fetid mist, in its charnel-house deadliness.

With ordinary fear goes always a physical terror, but with me in the presence of this unspeakable Thing was only the utter and awful terror of the mind, the mad fear of a prolonged and ghostly nightmare. Again and again I tried to shriek, to make some noise, but physically I was utterly dead. I could only feel myself go mad with the terror of hideous death. The eyes were close on me,—their movement so swift that they seemed to be but palpitating flames, the dead breath was around me like the depths of the deepest sea.

Suddenly a wet, icy mouth, like that of a dead cuttle-fish, shapeless, jelly-like, fell over mine. The horror began slowly to draw my life from me, but, as enormous and shuddering folds of palpitating jelly swept sinuously around me, my will came back, my body awoke with the reaction of final fear, and I closed with the nameless death that enfolded me.

What was it that I was fighting? My arms sunk through the unresisting mass that was turning me to ice. Moment by moment new folds of cold jelly swept round me, crushing me with the force of Titans. I fought to wrest my mouth from this awful Thing that sealed it, but, if ever I succeeded and caught a single breath, the wet, sucking mass closed over my face again before I could cry out. I think I fought for hours, desperately, insanely, in a silence that was more hideous than any sound,—fought until I felt final death at hand, until the memory of all my life rushed over me like a flood, until I no longer had strength to wrench my face from that hellish succubus, until with a last mechanical struggle I fell and yielded to death.

Then I heard a voice say, "If he is dead, I can never forgive myself; I was to blame."

Another replied, "He is not dead, I know we can save him if only we reach the hospital in time. Drive like hell, *cocher*! twenty francs for you, if you get there in three minutes."

Then there was night again, and nothingness, until I suddenly awoke and stared around. I lay in a hospital ward, very white and sunny, some yellow *fleurs-de-lis* stood beside the head of the pallet, and a tall sister of mercy sat by my side.

To tell the story in a few words, I was in the Hôtel Dieu, where the men had taken me that fearful night of the twelfth of June. I asked for Fargeau or Duchesne, and by and by the latter came, and sitting beside the bed told me all that I did not know.

It seems that they had sat, each in his room, hour after hour, hearing nothing, very much bored, and disappointed. Soon after two o'clock Fargeau, who was in the next room, called to me to ask if I was awake. I gave no reply, and, after shouting once or twice, he took his lantern and came to investigate. The door was locked on the inside! He instantly called d'Ardeche and Duchesne, and together they hurled themselves against the door. It resisted. Within they could hear irregular footsteps dashing here and there, with heavy breathing. Although frozen with terror, they fought to destroy the door and finally succeeded by using a great slab of marble that formed the shelf of the mantel in Fargeau's room. As the door crashed in, they were suddenly hurled back against the walls of the corridor, as though by an explosion, the lanterns were extinguished, and they found themselves in utter silence and darkness.

As soon as they recovered from the shock, they leaped into the room and fell over my body in the middle of the floor. They lighted one of the lanterns, and saw the strangest sight that can be imagined. The floor and walls to the height of about six feet were running with something that seemed like stagnant water, thick, glutinous, sickening. As for me, I was drenched with the same cursed liquid. The odor of musk was nauseating. They dragged me away, stripped off my clothing, wrapped me in their coats, and hurried to the hospital, thinking me perhaps dead. Soon after sunrise d'Ardeche left the hospital, being assured that I was in a fair way to recovery, with time, and with Fargeau went up to examine by daylight the traces of the adventure that was so nearly fatal. They were too late. Fire engines were coming down the street as they passed the Académie. A neighbor rushed up to d'Ardeche: "O Monsieur! what misfortune, yet what fortune! It is true *la Bouche d'Enfer*—I beg pardon, the residence of the lamented Mlle. de Tartas,—was burned, but not wholly, only the ancient building. The wings were saved, and for that great credit is due the brave firemen. Monsieur will remember them, no doubt."

It was quite true. Whether a forgotten lantern, overturned in the excitement, had done the work, or whether the origin of the fire was more supernatural, it was certain that "the Mouth of Hell" was no more. A last engine was pumping slowly as d'Ardeche came up; half a dozen limp, and one distended, hose stretched through the *porte cochère*, and within only the façade of Francis I. remained, draped still with the black stems of the wisteria. Beyond lay a great vacancy, where thin smoke was rising slowly. Every floor was gone, and the strange halls of Mlle. Blaye de Tartas were only a memory.

With d'Ardeche I visited the place last year, but in the stead of the ancient walls was then only a new and ordinary building, fresh and respectable; yet the wonderful stories of the old *Bouche d'Enfer* still lingered in the quarter, and will hold there, I do not doubt, until the Day of Judgment.

In Kropfsberg Keep

To the traveller from Innsbrück to Munich, up the lovely valley of the silver Inn, many castles appear, one after another, each on its beetling cliff or gentle hill,—appear and disappear, melting into the dark fir trees that grow so thickly on every side,—Laneck, Lichtwer, Ratholtz, Tratzberg, Matzen, Kropfsberg, gathering close around the entrance to the dark and wonderful Zillerthal.

But to us—Tom Rendel and myself—there are two castles only: not the gorgeous and princely Ambras, nor the noble old Tratzberg, with its crowded treasures of solemn and splendid mediævalism; but little Matzen, where eager hospitality forms the new life of a never-dead chivalry, and Kropfsberg, ruined, tottering, blasted by fire and smitten with grievous years,—a dead thing, and haunted,—full of strange legends, and eloquent of mystery and tragedy.

We were visiting the von C—s at Matzen, and gaining our first wondering knowledge of the courtly, cordial castle life in the Tyrol,—of the gentle and delicate hospitality of noble Austrians. Brixleg had ceased to be but a mark on a map, and had become a place of rest and delight, a home for homeless wanderers on the face of Europe, while Schloss Matzen was a synonym for all that was gracious and kindly and beautiful in life. The days moved on in a golden round of riding and driving and shooting: down to Landl and Thiersee for chamois, across the river to the magic Achensee, up the Zillerthal, across the Schmerner Joch, even to the railway station at Steinach. And in the evenings after the late dinners in the upper hall where the sleepy hounds leaned against our chairs

24

looking at us with suppliant eyes, in the evenings when the fire was dying away in the hooded fireplace in the library, stories. Stories, and legends, and fairy tales, while the stiff old portraits changed countenance constantly under the flickering firelight, and the sound of the drifting Inn came softly across the meadows far below.

If ever I tell the Story of Schloss Matzen, then will be the time to paint the too inadequate picture of this fair oasis in the desert of travel and tourists and hotels; but just now it is Kropfsberg the Silent that is of greater importance, for it was only in Matzen that the story was told by Fräulein E—, the gold-haired niece of Frau von C—, one hot evening in July, when we were sitting in the great west window of the drawing-room after a long ride up the Stallenthal. All the windows were open to catch the faint wind, and we had sat for a long time watching the Otzethaler Alps turn rose-color over distant Innsbrück, then deepen to violet as the sun went down and the white mists rose slowly until Lichtwer and Laneck and Kropfsberg rose like craggy islands in a silver sea.

And this is the story as Fräulein E— told it to us,—the Story of Kropfsberg Keep.

A great many years ago, soon after my grandfather died, and Matzen came to us, when I was a little girl, and so young that I remember nothing of the affair except as something dreadful that frightened me very much, two young men who had studied painting with my grandfather came down to Brixleg from Munich, partly to paint, and partly to amuse themselves,— "ghost-hunting" as they said, for they were very sensible young men and prided themselves on it, laughing at all kinds of "superstition," and particularly at that form which believed in ghosts and feared them. They had never seen a real ghost, you know, and they belonged to a certain set of people who believed nothing they had not seen themselves,—which always seemed to me *very* conceited. Well, they knew that we had lots of beautiful castles here in the "lower valley," and they assumed, and rightly, that every castle has at least *one* ghost story connected with it, so they chose this as their hunting ground, only

the game they sought was ghosts, not chamois. Their plan was to
visit every place that was supposed to be haunted, and to meet every reputed ghost, and prove that it really was no ghost at all.

There was a little inn down in the village then, kept by an old
man named Peter Rosskopf, and the two young men made this their
headquarters. The very first night they began to draw from the old
innkeeper all that he knew of legends and ghost stories connected
with Brixleg and its castles, and as he was a most garrulous old
gentleman he filled them with the wildest delight by his stories of
the ghosts of the castles about the mouth of the Zillerthal. Of course
the old man believed every word he said, and you can imagine his
horror and amazement when, after telling his guests the particularly blood-curdling story of Kropfsberg and its haunted keep, the
elder of the two boys, whose surname I have forgotten, but whose
Christian name was Rupert, calmly said, "Your story is most satis-
factory: we will sleep in Kropfsberg Keep to-morrow night, and
you must provide us with all that we may need to make ourselves
comfortable."

The old man nearly fell into the fire. "What for a blockhead are
you?" he cried, with big eyes. "The keep is haunted by Count
Albert's ghost, I tell you!"

"That is why we are going there to-morrow night; we wish to
make the acquaintance of Count Albert."

"But there was a man stayed there once, and in the morning he
was dead."

"Very silly of him; there are two of us, and we carry revolvers."

"But it's a *ghost*, I tell you," almost screamed the innkeeper;
"are ghosts afraid of firearms?"

"Whether they are or not, we are *not* afraid of *them*."

Here the younger boy broke in,—he was named Otto von Kleist.
I remember the name, for I had a music teacher once by that name.
He abused the poor old man shamefully; told him that they were
going to spend the night in Kropfsberg in spite of Count Albert
and Peter Rosskopf, and that he might as well make the most of it
and earn his money with cheerfulness.

In a word, they finally bullied the old fellow into submission, and when the morning came he set about preparing for the suicide, as he considered it, with sighs and mutterings and ominous shakings of the head.

You know the condition of the castle now,—nothing but scorched walls and crumbling piles of fallen masonry. Well, at the time I tell you of, the keep was still partially preserved. It was finally burned out only a few years ago by some wicked boys who came over from Jenbach to have a good time. But when the ghost hunters came, though the two lower floors had fallen into the crypt, the third floor remained. The peasants said it *could* not fall, but that it would stay until the Day of Judgment, because it was in the room above that the wicked Count Albert sat watching the flames destroy the great castle and his imprisoned guests, and where he finally hung himself in a suit of armor that had belonged to his mediæval ancestor, the first Count Kropfsberg.

No one dared touch him, and so he hung there for twelve years, and all the time venturesome boys and daring men used to creep up the turret steps and stare awfully through the chinks in the door at that ghostly mass of steel that held within itself the body of a murderer and suicide, slowly returning to the dust from which it was made. Finally it disappeared, none knew whither, and for another dozen years the room stood empty but for the old furniture and the rotting hangings.

So, when the two men climbed the stairway to the haunted room, they found a very different state of things from what exists now. The room was absolutely as it was left the night Count Albert burned the castle, except that all trace of the suspended suit of armor and its ghastly contents had vanished.

No one had dared to cross the threshold, and I suppose that for forty years no living thing had entered that dreadful room.

On one side stood a vast canopied bed of black wood, the damask hangings of which were covered with mould and mildew. All the clothing of the bed was in perfect order, and on it lay a book, open, and face downward. The only other furniture in the room consisted of several old chairs, a carved oak chest, and a big inlaid table covered with books and papers, and on one corner two or three bottles with dark solid sediment at the bottom, and a glass, also dark with the dregs of wine that had been poured out almost half a century before. The tapestry on the walls was green with mould, but hardly torn or otherwise defaced, for although the heavy dust of forty years lay on everything the room had been preserved from further harm. No spider web was to be seen, no trace of nibbling mice, not even a dead moth or fly on the sills of the diamond-paned windows; life seemed to have shunned the room utterly and finally.

The men looked at the room curiously, and, I am sure, not without some feelings of awe and unacknowledged fear; but, whatever they may have felt of instinctive shrinking, they said nothing, and quickly set to work to make the room passably inhabitable. They decided to touch nothing that had not absolutely to be changed, and therefore they made for themselves a bed in one corner with the mattress and linen from the inn. In the great fireplace they piled a lot of wood on the caked ashes of a fire dead for forty years, turned the old chest into a table, and laid out on it all their arrangements for the evening's amusement: food, two or three bottles of wine, pipes and tobacco, and the chess-board that was their inseparable travelling companion.

All this they did themselves: the innkeeper would not even come within the walls of the outer court; he insisted that he had washed his hands of the whole affair, the silly dunderheads might go to their death their own way. *He* would not aid and abet them. One of the stable boys brought the basket of food and the wood and the bed up the winding stone stairs, to be sure, but neither money nor prayers nor threats would bring him within the walls of the accursed place, and he stared fearfully at the hare-brained boys as they worked around the dead old room preparing for the night that was coming so fast.

At length everything was in readiness, and after a final visit to the inn for dinner Rupert and Otto started at sunset for the Keep. Half the village went with them, for Peter Rosskopf had babbled the whole story to an open-mouthed crowd of wondering men and women, and as to an execution the awe-struck crowd followed the two boys dumbly, curious to see if they surely would put their plan into execution. But none went farther than the outer doorway of the stairs, for it was already growing twilight. In absolute silence they watched the two foolhardy youths with their lives in their hands enter the terrible Keep, standing like a tower in the midst of the piles of stones that had once formed walls joining it with the mass of the castle beyond. When a moment later a light showed itself in the high windows above, they sighed resignedly and went their ways, to wait stolidly until morning should come and prove the truth of their fears and warnings.

In the mean time the ghost hunters built a huge fire, lighted their many candles, and sat down to await developments. Rupert afterwards told my uncle that they really felt no fear whatever, only a contemptuous curiosity, and they ate their supper with good appetite and an unusual relish. It was a long evening. They played many games of chess, waiting for midnight. Hour passed after hour, and nothing occurred to interrupt the monotony of the evening. Ten, eleven, came and went,—it was almost midnight. They piled more wood in the fireplace, lighted new candles, looked to their pistols—and waited. The clocks in the village struck twelve; the sound coming muffled through the high, deep-embrasured windows. Nothing happened, nothing to break the heavy silence; and with a feeling of disappointed relief they looked at each other and acknowledged that they had met another rebuff.

Finally they decided that there was no use in sitting up and boring themselves any longer, they had much better rest; so Otto threw himself down on the mattress, falling almost immediately asleep. Rupert sat a little longer, smoking, and watching the stars creep along behind the shattered glass and the bent leads of the lofty windows; watching the fire fall together, and the strange shadows move mysteriously on the mouldering walls. The iron hook in the oak beam, that crossed the ceiling midway, fascinated him, not with fear, but morbidly. So, it was from that hook that for twelve years, twelve long years of changing summer and winter, the body of Count Albert, murderer and suicide, hung in its strange casing of mediæval steel; moving a little at first, and turning gently while the fire died out on the hearth, while the ruins of the castle grew cold, and horrified peasants sought for the bodies of the score of gay, reckless, wicked guests whom Count Albert had gathered in Kropfsberg for a last debauch, gathered to their terrible and untimely death. What a strange and fiendish idea it was, the young, handsome noble who had ruined himself and his family in the society of the splendid debauchees, gathering them all together, men and women who had known only love and pleasure, for a glorious and awful riot of luxury, and then, when they were all dancing in the great ballroom, locking the doors and burning the whole castle about them, the while he sat in the great keep listening to their screams of agonized fear, watching the fire sweep from wing to wing until the whole mighty mass was one enormous and awful pyre, and then, clothing himself in his great-great-grandfather's armor, hanging himself in the midst of the ruins of what had been a proud and noble castle. So ended a great family, a great house.

But that was forty years ago.

He was growing drowsy; the light flickered and flared in the fireplace; one by one the candles went out; the shadows grew thick in the room. Why did that great iron hook stand out so plainly? why did that dark shadow dance and quiver so mockingly behind it?—why— But he ceased to wonder at anything. He was asleep.

It seemed to him that he woke almost immediately; the fire still burned, though low and fitfully on the hearth. Otto was sleeping, breathing quietly and regularly; the shadows had gathered close around him, thick and murky; with every passing moment the light died in the fireplace; he felt stiff with cold. In the utter silence he heard the clock in the village strike two. He shivered with a sudden and irresistible feeling of fear, and abruptly turned and looked towards the hook in the ceiling.

Yes, It was there. He knew that It would be. It seemed quite natural, he would have been disappointed had he seen nothing; but now he knew that the story was true, knew that he was wrong, and that the dead *do* sometimes return to earth, for there, in the fast-deepening shadow, hung the black mass of wrought steel, turning a little now and then, with the light flickering on the tarnished and rusty metal. He watched it quietly; he hardly felt afraid; it was rather a sentiment of sadness and fatality that filled him, of gloomy forebodings of something unknown, unimaginable. He sat and watched the thing disappear in the gathering dark, his hand on his pistol as it lay by him on the great chest. There was no sound but the regular breathing of the sleeping boy on the mattress.

It had grown absolutely dark; a bat fluttered against the broken glass of the window. He wondered if he was growing mad, for— he hesitated to acknowledge it to himself—he heard music; far, curious music, a strange and luxurious dance, very faint, very vague, but unmistakable.

Like a flash of lightning came a jagged line of fire down the blank wall opposite him, a line that remained, that grew wider, that let a pale cold light into the room, showing him now all its details,—the empty fireplace, where a thin smoke rose in a spiral from a bit of charred wood, the mass of the great bed, and, in the very middle, black against the curious brightness, the armored man, or ghost, or devil, standing, not suspended, beneath the rusty hook. And with the rending of the wall the music grew more distinct, though sounding still very, very far away.

Count Albert raised his mailed hand and beckoned to him; then turned, and stood in the riven wall.

Without a word, Rupert rose and followed him, his pistol in hand. Count Albert passed through the mighty wall and disappeared in the unearthly light. Rupert followed mechanically. He felt the crushing of the mortar beneath his feet, the roughness of the jagged wall where he rested his hand to steady himself.

The keep rose absolutely isolated among the ruins, yet on passing through the wall Rupert found himself in a long, uneven corridor, the floor of which was warped and sagging, while the walls were covered on one side with big faded portraits of an inferior quality, like those in the corridor that connects the Pitti and Uffizzi in Florence. Before him moved the figure of Count Albert,—a black silhouette in the ever-increasing light. And always the music grew stronger and stranger, a mad, evil, seductive dance that bewitched even while it disgusted.

In a final blaze of vivid, intolerable light, in a burst of hellish music that might have come from Bedlam, Rupert stepped from the corridor into a vast and curious room where at first he saw nothing, distinguished nothing but a mad, seething whirl of sweeping figures, white, in a white room, under white light, Count Albert standing before him, the only dark object to be seen. As his eyes grew accustomed to the fearful brightness, he knew that he was looking on a dance such as the damned might see in hell, but such as no living man had ever seen before.

Around the long, narrow hall, under the fearful light that came from nowhere, but was omnipresent, swept a rushing stream of unspeakable horrors, dancing insanely, laughing, gibbering hideously; the dead of forty years. White, polished skeletons, bare of flesh and vesture, skeletons clothed in the dreadful rags of dried and rattling sinews, the tags of tattering grave-clothes flaunting behind them. These were the dead of many years ago. Then the dead of more recent times, with yellow bones showing only here and there, the long and insecure hair of their hideous heads writhing in the beating air. Then green and gray horrors, bloated and shapeless, stained with earth or dripping with spattering water; and here and there white, beautiful things, like chiselled ivory, the dead of yesterday, locked it may be, in the mummy arms of rattling skeletons.

Round and round the cursed room, a swaying, swirling maelstrom of death, while the air grew thick with miasma, the floor foul with shreds of shrouds, and yellow parchment, clattering bones, and wisps of tangled hair.

And in the very midst of this ring of death, a sight not for words nor for thought, a sight to blast forever the mind of the man who looked upon it: a leaping, writhing dance of Count Albert's victims, the score of beautiful women and reckless men who danced to their awful death while the castle burned around them, charred and shapeless now, a living charnel-house of nameless horror.

Count Albert, who had stood silent and gloomy, watching the dance of the damned, turned to Rupert, and for the first time spoke.

"We are ready for you now; dance!"

A prancing horror, dead some dozen years, perhaps, flaunted from the rushing river of the dead, and leered at Rupert with eyeless skull.

"Dance!"

Rupert stood frozen, motionless.

"Dance!"

His hard lips moved. "Not if the devil came from hell to make me."

Count Albert swept his vast two-handed sword into the fœtid air while the tide of corruption paused in its swirling, and swept down on Rupert with gibbering grins.

The room, and the howling dead, and the black portent before him circled dizzily around, as with a last effort of departing consciousness he drew his pistol and fired full in the face of Count Albert.

Perfect silence, perfect darkness; not a breath, not a sound: the dead stillness of a long-sealed tomb. Rupert lay on his back, stunned, helpless, his pistol clenched in his frozen hand, a smell of powder in the black air. Where was he? Dead? In hell? He reached his hand out cautiously; it fell on dusty boards. Outside, far away, a clock struck three. Had he dreamed? Of course; but how ghastly a dream! With chattering teeth he called softly,—

"Otto!"

There was no reply, and none when he called again and again. He staggered weakly to his feet, groping for matches and candles. A panic of abject terror came on him; the matches were gone! He turned towards the fireplace: a single coal glowed in the white ashes. He swept a mass of papers and dusty books from the table, and with trembling hands cowered over the embers, until he succeeded in lighting the dry tinder. Then he piled the old books on the blaze, and looked fearfully around.

No: It was gone,—thank God for that; the hook was empty.

But why did Otto sleep so soundly; why did he not awake?

He stepped unsteadily across the room in the flaring light of the burning books, and knelt by the mattress.

So they found him in the morning, when no one came to the inn from Kropfsberg Keep, and the quaking Peter Rosskopf arranged a relief party;—found him kneeling beside the mattress where Otto lay, shot in the throat and quite dead.

THE WHITE VILLA

WHEN we left Naples on the 8.10 train for Pæstum, Tom and I, we fully intended returning by the 2.46. Not because two hours time seemed enough wherein to exhaust the interests of those deathless ruins of a dead civilization, but simply for the reason that, as our *Indicatore* informed us, there was but one other train, and that at 6.11, which would land us in Naples too late for the dinner at the Turners and the San Carlo afterwards. Not that I cared in the least for the dinner or the theatre; but then, I was not so obviously in Miss Turner's good graces as Tom Rendel was, which made a difference.

However, we had promised, so that was an end of it.

This was in the spring of '88, and at that time the railroad, which was being pushed onward to Reggio, whereby travellers to Sicily might be spared the agonies of a night on the fickle Mediterranean, reached no farther than Agropoli, some twenty miles beyond Pæstum; but although the trains were as yet few and slow, we accepted the half-finished road with gratitude, for it penetrated the very centre of Campanian brigandage, and made it possible for us to see the matchless temples in safety, while a few years before it was necessary for intending visitors to obtain a military escort from the Government; and military escorts are not for young architects.

So we set off contentedly, that white May morning, determined to make the best of our few hours, little thinking that before we saw

35

Naples again we were to witness things that perhaps no American
had ever seen before.

For a moment, when we left the train at "Pesto," and started to
walk up the flowery lane leading to the temples, we were almost
inclined to curse this same railroad. We had thought, in our innocence, that we should be alone, that no one else would think of
enduring the long four hours' ride from Naples just to spend two
hours in the ruins of these temples; but the event proved our
unwisdom. We were *not* alone. It was a compact little party of con-
ventional sight-seers that accompanied us. The inevitable English
family with the three daughters, prominent of teeth, flowing of hair,
aggressive of scarlet Murrays and Baedekers; the two blond and
untidy Germans; a French couple from the pages of *La Vie Paris-
ienne*; and our "old man of the sea," the white-bearded Presbyte-
rian minister from Pennsylvania who had made our life miserable
in Rome at the time of the Pope's Jubilee. Fortunately for us, this
terrible old man had fastened himself upon a party of American
school-teachers travelling *en Cook*, and for the time we were safe;
but our vision of two hours of dreamy solitude faded lamentably
away.

Yet how beautiful it was! this golden meadow walled with far,
violet mountains, breathless under a May sun; and in the midst,
rising from tangles of asphodel and acanthus, vast in the vacant
plain, three temples, one silver gray, one golden gray, and one
flushed with intangible rose. And all around nothing but velvet
meadows stretching from the dim mountains behind, away to the
sea, that showed only as a thin line of silver just over the edge of
the still grass.

The tide of tourists swept noisily through the Basilica and the
temple of Poseidon across the meadow to the distant temple of
Ceres, and Tom and I were left alone to drink in all the fine wine
of dreams that was possible in the time left us. We gave but little
space to examining the temples the tourists had left, but in a few
moments found ourselves lying in the grass to the east of Poseidon,
looking dimly out towards the sea, heard now, but not seen,—a

vague and pulsating murmur that blended with the humming of bees all about us.

A small shepherd boy, with a woolly dog, made shy advances of friendship, and in a little time we had set him to gathering flowers for us: asphodels and bee-orchids, anemones, and the little thin green iris so fairylike and frail. The murmur of the tourist crowd had merged itself in the moan of the sea, and it was very still; suddenly I heard the words I had been waiting for,—the suggestion I had refrained from making myself, for I knew Thomas.

"I say, old man, shall we let the 2.46 go to thunder?"

I chuckled to myself. "But the Turners?"

"They be blowed, we can tell them we missed the train."

"That is just exactly what we shall do," I said, pulling out my watch, "unless we start for the station right now."

But Tom drew an acanthus leaf across his face and showed no signs of moving; so I filled my pipe again, and we missed the train.

As the sun dropped lower towards the sea, changing its silver line to gold, we pulled ourselves together, and for an hour or more sketched vigorously; but the mood was not on us. It was "too jolly fine to waste time working," as Tom said; so we started off to explore the single street of the squalid town of Pesto that was lost within the walls of dead Poseidonia. It was not a pretty village,—if you can call a rut-riven lane and a dozen houses a village,—nor were the inhabitants thereof reassuring in appearance. There was no sign of a church,—nothing but dirty huts, and in the midst, one of two stories, rejoicing in the name of *Albergo del Sole*, the first story of which was a black and cavernous smithy, where certain swarthy knaves, looking like banditti out of a job, sat smoking sulkily.

"We might stay here all night," said Tom, grinning askance at this choice company; but his suggestion was not received with enthusiasm.

Down where the lane from the station joined the main road stood the only sign of modern civilization,—a great square structure, half villa, half fortress, with round turrets on its four corners, and a ten-foot wall surrounding it. There were no windows in its first story, so far as we could see, and it had evidently been at one time the fortified villa of some Campanian noble. Now, however, whether because brigandage had been stamped out, or because the villa was empty and deserted, it was no longer formidable; the gates of the great wall hung sagging on their hinges, brambles growing all over them, and many of the windows in the upper story were broken and black. It was a strange place, weird and mysterious, and we looked at it curiously. "There is a story about that place," said Tom, with conviction.

It was growing late: the sun was near the edge of the sea as we walked down the ivy-grown walls of the vanished city for the last time, and as we turned back, a red flush poured from the west, and painted the Doric temples in pallid rose against the evanescent purple of the Apennines. Already a thin mist was rising from the meadows, and the temples hung pink in the misty grayness.

It was a sorrow to leave the beautiful things, but we could run no risk of missing this last train, so we walked slowly back towards the temples.

"What is that Johnny waving his arm at us for?" asked Tom, suddenly.

"How should I know? We are not on his land, and the walls don't matter."

We pulled out our watches simultaneously.

"What time are you?" I said.

"Six minutes before six."

"And I am seven minutes. It can't take us all that time to walk to the station."

"Are you sure the train goes at 6.11?"

"Dead sure," I answered; and showed him the *Indicatore*.

By this time a woman and two children were shrieking at us hysterically; but what they said I had no idea, their Italian being of a strange and awful nature.

"Look here," I said, "let's run; perhaps our watches are both slow."

"Or—perhaps the time-table is changed."

Then we ran, and the populace cheered and shouted with enthusiasm; our dignified run became a panic-stricken rout, for as we turned into the lane, smoke was rising from beyond the bank that hid the railroad; a bell rang; we were so near that we could hear the interrogative *Pronte?* the impatient *Partenza!* and the definitive *Andiamo!* But the train was five hundred yards away, steaming towards Naples, when we plunged into the station as the clock struck six, and yelled for the station-master.

He came, and we indulged in crimination and recrimination.

When we could regard the situation calmly, it became apparent that the time-table *had* been changed two days before, the 6.11 now leaving at 5.58. A *facchino* came in, and we four sat down and regarded the situation judicially.

"Was there any other train?"

"No."

"Could we stay at the Albergo del Sole?"

A forefinger drawn across the throat by the Capo Stazione with a significant "cluck" closed that question.

"Then we must stay with you here at the station."

"But, Signori, I am not married. I live here only with the *facchini*. I have only one room to sleep in. It is impossible!"

"But we must sleep somewhere, likewise eat. What can we do?" and we shifted the responsibility deftly on the shoulders of the poor old man, who was growing excited again.

He trotted nervously up and down the station for a minute, then he called the *facchino*. "Giuseppe, go up to the villa and ask if two *forestieri* who have missed the last train can stay there all night!"

Protests were useless. The *facchino* was gone, and we waited anxiously for his return. It seemed as though he would never come. Darkness had fallen, and the moon was rising over the mountains. At last he appeared.

"The Signori may stay all night, and welcome; but they cannot come to dinner, for there is nothing in the house to eat!"

This was not reassuring, and again the old station-master lost himself in meditation. The results were admirable, for in a little time the table in the waiting-room had been transformed into a

dining-table, and Tom and I were ravenously devouring a big
omelette, and bread and cheese, and drinking a most shocking sour
wine as though it were Château Yquem. A *facchino* served us, with
clumsy good-will; and when we had induced our nervous old host
to sit down with us and partake of his own hospitality, we succeeded in forming a passably jolly dinner-party, forgetting over
our sour wine and cigarettes the coming hours from ten until sunrise, which lay before us in a dubious mist.

It was with crowding apprehensions which we strove in vain to
joke away that we set out at last to retrace our steps to the mysterious villa, the *facchino* Giuseppe leading the way. By this time
the moon was well overhead, and just behind us as we tramped up
the dewy lane, white in the moonlight between the ink-black
hedgerows on either side. How still it was! Not a breath of air, not
a sound of life; only the awful silence that had lain almost unbroken for two thousand years over this vast graveyard of a dead world.

As we passed between the shattered gates and wound our way
in the moonlight through the maze of gnarled fruit-trees, decay-
ing farm implements and piles of lumber, towards the small door
that formed the only opening in the first story of this deserted fortress, the cold silence was shattered by the harsh baying of dogs
somewhere in the distance to the right, beyond the barns that
formed one side of the court. From the villa came neither light nor
sound. Giuseppe knocked at the weather-worn door, and the sound
echoed cavernously within; but there was no other reply. He
knocked again and again, and at length we heard the rasping jar of
sliding bolts, and the door opened a little, showing an old, old man,
bent with age and gaunt with malaria. Over his head he held a big
Roman lamp, with three wicks, that cast strange shadows on his
face,—a face that was harmless in its senility, but intolerably sad.
He made no reply to our timid salutations, but motioned
tremblingly to us to enter; and with a last "good-night" to Giuseppe
we obeyed, and stood half-way up the stone stairs that led directly
from the door, while the old man tediously shot every bolt and
adjusted the heavy bar.

Then we followed him in the semi-darkness up the steps into what had been the great hall of the villa. A fire was burning in a great fireplace so beautiful in design that Tom and I looked at each other with interest. By its fitful light we could see that we were in a huge circular room covered by a flat, saucer-shaped dome,—a room that must once have been superb and splendid, but that now was a lamentable wreck. The frescoes on the dome were stained and mildewed, and here and there the plaster was gone altogether; the carved doorways that led out on all sides had lost half the gold with which they had once been covered, and the floor was of brick, sunken into treacherous valleys. Rough chests, piles of old newspapers, fragments of harnesses, farm implements, a heap of rusty carbines and cutlasses, nameless litter of every possible kind, made the room into a wilderness which under the firelight seemed even more picturesque than it really was. And on this inexpressible confusion of lumber the pale shapes of the seventeenth-century nymphs, startling in their weather-stained nudity, looked down with vacant smiles.

For a few moments we warmed ourselves before the fire; and then, in the same dejected silence, the old man led the way to one of the many doors, handed us a brass lamp, and with a stiff bow turned his back on us.

Once in our room alone, Tom and I looked at each other with faces that expressed the most complex emotions.

"Well, of all the rum goes," said Tom, "this is the rummiest go I ever experienced!"

"Right, my boy; as you very justly remark, we are in for it. Help me shut this door, and then we will reconnoitre, take account of stock, and size up our chances."

But the door showed no sign of closing; it grated on the brick floor and stuck in the warped casing, and it took our united efforts to jam the two inches of oak into its place, and turn the enormous old key in its rusty lock.

"Better now, much better now," said Tom; "now let us see where we are."

The room was easily twenty-five feet square, and high in proportion; evidently it had been a state apartment, for the walls were covered with carved panelling that had once been white and gold, with mirrors in the panels, the wood now stained every imaginable color, the mirrors cracked and broken, and dull with mildew. A big fire had just been lighted in the fireplace, the shutters were closed, and although the only furniture consisted of two massive bedsteads, and a chair with one leg shorter than the others, the room seemed almost comfortable.

I opened one of the shutters, that closed the great windows that ran from the floor almost to the ceiling, and nearly fell through the cracked glass into the floorless balcony. "Tom, come here, quick," I cried; and for a few minutes neither of us thought about our dubious surroundings, for we were looking at Pæstum by moonlight.

A flat, white mist, like water, lay over the entire meadow; from the midst rose against the blue-black sky the three ghostly temples, black and silver in the vivid moonlight, floating, it seemed, in the fog; and behind them, seen in broken glints between the pallid shafts, stretched the line of the silver sea.

Perfect silence,—the silence of implacable death.

We watched the white tide of mist rise around the temples, until we were chilled through, and so presently went to bed. There was but one door in the room, and that was securely locked; the great windows were twenty feet from the ground, so we felt reasonably safe from all possible attack.

In a few minutes Tom was asleep and breathing audibly; but my constitution is more nervous than his, and I lay awake for some little time, thinking of our curious adventure and of its possible outcome. Finally, I fell asleep,—for how long I do not know: but I woke with the feeling that some one had tried the handle of the door. The fire had fallen into a heap of coals which cast a red glow in the room, whereby I could see dimly the outline of Tom's bed, the broken-legged chair in front of the fireplace, and the door in its deep casing by the chimney, directly in front of my bed. I sat up, nervous from my sudden awakening under these strange circumstances, and stared at the door. The latch rattled, and the door swung smoothly open. I began to shiver coldly. That door was locked; Tom and I had all we could do to jam it together and lock it. But we *did* lock it; and now it was opening silently. In a minute more it as silently closed.

Then I heard a footstep,—I swear I heard a footstep *in the room*, and with it the *frou-frou* of trailing skirts; my breath stopped and my teeth grated against each other as I heard the soft footfalls and the feminine rustle pass along the room towards the fireplace. My eyes saw nothing; yet there was enough light in the room for me to distinguish the pattern on the carved panels of the door. The steps stopped by the fire, and I saw the broken-legged chair lean to the left, with a little jar as its short leg touched the floor.

I sat still, frozen, motionless, staring at the vacancy that was filled with such terror for me; and as I looked, the seat of the chair creaked, and it came back to its upright position again.

And then the footsteps came down the room lightly, towards the window; there was a pause, and then the great shutters swung back, and the white moonlight poured in. Its brilliancy was unbroken by any shadow, by any sign of material substance.

I tried to cry out, to make some sound, to awaken Tom; this sense of utter loneliness in the presence of the Inexplicable was maddening. I don't know whether my lips obeyed my will or no; at all events, Tom lay motionless, with his deaf ear up, and gave no sign.

The shutters closed as silently as they had opened; the moonlight was gone, the firelight also, and in utter darkness I waited. If I could only *see*! If something were visible, I should not mind it so much; but this ghastly hearing of every little sound, every rustle of a gown, every breath, yet seeing nothing, was soul-destroying. I think in my abject terror I prayed that I might see, only see; but the darkness was unbroken.

Then the footsteps began to waver fitfully, and I heard the rustle of garments sliding to the floor, the clatter of little shoes flung down, the rattle of buttons, and of metal against wood.

Rigors shot over me, and my whole body shivered with collapse as I sank back on the pillow, waiting with every nerve tense, listening with all my life.

The coverlid was turned back beside me, and in another moment the great bed sank a little as something slipped between the sheets with an audible sigh.

I called to my aid every atom of remaining strength, and, with a cry that shivered between my clattering teeth, I hurled myself headlong from the bed on to the floor.

I must have lain for some time stunned and unconscious, for when I finally came to myself it was cold in the room, there was no last glow of lingering coals in the fireplace, and I was stiff with chill.

It all flashed over me like the haunting of a heavy dream. I laughed a little at the dim memory, with the thought, "I must try to recollect all the details; they will do to tell Tom," and rose stiffly to return to bed, when—there it was again, and my heart stopped,—the hand on the door.

I paused and listened. The door opened with a muffled creak, closed again, and I heard the lock turn rustily. I would have died now before getting into that bed again; but there was terror equally without; so I stood trembling and listened,—listened to heavy, stealthy steps creeping along on the other side of the bed. I clutched the coverlid, staring across into the dark.

There was a rush in the air by my face, the sound of a blow, and simultaneously a shriek, so awful, so despairing, so blood-curdling that I felt my senses leaving me again as I sank crouching on the floor by the bed.

And then began the awful duel, the duel of invisible, audible shapes; of things that shrieked and raved, mingling thin, feminine cries with low, stifled curses and indistinguishable words. Round and round the room, footsteps chasing footsteps in the ghastly night, now away by Tom's bed, now rushing swiftly down the great room until I felt the flash of swirling drapery on my hard lips. Round and round, turning and twisting till my brain whirled with the mad cries.

They were coming nearer. I felt the jar of their feet on the floor beside me. Came one long, gurgling moan close over my head, and then, crushing down upon me, the weight of a collapsing body; there was long hair over my face, and in my staring eyes; and as awful silence succeeded the less awful tumult, life went out, and I fell unfathomable miles into nothingness.

The gray dawn was sifting through the chinks in the shutters when I opened my eyes again. I lay stunned and faint, staring up at the mouldy frescoes on the ceiling, struggling to gather together my wandering senses and knit them into something like consciousness. But now as I pulled myself little by little together there was no thought of dreams before me. One after another the awful incidents of that unspeakable night came back, and I lay incapable of movement, of action, trying to piece together the whirling fragments of memory that circled dizzily around me.

Little by little it grew lighter in the room. I could see the pallid lines struggling through the shutters behind me, grow stronger along the broken and dusty floor. The tarnished mirrors reflected dirtily the growing daylight; a door closed, far away, and I heard the crowing of a cock; then by and by the whistle of a passing train.

Years seemed to have passed since I first came into this terrible room. I had lost the use of my tongue, my voice refused to obey my panic-stricken desire to cry out; once or twice I tried in vain to force an articulate sound through my rigid lips; and when at last a broken whisper rewarded my feverish struggles, I felt a strange sense of great victory. How soundly he slept! Ordinarily, rousing him was no easy task, and now he revolted steadily against being awakened at this untimely hour. It seemed to me that I had called him for ages almost, before I heard him grunt sleepily and turn in bed.

"Tom," I cried weakly, "Tom, come and help me!"

"What do you want? what is the matter with you?"

"Don't ask, come and help me!"

"Fallen out of bed I guess;" and he laughed drowsily.

My abject terror lest he should go to sleep again gave me new strength. Was it the actual physical paralysis born of killing fear that held me down? I could not have raised my head from the floor on my life; I could only cry out in deadly fear for Tom to come and help me.

"Why don't you get up and get into bed?" he answered, when I implored him to come to me. "You have got a bad nightmare; wake up!"

But something in my voice roused him at last, and he came chuckling across the room, stopping to throw open two of the great shutters and let a burst of white light into the room. He climbed up on the bed and peered over jeeringly. With the first glance the laugh died, and he leaped the bed and bent over me.

"My God, man, what is the matter with you? You are hurt!"

"I don't know what is the matter; lift me up, get me away from here, and I'll tell you all I know."

"But, old chap, you must be hurt awfully; the floor is covered with blood!"

He lifted my head and held me in his powerful arms. I looked down: a great red stain blotted the floor beside me.

But, apart from the black bruise on my head, there was no sign of a wound on my body, nor stain of blood on my lips. In as few words as possible I told him the whole story.

"Let's get out of this," he said when I had finished; "this is no place for us. Brigands I can stand, but—"

He helped me to dress, and as soon as possible we forced open the heavy door, the door I had seen turn so softly on its hinges only a few hours before, and came out into the great circular hall, no less strange and mysterious now in the half light of dawn than it had been by firelight. The room was empty, for it must have been very early, although a fire already blazed in the fireplace. We sat by the fire some time, seeing no one. Presently slow footsteps sounded in the stairway, and the old man entered, silent as the night before, nodding to us civilly, but showing by no sign any surprise which he may have felt at our early rising. In absolute silence he moved around, preparing coffee for us; and when at last the frugal breakfast was ready, and we sat around the rough table munching coarse bread and sipping the black coffee, he would reply to our overtures only by monosyllables.

Any attempt at drawing from him some facts as to the history of the villa was received with a grave and frigid repellence that baffled us; and we were forced to say *addio* with our hunger for some explanation of the events of the night still unsatisfied.

But we saw the temples by sunrise, when the mistlike lambent opals bathed the bases of the tall columns salmon in the morning light! It was a rhapsody in the pale and unearthly colors of Puvis de Chavannes vitalized and made glorious with splendid sunlight; the apotheosis of mist; a vision never before seen, never to be forgotten. It was so beautiful that the memory of my ghastly night paled and faded, and it was Tom who assailed the station-master with questions while we waited for the train from Agropoli.

Luckily he was more than loquacious, he was voluble under the ameliorating influence of the money we forced upon him; and this, in few words, was the story he told us while we sat on the platform smoking, marvelling at the mists that rose to the east, now veiling, now revealing the lavender Apennines.

"Is there a story of *La Villa Bianca*?"

"Ah, Signori, certainly; and a story very strange and very terrible. It was much time ago, a hundred,—two hundred years; I do not know. Well, the Duca di San Damiano married a lady so fair, so most beautiful that she was called *La Luna di Pesto*; but she was of the people,—more, she was of the banditti: her father was of Calabria, and a terror of the Campagna. But the Duke was young, and he married her, and for her built the white villa; and it was a wonder throughout Campania,—you have seen? It is splendid now, even if a ruin. Well, it was less than a year after they came to the villa before the Duke grew jealous,—jealous of the new captain of the banditti who took the place of the father of *La Luna*, himself killed in a great battle up there in the mountains. Was there cause? Who shall know? But there were stories among the people of terrible things in the villa, and how *La Luna* was seen almost never outside the walls. Then the Duke would go for many days to Napoli, coming home only now and then to the villa that was become a

fortress, so many men guarded its never-opening gates. And once—
it was in the spring—the Duke came silently down from Napoli,
and there, by the three poplars you see away towards the north,
his carriage was set upon by armed men, and he was almost killed;
but he had with him many guards, and after a terrible fight the
brigands were beaten off; but before him, wounded, lay the captain,—the man whom he feared and hated. He looked at him, lying
there under the torchlight, and in his hand saw *his own sword.*
Then he became a devil: with the same sword he ran the brigand
through, leaped in the carriage, and, entering the villa, crept to
the chamber of *La Luna,* and killed her with the sword she had
given to her lover.

"This is all the story of the White Villa, except that the Duke
came never again to Pesto. He went back to the king at Napoli, and
for many years he was the scourge of the banditti of Campania; for
the King made him a general, and San Damiano was a name feared
by the lawless and loved by the peaceful, until he was killed in a
battle down by Mormanno.

"And *La Luna?* Some say she comes back to the villa, once a
year, when the moon is full, in the month when she was slain; for
the Duke buried her, they say, with his own hands, in the garden
that was once under the window of her chamber; and as she died
unshriven, so was she buried without the pale of the Church. Therefore she cannot sleep in peace,—*non è vero?* I do not know if the
story is true, but this is the story, Signori, and there is the train
for Napoli. *Ah, grazie! Signori, grazie tanto! A rivederci! Signori,
a rivederci!*"

Sister Maddelena

Across the valley of the Oreto from Monreale, on the slopes of the mountains just above the little village of Parco, lies the old convent of Sta. Catarina. From the cloister terrace at Monreale you can see its pale walls and the slim campanile of its chapel rising from the crowded citron and mulberry orchards that flourish, rank and wild, no longer cared for by pious and loving hands. From the rough road that climbs the mountains to Assunto, the convent is invisible, a gnarled and ragged olive grove intervening, and a spur of cliffs as well, while from Palermo one sees only the speck of white, flashing in the sun, indistinguishable from the many similar gleams of desert monastery or pauper village.

Partly because of this seclusion, partly by reason of its extreme beauty, partly, it may be, because the present owners are more than charming and gracious in their pressing hospitality, Sta. Catarina seems to preserve an element of the poetic, almost magical; and as I drove with the Cavaliere Valguanera one evening in March out of Palermo, along the garden valley of the Oreto, then up the mountain side where the warm light of the spring sunset swept across from Monreale, lying golden and mellow on the luxuriant growth of figs, and olives, and orange-trees, and fantastic cacti, and so up to where the path of the convent swung off to the right round a dizzy point of cliff that reached out gaunt and gray from the olives below,—as I drove thus in the balmy air, and saw of a sudden a vision of creamy walls and orange roofs, draped in fantastic festoons of roses, with a single curving palm-tree stuck black and

49

feathery against the gold sunset, it is hardly to be wondered at that I should slip into a mood of visionary enjoyment, looking for a time on the whole thing as the misty phantasm of a summer dream.

The Cavaliere had introduced himself to us,—Tom Rendel and me,—one morning soon after we reached Palermo, when, in the first bewilderment of architects in this paradise of art and color, we were working nobly at our sketches in that dream of delight, the Capella Palatina. He was himself an amateur archæologist, he told us, and passionately devoted to his island; so he felt impelled to speak to any one whom he saw appreciating the almost—and in a way fortunately—unknown beauties of Palermo. In a little time we were fully acquainted, and talking like the oldest friends. Of course he knew acquaintances of Rendel's,—some one always does: this time they were officers on the tubby U. S. S. "Quinebaug," that, during the summer of 1888, was trying to uphold the maritime honor of the United States in European waters. Luckily for us, one of the officers was a kind of cousin of Rendel's, and came from Baltimore as well, so, as he had visited at the Cavaliere's place, we were soon invited to do the same. It was in this way that, with the luck that attends Rendel wherever he goes, we came to see something of domestic life in Italy, and that I found myself involved in another of those adventures for which I naturally sought so little.

I wonder if there is any other place in Sicily so faultless as Sta. Catarina? Taormina is a paradise, an epitome of all that is beautiful in Italy,—Venice excepted. Girgenti is a solemn epic, with its golden temples between the sea and hills. Cefalù is wild and strange, and Monreale a vision out of a fairy tale; but Sta. Catarina!—

Fancy a convent of creamy stone and rose-red brick perched on a ledge of rock midway between earth and heaven, the cliff falling almost sheer to the valley two hundred feet and more, the mountain rising behind straight towards the sky; all the rocks covered with cactus and dwarf fig-trees, the convent draped in smothering roses, and in front a terrace with a fountain in the midst; and then—nothing—between you and the sapphire sea, six miles away. Below stretches the Eden valley, the Concha d'Oro, gold-green fig orchards alternating with smoke-blue olives, the mountains rising on either hand and sinking undulously away towards the bay where, like a magic city of ivory and nacre, Palermo lies guarded by the twin mountains, Monte Pellegrino and Capo Zafferano, arid rocks like dull amethysts, rose in sunlight, violet in shadow: lions couchant, guarding the sleeping town.

Seen as we saw it for the first time that hot evening in March, with the golden lambent light pouring down through the valley, making it in verity a "shell of gold," sitting in Indian chairs on the terrace, with the perfume of roses and jasmines all around us, the valley of the Oreto, Palermo, Sta. Catarina, Monreale,—all were but parts of a dreamy vision, like the heavenly city of Sir Percivale, to attain which he passed across the golden bridge that burned after him as he vanished in the intolerable light of the Beatific Vision.

It was all so unreal, so phantasmal, that I was not surprised in the least when, late in the evening after the ladies had gone to their rooms, and the Cavaliere, Tom, and I were stretched out in chairs on the terrace, smoking lazily under the multitudinous stars, the Cavaliere said, "There is something I really must tell you both before you go to bed, so that you may be spared any unnecessary alarm."

"You are going to say that the place is haunted," said Rendel, feeling vaguely on the floor beside him for his glass of Amaro: "thank you; it is all it needs."

The Cavaliere smiled a little: "Yes, that is just it. Sta. Catarina is really haunted; and much as my reason revolts against the idea as superstitious and savoring of priestcraft, yet I must acknowledge I see no way of avoiding the admission. I do not presume to offer any explanations, I only state the fact; and the fact is that to-night one or other of you will, in all human—or unhuman— probability, receive a visit from Sister Maddelena. You need not be in the least afraid, the apparition is perfectly gentle and harmless; and, moreover, having seen it once, you will never see it again. No one sees the ghost, or whatever it is, but once, and that usually the first night he spends in the house. I myself saw the thing eight—

nine years ago, when I first bought the place from the Marchese di
Muxaro; all my people have seen it, nearly all my guests, so I think
you may as well be prepared."

"Then tell us what to expect," I said; "what kind of a ghost is
this nocturnal visitor?"

"It is simple enough. Some time to-night you will suddenly
awake and see before you a Carmelite nun who will look fixedly at
you, say distinctly and very sadly, 'I cannot sleep,' and then van-
ish. That is all, it is hardly worth speaking of, only some people
are terribly frightened if they are visited unwarned by strange
apparitions; so I tell you this that you may be prepared."

"This was a Carmelite convent, then?" I said.

"Yes; it was suppressed after the unification of Italy, and given
to the House of Muxaro; but the family died out, and I bought it.
There is a story about the ghostly nun, who was only a novice, and
even that unwillingly, which gives an interest to an otherwise very
commonplace and uninteresting ghost."

"I beg that you will tell it us," cried Rendel.

"There is a storm coming," I added. "See, the lightning is flashing already up among the mountains at the head of the valley; if
the story is tragic, as it must be, now is just the time for it. You
will tell it, will you not?"

The Cavaliere smiled that slow, cryptic smile of his that was so
unfathomable.

"As you say, there is a shower coming, and as we have fierce
tempests here, we might not sleep; so perhaps we may as well sit
up a little longer, and I will tell you the story."

The air was utterly still, hot and oppressive; the rich, sick odor
of the oranges just bursting into bloom came up from the valley in
a gently rising tide. The sky, thick with stars, seemed mirrored in
the rich foliage below, so numerous were the glow-worms under
the still trees, and the fireflies that gleamed in the hot air. Lightning flashed fitfully from the darkening west; but as yet no thunder broke the heavy silence.

The Cavaliere lighted another cigar, and pulled a cushion under
his head so that he could look down to the distant lights of the
city. "This is the story," he said.

"Once upon a time, late in the last century, the Duca di Castiglione was attached to the court of Charles III., King of the Two Sicilies, down at Palermo. They tell me he was very ambitious, and, not content with marrying his son to one of the ladies of the House of Tuscany, had betrothed his only daughter, Rosalia, to Prince Antonio, a cousin of the king. His whole life was wrapped up in the fame of his family, and he quite forgot all domestic affection in his madness for dynastic glory. His son was a worthy scion, cold and proud; but Rosalia was, according to legend, utterly the reverse,—a passionate, beautiful girl, wilful and headstrong, and careless of her family and the world.

"The time had nearly come for her to marry Prince Antonio, a typical *roué* of the Spanish court, when, through the treachery of a servant, the Duke discovered that his daughter was in love with a young military officer whose name I don't remember, and that an elopement had been planned to take place the next night. The fury and dismay of the old autocrat passed belief; he saw in a flash the downfall of all his hopes of family aggrandizement through union with the royal house, and, knowing well the spirit of his daughter, despaired of ever bringing her to subjection. Nevertheless, he attacked her unmercifully, and, by bullying and threats, by imprisonment, and even bodily chastisement, he tried to break her spirit and bend her to his indomitable will. Through his power at court he had the lover sent away to the mainland, and for more than a year he held his daughter closely imprisoned in his palace on the Toledo,—that one, you may remember, on the right, just beyond the Via del Collegio dei Gesuiti, with the beautiful iron-work grilles at all the windows, and the painted frieze. But nothing could move her, nothing bend her stubborn will; and at last, furious at the girl he could not govern, Castiglione sent her to this convent, then one of the few houses of barefoot Carmelite nuns in Italy. He stipulated that she should take the name of Maddelena, that he should never hear of her again, and that she should be held an absolute prisoner in this conventual castle.

"Rosalia—or Sister Maddelena, as she was now—believed her lover dead, for her father had given her good proofs of this, and she believed him; nevertheless she refused to marry another, and seized upon the convent life as a blessed relief from the tyranny of her maniacal father.

"She lived here for four or five years; her name was forgotten at court and in her father's palace. Rosalia di Castiglione was dead, and only Sister Maddelena lived, a Carmelite nun, in her place.

"In 1798 Ferdinand IV. found himself driven from his throne on the mainland, his kingdom divided, and he himself forced to flee to Sicily. With him came the lover of the dead Rosalia, now high in military honor. He on his part had thought Rosalia dead, and it was only by accident that he found that she still lived, a Carmelite nun. Then began the second act of the romance that until then had been only sadly commonplace, but now became dark and tragic. Michele—Michele Biscari,—that was his name; I remember now—haunted the region of the convent, striving to communicate with Sister Maddelena; and at last, from the cliffs over us, up there among the citrons—you will see by the next flash of lightning—he saw her in the great cloister, recognized her in her white habit, found her the same dark and splendid beauty of six years before, only made more beautiful by her white habit and her rigid life. By and by he found a day when she was alone, and tossed a ring to her as she stood in the midst of the cloister. She looked up, saw him, and from that moment lived only to love him in life as she had loved his memory in the death she had thought had overtaken him.

"With the utmost craft they arranged their plans together. They could not speak, for a word would have aroused the other inmates of the convent. They could make signs only when Sister Maddelena was alone. Michele could throw notes to her from the cliff,—a feat demanding a strong arm, as you will see, if you measure the distance with your eye,—and she could drop replies from the window over the cliff, which he picked up at the bottom. Finally he succeeded in casting into the cloister a coil of light rope. The girl fastened it to the bars of one of the windows, and—so great is the madness of love—Biscari actually climbed the rope from the valley to the window of the cell, a distance of almost two hundred feet, with but three little craggy resting-places in all that height. For nearly a month these nocturnal visits were undiscovered, and Michele had almost completed his arrangements for carrying the girl from Sta. Catarina and away to Spain, when unfortunately one of the sisters, suspecting some mystery, from the changed face of Sister Maddelena, began investigating, and at length discovered the rope neatly coiled up by the nun's window, and hidden under some clinging vines. She instantly told the Mother Superior; and together they watched from a window in the crypt of the chapel,— the only place, as you will see to-morrow, from which one could see the window of Sister Maddelena's cell. They saw the figure of Michele daringly ascending the slim rope; watched hour after hour, the Sister remaining while the Superior went to say the hours in the chapel, at each of which Sister Maddelena was present; and at last, at prime, just as the sun was rising, they saw the figure slip down the rope, watched the rope drawn up and concealed, and knew that Sister Maddelena was in their hands for vengeance and punishment,—a criminal.

"The next day, by the order of the Mother Superior, Sister Maddelena was imprisoned in one of the cells under the chapel, charged with her guilt, and commanded to make full and complete confession. But not a word would she say, although they offered her forgiveness if she would tell the name of her lover. At last the Superior told her that after this fashion would they act the coming night: she herself would be placed in the crypt, tied in front of the window, her mouth gagged; that the rope would be lowered, and the lover allowed to approach even to the sill of her window, and at that moment the rope would be cut, and before her eyes her lover would be dashed to death on the ragged cliffs. The plan was feasible, and Sister Maddelena knew that the Mother was perfectly capable of carrying it out. Her stubborn spirit was broken, and in the only way possible; she begged for mercy, for the sparing of her lover. The Mother Superior was deaf at first; at last she said, 'It is your life or his. I will spare him on condition that you sacrifice your own life.' Sister Maddelena accepted the terms joyfully, wrote a last farewell to Michele, fastened the note to the rope, and with her own hands cut the rope and saw it fall coiling down to the valley bed far below.

"Then she silently prepared for death; and at midnight, while her lover was wandering, mad with the horror of impotent fear, around the white walls of the convent, Sister Maddelena, for love of Michele, gave up her life. How, was never known. That she was indeed dead was only a suspicion, for when Biscari finally compelled the civil authorities to enter the convent, claiming that murder had been done there, they found no sign. Sister Maddelena had been sent to the parent house of the barefoot Carmelites at Avila in Spain, so the Superior stated, because of her incorrigible contumacy. The old Duke of Castiglione refused to stir hand or foot in the matter, and Michele, after fruitless attempts to prove that the Superior of Sta. Catarina had caused the death, was forced to leave Sicily. He sought in Spain for very long; but no sign of the girl was to be found, and at last he died, exhausted with suffering and sorrow.

"Even the name of Sister Maddelena was forgotten, and it was not until the convents were suppressed, and this house came into the hands of the Muxaros, that her story was remembered. It was then that the ghost began to appear; and, an explanation being necessary, the story, or legend, was obtained from one of the nuns who still lived after the suppression. I think the fact—for it is a fact— of the ghost rather goes to prove that Michele was right, and that poor Rosalia gave her life a sacrifice for love,—whether in accordance with the terms of the legend or not, I cannot say. One or the other of you will probably see her to-night. You might ask her for the facts. Well, that is all the story of Sister Maddelena, known in the world as Rosalia di Castiglione. Do you like it?"

"It is admirable," said Rendel, enthusiastically. "But I fancy I should rather look on it simply as a story, and not as a warning of what is going to happen. I don't much fancy real ghosts myself."

"But the poor Sister is quite harmless;" and Valguanera rose, stretching himself. "My servants say she wants a mass said over her, or something of that kind; but I haven't much love for such priestly hocus-pocus,—I beg your pardon" (turning to me), "I had forgotten that you were a Catholic: forgive my rudeness."

"My dear Cavaliere, I beg you not to apologize. I am sorry you cannot see things as I do; but don't for a moment think I am hypersensitive."

"I have an excuse,—perhaps you will say only an explanation; but I live where I see all the absurdities and corruptions of the Church."

"Perhaps you let the accidents blind you to the essentials; but do not let us quarrel to-night,—see, the storm is close on us. Shall we go in?"

The stars were blotted out through nearly all the sky; low, thunderous clouds, massed at the head of the valley, were sweeping over so close that they seemed to brush the black pines on the mountain above us. To the south and east the storm-clouds had shut down almost to the sea, leaving a space of black sky where the moon in its last quarter was rising just to the left of Monte Pellegrino,—a black silhouette against the pallid moonlight. The rosy lightning flashed almost incessantly, and through the fitful darkness came the sound of bells across the valley, the rushing torrent below, and the dull roar of the approaching rain, with a deep organ point of solemn thunder through it all.

We fled indoors from the coming tempest, and taking our candles, said "good-night," and sought each his respective room.

My own was in the southern part of the old convent, giving on the terrace we had just quitted, and about over the main doorway. The rushing storm, as it swept down the valley with the swelling torrent beneath, was very fascinating, and after wrapping myself in a dressing-gown I stood for some time by the deeply embrasured window, watching the blazing lightning and the beating rain whirled by fitful gusts of wind around the spurs of the mountains. Gradually the violence of the shower seemed to decrease, and I threw myself down on my bed in the hot air, wondering if I really was to experience the ghostly visit the Cavaliere so confidently predicted.

I had thought out the whole matter to my own satisfaction, and fancied I knew exactly what I should do, in case Sister Maddelena came to visit me. The story touched me: the thought of the poor faithful girl who sacrificed herself for her lover,—himself, very likely, quite unworthy,—and who now could never sleep for reason of her unquiet soul, sent out into the storm of eternity without spiritual aid or counsel. I could not sleep; for the still vivid lightning, the crowding thoughts of the dead nun, and the shivering anticipation of my possible visitation, made slumber quite out of the question. No suspicion of sleepiness had visited me, when, perhaps an hour after midnight, came a sudden vivid flash of lightning, and, as my dazzled eyes began to regain the power of sight, I saw her as plainly as in life,—a tall figure, shrouded in the white habit of the Carmelites, her head bent, her hands clasped before her. In another flash of lightning she slowly raised her head and looked at me long and earnestly. She was very beautiful, like the Virgin of Beltraffio in the National Gallery,—more beautiful than I had supposed possible, her deep, passionate eyes very tender and pitiful in their pleading, beseeching glance. I hardly think I was frightened, or even startled, but lay looking steadily at her as she stood in the beating lightning.

Then she breathed, rather than articulated, with a voice that almost brought tears, so infinitely sad and sorrowful was it, "I cannot sleep!" and the liquid eyes grew more pitiful and questioning as bright tears fell from them down the pale dark face.

The figure began to move slowly towards the door, its eyes fixed on mine with a look that was weary and almost agonized. I leaped from the bed and stood waiting. A look of utter gratitude swept over the face, and, turning, the figure passed through the doorway.

Out into the shadow of the corridor it moved, like a drift of pallid storm-cloud, and I followed, all natural and instinctive fear or nervousness quite blotted out by the part I felt I was to play in giving rest to a tortured soul. The corridors were velvet black; but the pale figure floated before me always, an unerring guide, now but a thin mist on the utter night, now white and clear in the bluish lightning through some window or doorway.

Down the stairway into the lower hall, across the refectory, where the great frescoed Crucifixion flared into sudden clearness under the fitful lightning, out into the silent cloister.

It was very dark. I stumbled along the heaving bricks, now guiding myself by a hand on the whitewashed wall, now by a touch on a column wet with the storm. From all the eaves the rain was dripping on to the pebbles at the foot of the arcade: a pigeon, startled from the capital where it was sleeping, beat its way into the cloister close. Still the white thing drifted before me to the farther side of the court, then along the cloister at right angles, and paused before one of the many doorways that led to the cells.

A sudden blaze of fierce lightning, the last now of the fleeting trail of storm, leaped around us, and in the vivid light I saw the white face turned again with the look of overwhelming desire, of beseeching pathos, that had choked my throat with an involuntary sob when first I saw Sister Maddelena. In the brief interval that ensued after the flash, and before the roaring thunder burst like the crash of battle over the trembling convent, I heard again the sorrowful words, "I cannot sleep," come from the impenetrable darkness. And when the lightning came again, the white figure was gone.

I wandered around the courtyard, searching in vain for Sister Maddelena, even until the moonlight broke through the torn and sweeping fringes of the storm. I tried the door where the white figure vanished: it was locked; but I had found what I sought, and, carefully noting its location, went back to my room, but not to sleep.

In the morning the Cavaliere asked Rendel and me which of us had seen the ghost, and I told him my story; then I asked him to grant me permission to sift the thing to the bottom; and he courteously gave the whole matter into my charge, promising that he would consent to anything.

I could hardly wait to finish breakfast; but no sooner was this done than, forgetting my morning pipe, I started with Rendel and the Cavaliere to investigate.

"I am sure there is nothing in that cell," said Valguanera, when we came in front of the door I had marked. "It is curious that you should have chosen the door of the very cell that tradition assigns to Sister Maddelena; but I have often examined that room myself, and I am sure that there is no chance for anything to be concealed. In fact, I had the floor taken up once, soon after I came here, knowing the room was that of the mysterious Sister, and thinking that there, if anywhere, the monastic crime would have taken place; still, we will go in, if you like."

He unlocked the door, and we entered, one of us, at all events, with a beating heart. The cell was very small, hardly eight feet square. There certainly seemed no opportunity for concealing a body in the tiny place; and although I sounded the floor and walls, all gave a solid, heavy answer,—the unmistakable sound of masonry.

For the innocence of the floor the Cavaliere answered. He had, he said, had it all removed, even to the curving surfaces of the vault below; yet somewhere in this room the body of the murdered girl was concealed,—of this I was certain. But where? There seemed no answer; and I was compelled to give up the search for the moment, somewhat to the amusement of Valguanera, who had watched curiously to see if I could solve the mystery.

But I could not forget the subject, and towards noon started on another tour of investigation. I procured the keys from the Cavaliere, and examined the cells adjoining; they were apparently the same, each with its window opposite the door, and nothing— Stay, were they the same? I hastened into the suspected cell; it was as I thought: this cell, being on the corner, could have had two windows, yet only one was visible, and that to the left, at right angles with the doorway. Was it imagination? As I sounded the wall opposite the door, where the other window should be, I fancied that the sound was a trifle less solid and dull. I was becoming excited. I dashed back to the cell on the right, and, forcing open the little window, thrust my head out.

It was found at last! In the smooth surface of the yellow wall was a rough space, following approximately the shape of the other cell windows, not plastered like the rest of the wall, but showing the shapes of bricks through its thick coatings of whitewash. I turned with a gasp of excitement and satisfaction: yes, the embrasure of the wall was deep enough; what a wall it was!—four feet at least, and the opening of the window reached to the floor, though the window itself was hardly three feet square. I felt absolutely certain that the secret was solved, and called the Cavaliere and Rendel, too excited to give them an explanation of my theories.

They must have thought me mad when I suddenly began scraping away at the solid wall in front of the door; but in a few minutes they understood what I was about, for under the coatings of paint and plaster appeared the original bricks; and as my architectural knowledge had led me rightly, the space I had cleared was directly over a vertical joint between firm, workmanlike masonry on one hand, and rough amateurish work on the other, bricks laid anyway, and without order or science.

Rendel seized a pick, and was about to assail the rude wall, when I stopped him.

"Let us be careful," I said; "who knows what we may find?" So we set to work digging out the mortar around a brick at about the level of our eyes.

How hard the mortar had become! But a brick yielded at last, and with trembling fingers I detached it. Darkness within, yet beyond question there was a cavity there, not a solid wall; and with infinite care we removed another brick. Still the hole was too small to admit enough light from the dimly illuminated cell. With a chisel we pried at the sides of a large block of masonry, perhaps eight bricks in size. It moved, and we softly slid it from its bed.

Valguanera, who was standing watching us as we lowered the bricks to the floor, gave a sudden cry, a cry like that of a frightened woman,—terrible, coming from him. Yet there was cause.

Framed by the ragged opening of the bricks, hardly seen in the dim light, was a face, an ivory image, more beautiful than any antique bust, but drawn and distorted by unspeakable agony: the lovely mouth half open, as though gasping for breath; the eyes cast upward; and below, slim chiselled hands crossed on the breast, but clutching the folds of the white Carmelite habit, torture and

agony visible in every tense muscle, fighting against the determination of the rigid pose.

We stood there breathless, staring at the pitiful sight, fascinated, bewitched. So this was the secret. With fiendish ingenuity,
the rigid ecclesiastics had blocked up the window, then forced the
beautiful creature to stand in the alcove, while with remorseless
hands and iron hearts they had shut her into a living tomb. I had
read of such things in romance; but to find the verity here, before
my eyes—

Steps came down the cloister, and with a simultaneous thought
we sprang to the door and closed it behind us. The room was
sacred; that awful sight was not for curious eyes. The gardener was
coming to ask some trivial question of Valguanera. The Cavaliere
cut him short. "Pietro, go down to Parco and ask Padre Stefano to
come here at once." (I thanked him with a glance.) "Stay!" He
turned to me: "Signore, it is already two o'clock and too late for
mass, is it not?"

I nodded.

Valguanera thought a moment, then he said, "Bring two horses;
the Signor Americano will go with you,—do you understand?" Then,
turning to me, "You will go, will you not? I think you can explain
matters to Padre Stefano better than I."

"Of course I will go, more than gladly." So it happened that
after a hasty luncheon I wound down the mountain to Parco, found
Padre Stefano, explained my errand to him, found him intensely
eager and sympathetic, and by five o'clock had him back at the
convent with all that was necessary for the resting of the soul of
the dead girl.

In the warm twilight, with the last light of the sunset pouring
into the little cell through the window where almost a century ago
Rosalia had for the last time said farewell to her lover, we gathered together to speed her tortured soul on its journey, so long
delayed. Nothing was omitted; all the needful offices of the Church
were said by Padre Stefano, while the light in the window died
away, and the flickering flames of the candles carried by two of
the acolytes from San Francesco threw fitful flashes of pallid light

into the dark recess where the white face had prayed to Heaven for a hundred years.

Finally, the Padre took the asperge from the hands of one of the acolytes, and with a sign of the cross in benediction while he chanted the *Asperges*, gently sprinkled the holy water on the up-turned face. Instantly the whole vision crumbled to dust, the face was gone, and where once the candlelight had flickered on the perfect semblance of the girl dead so very long, it now fell only on the rough bricks which closed the window, bricks laid with frozen hearts by pitiless hands.

But our task was not done yet. It had been arranged that Padre Stefano should remain at the convent all night, and that as soon as midnight made it possible he should say the first mass for the repose of the girl's soul. We sat on the terrace talking over the strange events of the last crowded hours, and I noted with satisfaction that the Cavaliere no longer spoke of the Church with that hardness, which had hurt me so often. It is true that the Padre was with us nearly all the time; but not only was Valguanera courteous, he was almost sympathetic; and I wondered if it might not prove that more than one soul benefited by the untoward events of the day.

With the aid of the astonished and delighted servants, and no little help as well from Signora Valguanera, I fitted up the long cold Altar in the chapel, and by midnight we had the gloomy sanctuary beautiful with flowers and candles. It was a curiously solemn service, in the first hour of the new day, in the midst of blazing candles and the thick incense, the odor of the opening orange-blooms drifting up in the fresh morning air, and mingling with the incense smoke and the perfume of flowers within. Many prayers were said that night for the soul of the dead girl, and I think many afterwards; for after the benediction I remained for a little time in my place, and when I rose from my knees and went towards the chapel door, I saw a figure kneeling still, and, with a start, recognized the form of the Cavaliere. I smiled with quiet satisfaction and gratitude, and went away softly, content with the chain of events that now seemed finished.

The next day the alcove was again walled up, for the precious dust could not be gathered together for transportation to consecrated ground; so I went down to the little cemetery at Parco for a basket of earth, which we cast in over the ashes of Sister Maddelena.

By and by, when Rendel and I went away, with great regret, Valguanera came down to Palermo with us; and the last act that we performed in Sicily was assisting him to order a tablet of marble, whereon was carved this simple inscription:—

HERE LIES THE BODY OF
ROSALIA DI CASTIGLIONI,
CALLED
SISTER MADDELENA.
HER SOUL
IS WITH HIM WHO GAVE IT.

To this I added in thought:—
"Let him that is without sin among you cast the first stone."

Notre Dame des Eaux

West of St. Pol de Leon, on the sea-cliffs of Finisterre, stands the ancient church of Notre Dame des Eaux. Five centuries of beating winds and sweeping rains have moulded its angles, and worn its carvings and sculpture down to the very semblance of the ragged cliffs themselves, until even the Breton fisherman, looking lovingly from his boat as he makes for the harbor of Morlaix, hardly can say where the crags end, and where the church begins. The teeth of the winds of the sea have devoured, bit by bit, the fine sculpture of the doorway and the thin cusps of the window tracery; gray moss creeps caressingly over the worn walls in ineffectual protection; gentle vines, turned crabbed by the harsh beating of the fierce winds, clutch the crumbling buttresses, climb up over the sinking roof, reach in even at the louvres of the belfry, holding the little sanctuary safe in desperate arms against the savage warfare of the sea and sky.

Many a time you may follow the rocky highway from St. Pol even around the last land of France, and so to Brest, yet never see sign of Notre Dame des Eaux; for it clings to a cliff somewhat lower than the road, and between grows a stunted thicket of harsh and ragged trees, their skeleton white branches, tortured and contorted, thrusting sorrowfully out of the hard, dark foliage that still grows below, where the rise of land below the highway gives some protection. You must leave the wood by the two cottages of yellow stone, about twenty miles beyond St. Pol, and go down to the right, around the old stone quarry; then, bearing to the left by the little cliff path, you will, in a moment, see the pointed roof of the tower of Notre Dame, and, later, come down to the side porch among the crosses of the arid little graveyard.

It is worth the walk, for though the church has outwardly little but its sad picturesqueness to repay the artist, within it is a dream and a delight. A Norman nave of round, red stone piers and arches, a delicate choir of the richest flamboyant, a High Altar of the time of Francis I., form only the mellow background and frame for carven tombs and dark old pictures, hanging lamps of iron and brass, and black, heavily carved choir-stalls of the Renaissance.

So has the little church lain unnoticed for many centuries; for the horrors and follies of the Revolution have never come near, and the hardy and faithful people of Finisterre have feared God and loved Our Lady too well to harm her church. For many years it was the church of the Comtes de Jarleuc; and these are their tombs that mellow year by year under the warm light of the painted windows, given long ago by Comte Robert de Jarleuc, when the heir of Poullaouen came safely to shore in the harbor of Morlaix, having escaped from the Isle of Wight, where he had lain captive after the awful defeat of the fleet of Charles of Valois at Sluys. And now the heir of Poullaouen lies in a carven tomb, forgetful of the world where he fought so nobly: the dynasty he fought to establish, only a memory; the family he made glorious, a name; the Château Poullaouen a single crag of riven masonry in the fields of M. du Bois, mayor of Morlaix.

It was Julien, Comte de Bergerac, who rediscovered Notre Dame des Eaux, and by his picture of its dreamy interior in the Salon of '86 brought once more into notice this forgotten corner of the world. The next year a party of painters settled themselves near by, roughing it as best they could, and in the year following, Mme. de Bergerac and her daughter Héloïse came with Julien, and, buying the old farm of Pontivy, on the highway over Notre Dame, turned it into a summer house that almost made amends for their lost château on the Dordogne, stolen from them as virulent Royalists by the triumphant Republic in 1794.

Little by little a summer colony of painters gathered around Pontivy, and it was not until the spring of 1890 that the peace of the colony was broken. It was a sorrowful tragedy. Jean d'Yriex, the youngest and merriest devil of all the jolly crew, became suddenly moody and morose. At first this was attributed to his undisguised admiration for Mlle. Héloïse, and was looked on as one of the vagaries of boyish passion; but one day, while riding with M. de Bergerac, he suddenly seized the bridle of Julien's horse, wrenched it from his hand, and, turning his own horse's head towards the cliffs, lashed the terrified animals into a gallop straight towards the brink. He was only thwarted in his mad object by Julien, who with a quick blow sent him headlong in the dry grass, and reined in the terrified animals hardly a yard from the cliffs. When this happened, and no word of explanation was granted, only a sullen silence that lasted for days, it became clear that poor Jean's brain was wrong in some way. Héloïse devoted herself to him with infinite patience,—though she felt no special affection for him, only pity,—and while he was with her he seemed sane and quiet. But at night some strange mania took possession of him. If he had worked on his Prix de Rome picture in the daytime, while Héloïse sat by him, reading aloud or singing a little, no matter how good the work, it would have vanished in the morning, and he would again begin, only to erase his labor during the night.

At last his growing insanity reached its climax; and one day in Notre Dame, when he had painted better than usual, he suddenly stopped, seized a palette knife, and slashed the great canvas in strips. Héloïse sprang forward to stop him, and in crazy fury he turned on her, striking at her throat with the palette knife. The thin steel snapped, and the white throat showed only a scarlet scratch. Héloïse, without that ordinary terror that would crush most women, grasped the thin wrists of the madman, and, though he could easily have wrenched his hands away, d'Yriex sank on his knees in a passion of tears. He shut himself in his room at Pontivy, refusing to see any one, walking for hours up and down, fighting against growing madness. Soon Dr. Charpentier came from Paris,

summoned by Mme. de Bergerac; and after one short, forced
interview, left at once for Paris, taking M. d'Yriex with him.

A few days later came a letter for Mme. de Bergerac, in which
Dr. Charpentier confessed that Jean had disappeared, that he had
allowed him too much liberty, owing to his apparent calmness, and
that when the train stopped at Le Mans he had slipped from him
and utterly vanished.

During the summer, word came occasionally that no trace had
been found of the unhappy man, and at last the Pontivy colony
realized that the merry boy was dead. Had he lived he *must* have
been found, for the exertions of the police were perfect; yet not
the slightest trace was discovered, and his lamentable death was
acknowledged, not only by Mme. de Bergerac and Jean's family,—
sorrowing for the death of their first-born, away in the warm hills
of Lozère,—but by Dr. Charpentier as well.

So the summer passed, and the autumn came, and at last the
cold rains of November—the skirmish line of the advancing army
of winter—drove the colony back to Paris.

It was the last day at Pontivy, and Mlle. Héloïse had come down
to Notre Dame for a last look at the beautiful shrine, a last prayer
for the repose of the tortured soul of poor Jean d'Yriex. The rains
had ceased for a time, and a warm stillness lay over the cliffs and
on the creeping sea, swaying and lapping around the ragged shore.
Héloïse knelt very long before the Altar of Our Lady of the Waters;
and when she finally rose, could not bring herself to leave as yet
that place of sorrowful beauty, all warm and golden with the last
light of the declining sun. She watched the old verger, Pierre Polou,
stumping softly around the darkening building, and spoke to him
once, asking the hour; but he was very deaf, as well as nearly blind,
and he did not answer.

So she sat in the corner of the aisle by the Altar of Our Lady of
the Waters, watching the checkered light fade in the advancing
shadows, dreaming sad day-dreams of the dead summer, until the
day-dreams merged in night-dreams, and she fell asleep.

Then the last light of the early sunset died in the gleaming quar-
ries of the west window; Pierre Polou stumbled uncertainly through

the dusky shadow, locked the sagging doors of the mouldering south porch, and took his way among the leaning crosses up to the highway and his little cottage, a good mile away,—the nearest house to the lonely Church of Notre Dame des Eaux.

With the setting of the sun great clouds rose swiftly from the sea; the wind freshened, and the gaunt branches of the weather-worn trees in the churchyard lashed themselves beseechingly before the coming storm. The tide turned, and the waters at the foot of the rocks swept uneasily up the narrow beach and caught at the weary cliffs, their sobbing growing and deepening to a threatening, solemn roar. Whirls of dead leaves rose in the churchyard, and threw themselves against the blank windows. The winter and the night came down together.

Héloïse awoke, bewildered and wondering; in a moment she realized the situation, and without fear or uneasiness. There was nothing to dread in Notre Dame by night; the ghosts, if there were ghosts, would not trouble her, and the doors were securely locked. It was foolish of her to fall asleep, and her mother would be most uneasy at Pontivy if she realized before dawn that Héloïse had not returned. On the other hand, she was in the habit of wandering off to walk after dinner, often not coming home until late, so it was quite possible that she might return before Madame knew of her absence, for Polou came always to unlock the church for the low mass at six o'clock; so she arose from her cramped position in the aisle, and walked slowly up to the choir-rail, entered the chancel, and felt her way to one of the stalls, on the south side, where there were cushions and an easy back.

It was really very beautiful in Notre Dame by night; she had never suspected how strange and solemn the little church could be when the moon shone fitfully through the south windows, now bright and clear, now blotted out by sweeping clouds. The nave was barred with the long shadows of the heavy pillars, and when the moon came out she could see far down almost to the west end. How still it was! Only a soft low murmur without of the restless limbs of the trees, and of the creeping sea.

It was very soothing, almost like a song; and Héloïse felt sleep coming back to her as the clouds shut out the moon, and all the church grew black.

She was drifting off into the last delicious moment of vanishing consciousness, when she suddenly came fully awake, with a shock that made every nerve tingle. In the midst of the far faint sounds of the tempestuous night she had heard a footstep! Yet the church was utterly empty, she was sure. And again! A footstep dragging and uncertain, stealthy and cautious, but an unmistakable step, away in the blackest shadow at the end of the church.

She sat up, frozen with the fear that comes at night and that is overwhelming, her hands clutching the coarse carving of the arms of the stall, staring down into the dark.

Again the footstep, and again,—slow, measured, one after another at intervals of perhaps half a minute, growing a little louder each time, a little nearer.

Would the darkness never be broken? Would the cloud never pass? Minute after minute went like weary hours, and still the moon was hid, still the dead branches rattled clatteringly on the high windows. Unconsciously she moved, as under a magician's spell, down to the choir-rail, straining her eyes to pierce the thick night. And the step, it was very near! Ah, the moon at last! A white ray fell through the westernmost window, painting a bar of light on the floor of sagging stone. Then a second bar, then a third, and a fourth, and for a moment Héloïse could have cried out with relief, for nothing broke the lines of light,—no figure, no shadow. In another moment came a step, and from the shadow of the last column appeared in the pallid moonlight the figure of a man. The girl stared breathless, the moonlight falling on her as she stood rigid against the low parapet. Another step and another, and she saw before her—was it ghost or living man?—a white mad face staring from matted hair and beard, a tall thin figure half clothed in rags, limping as it stepped towards her with wounded feet. From the dead face stared mad eyes that gleamed like the eyes of a cat, fixed on hers with insane persistence, holding her, fascinating her as a cat fascinates a bird.

One more step,—it was close before her now! those awful, luminous eyes dilating and contracting in awful palpitations. And the moon was going out; the shadows swept one by one over the windows; she stared at the moonlit face for a last fascinated glance— Mother of God! it was— The shadow swept over them, and now only remained the blazing eyes and the dim outline of a form that crouched waveringly before her as a cat crouches, drawing its vibrating body together for the spring that blots out the life of the victim.

In another instant the mad thing would leap; but just as the quiver swept over the crouching body, Héloïse gathered all her strength into one action of desperate terror.

"Jean, stop!"

The thing crouched before her paused, chattering softly to itself; then it articulated dryly, and with all the trouble of a learning child, the one word, "*Chantez!*"

Without a thought, Héloïse sang; it was the first thing that she remembered, an old Provençal song that d'Yriex had always loved. While she sang, the poor mad creature lay huddled at her feet, separated from her only by the choir parapet, its dilating, contracting eyes never moving for an instant. As the song died away, came again that awful tremor, indicative of the coming death-spring, and again she sang,—this time the old *Pange lingua*, its sonorous Latin sounding in the deserted church like the voice of dead centuries.

And so she sang, on and on, hour after hour,—hymns and *chansons*, folk-songs and bits from comic operas, songs of the boulevards alternating with the *Tantum ergo* and the *O Filii et Filiæ*. It mattered little what she sang. At last it seemed to her that it mattered little whether she sang or no; for her brain whirled round and round like a dizzy maelstrom, her icy hands, griping the hard rail, alone supported her dying body. She could hear no sound of her song; her body was numb, her mouth parched, her lips cracked and bleeding; she felt the drops of blood fall from her chin. And still she sang, with the yellow palpitating eyes holding her as in a vice. If only she could continue until dawn! It must be dawn so soon! The windows were growing gray, the rain lashed outside, she could distinguish the features of the horror before her; but the night of death was growing with the coming day, blackness swept down upon her; she could sing no more, her tortured lips made one last effort to form the words, "Mother of God, save me!" and night and death came down like a crushing wave.

But her prayer was heard; the dawn had come, and Polou unlocked the porch-door for Father Augustin just in time to hear the last agonized cry. The maniac turned in the very act of leaping on his victim, and sprang for the two men, who stopped in dumb amazement. Poor old Pierre Polou went down at a blow; but Father Augustin was young and fearless, and he grappled the mad animal with all his strength and will. It would have gone ill even with him,—for no one can stand against the bestial fury of a man in whom reason is dead,—had not some sudden impulse seized the maniac, who pitched the priest aside with a single movement, and, leaping through the door, vanished forever.

Did he hurl himself from the cliffs in the cold wet morning, or was he doomed to wander, a wild beast, until, captured, he beat himself in vain against the walls of some asylum, an unknown pauper lunatic? None ever knew.

The colony at Pontivy was blotted out by the dreary tragedy, and Notre Dame des Eaux sank once more into silence and solitude. Once a year Father Augustin said mass for the repose of the soul of Jean d'Yriex; but no other memory remained of the horror that blighted the lives of an innocent girl and of a gray-haired mother mourning for her dead boy in far Lozère.

THE DEAD VALLEY

I have a friend, Olof Ehrensvärd, a Swede by birth, who yet, by reason of a strange and melancholy mischance of his early boyhood, has thrown his lot with that of the New World. It is a curious story of a headstrong boy and a proud and relentless family: the details do not matter here, but they are sufficient to weave a web of romance around the tall yellow-bearded man with the sad eyes and the voice that gives itself perfectly to plaintive little Swedish songs remembered out of childhood. In the winter evenings we play chess together, he and I, and after some close, fierce battle has been fought to a finish—usually with my own defeat—we fill our pipes again, and Ehrensvärd tells me stories of the far, half-remembered days in the fatherland, before he went to sea: stories that grow very strange and incredible as the night deepens and the fire falls together, but stories that, nevertheless, I fully believe.

One of them made a strong impression on me, so I set it down here, only regretting that I cannot reproduce the curiously perfect English and the delicate accent which to me increased the fascination of the tale. Yet, as best I can remember it, here it is.

"I never told you how Nils and I went over the hills to Hallsberg, and how we found the Dead Valley, did I? Well, this is the way it happened. I must have been about twelve years old, and Nils Sjöberg, whose father's estate joined ours, was a few months younger. We were inseparable just at that time, and whatever we did, we did together.

73

"Once a week it was market day in Engelholm, and Nils and I went always there to see the strange sights that the market gathered from all the surrounding country. One day we quite lost our hearts, for an old man from across the Elfborg had brought a little dog to sell, that seemed to us the most beautiful dog in all the world. He was a round, woolly puppy, so funny that Nils and I sat down on the ground and laughed at him, until he came and played with us in so jolly a way that we felt that there was only one really desirable thing in life, and that was the little dog of the old man from across the hills. But alas! we had not half money enough wherewith to buy him, so we were forced to beg the old man not to sell him before the next market day, promising that we would bring the money for him then. He gave us his word, and we ran home very fast and implored our mothers to give us money for the little dog.

"We got the money, but we could not wait for the next market day. Suppose the puppy should be sold! The thought frightened us so that we begged and implored that we might be allowed to go over the hills to Hallsberg where the old man lived, and get the little dog ourselves, and at last they told us we might go. By starting early in the morning we should reach Hallsberg by three o'clock, and it was arranged that we should stay there that night with Nils's aunt, and, leaving by noon the next day, be home again by sunset.

"Soon after sunrise we were on our way, after having received minute instructions as to just what we should do in all possible and impossible circumstances, and finally a repeated injunction that we should start for home at the same hour the next day, so that we might get safely back before nightfall.

"For us, it was magnificent sport, and we started off with our rifles, full of the sense of our very great importance: yet the journey was simple enough, along a good road, across the big hills we knew so well, for Nils and I had shot over half the territory this side of the dividing ridge of the Elfborg. Back of Engelholm lay a long valley, from which rose the low mountains, and we had to cross this, and then follow the road along the side of the hills for three or four miles, before a narrow path branched off to the left, leading up through the pass.

"Nothing occurred of interest on the way over, and we reached Hallsberg in due season, found to our inexpressible joy that the little dog was not sold, secured him, and so went to the house of Nils's aunt to spend the night.

"Why we did not leave early on the following day, I can't quite remember; at all events, I know we stopped at a shooting range just outside of the town, where most attractive pasteboard pigs were sliding slowly through painted foliage, serving so as beautiful marks. The result was that we did not get fairly started for home until afternoon, and as we found ourselves at last pushing up the side of the mountain with the sun dangerously near their summits, I think we were a little scared at the prospect of the examination and possible punishment that awaited us when we got home at midnight.

"Therefore we hurried as fast as possible up the mountain side, while the blue dusk closed in about us, and the light died in the purple sky. At first we had talked hilariously, and the little dog had leaped ahead of us with the utmost joy. Latterly, however, a curious oppression came on us; we did not speak or even whistle, while the dog fell behind, following us with hesitation in every muscle.

"We had passed through the foothills and the low spurs of the mountains, and were almost at the top of the main range, when life seemed to go out of everything, leaving the world dead, so suddenly silent the forest became, so stagnant the air. Instinctively we halted to listen.

"Perfect silence,—the crushing silence of deep forests at night; and more, for always, even in the most impenetrable fastnesses of the wooded mountains, is the multitudinous murmur of little lives, awakened by the darkness, exaggerated and intensified by the stillness of the air and the great dark: but here and now the silence seemed unbroken even by the turn of a leaf, the movement of a twig, the note of night bird or insect. I could hear the blood beat through my veins; and the crushing of the grass under our feet as we advanced with hesitating steps sounded like the falling of trees.

"And the air was stagnant,—dead. The atmosphere seemed to lie upon the body like the weight of sea on a diver who has ventured too far into its awful depths. What we usually call silence seems so only in relation to the din of ordinary experience. This was silence in the absolute, and it crushed the mind while it intensified the senses, bringing down the awful weight of inextinguishable fear.

"I know that Nils and I stared towards each other in abject terror, listening to our quick, heavy breathing, that sounded to our acute senses like the fitful rush of waters. And the poor little dog we were leading justified our terror. The black oppression seemed to crush him even as it did us. He lay close on the ground, moaning feebly, and dragging himself painfully and slowly closer to Nils's feet. I think this exhibition of utter animal fear was the last touch, and must inevitably have blasted our reason—mine anyway; but just then, as we stood quaking on the bounds of madness, came a sound, so awful, so ghastly, so horrible, that it seemed to rouse us from the dead spell that was on us.

"In the depth of the silence came a cry, beginning as a low, sorrowful moan, rising to a tremulous shriek, culminating in a yell that seemed to tear the night in sunder and rend the world as by a cataclysm. So fearful was it that I could not believe it had actual existence: it passed previous experience, the powers of belief, and for a moment I thought it the result of my own animal terror, an hallucination born of tottering reason.

"A glance at Nils dispelled this thought in a flash. In the pale light of the high stars he was the embodiment of all possible human fear, quaking with an ague, his jaw fallen, his tongue out, his eyes protruding like those of a hanged man. Without a word we fled, the panic of fear giving us strength, and together, the little dog caught close in Nils's arms, we sped down the side of the cursed mountains,—anywhere, goal was of no account: we had but one impulse—to get away from that place.

"So under the black trees and the far white stars that flashed through the still leaves overhead, we leaped down the mountain side, regardless of path or landmark, straight through the tangled underbrush, across mountain streams, through fens and copses, anywhere, so only that our course was downward.

"How long we ran thus, I have no idea, but by and by the forest fell behind, and we found ourselves among the foothills, and fell exhausted on the dry short grass, panting like tired dogs.

"It was lighter here in the open, and presently we looked around to see where we were, and how we were to strike out in order to find the path that would lead us home. We looked in vain for a familiar sign. Behind us rose the great wall of black forest on the flank of the mountain: before us lay the undulating mounds of low foothills, unbroken by trees or rocks, and beyond, only the fall of black sky bright with multitudinous stars that turned its velvet depth to a luminous gray.

"As I remember, we did not speak to each other once: the terror was too heavy on us for that, but by and by we rose simultaneously and started out across the hills.

"Still the same silence, the same dead, motionless air—air that was at once sultry and chilling: a heavy heat struck through with an icy chill that felt almost like the burning of frozen steel. Still carrying the helpless dog, Nils pressed on through the hills, and I followed close behind. At last, in front of us, rose a slope of moor touching the white stars. We climbed it wearily, reached the top, and found ourselves gazing down into a great, smooth valley, filled half way to the brim with—what?

"As far as the eye could see stretched a level plain of ashy white, faintly phosphorescent, a sea of velvet fog that lay like motionless water, or rather like a floor of alabaster, so dense did it appear, so seemingly capable of sustaining weight. If it were possible, I think that sea of dead white mist struck even greater terror into my soul than the heavy silence or the deadly cry—so ominous was it, so utterly unreal, so phantasmal, so impossible, as it lay there like a dead ocean under the steady stars. Yet through that mist *we must go*! there seemed no other way home, and, shattered with abject fear, mad with the one desire to get back, we started down the slope to where the sea of milky mist ceased, sharp and distinct around the stems of the rough grass.

"I put one foot into the ghostly fog. A chill as of death struck through me, stopping my heart, and I threw myself backward on the slope. At that instant came again the shriek, close, close, right in our ears, in ourselves, and far out across that damnable sea I saw the cold fog lift like a water-spout and toss itself high in writhing convolutions towards the sky. The stars began to grow dim as thick vapor swept across them, and in the growing dark I saw a great, watery moon lift itself slowly above the palpitating sea, vast and vague in the gathering mist.

"This was enough: we turned and fled along the margin of the white sea that throbbed now with fitful motion below us, rising, rising, slowly and steadily, driving us higher and higher up the side of the foothills.

"It was a race for life; that we knew. How we kept it up I cannot understand, but we did, and at last we saw the white sea fall behind us as we staggered up the end of the valley, and then down into a region that we knew, and so into the old path. The last thing I remember was hearing a strange voice, that of Nils, but horribly changed, stammer brokenly, 'The dog is dead!' and then the whole world turned around twice, slowly and resistlessly, and consciousness went out with a crash.

"It was some three weeks later, as I remember, that I awoke in my own room, and found my mother sitting beside the bed. I could not think very well at first, but as I slowly grew strong again, vague flashes of recollection began to come to me, and little by little the whole sequence of events of that awful night in the Dead Valley came back. All that I could gain from what was told me was that three weeks before I had been found in my own bed, raging sick, and that my illness grew fast into brain fever. I tried to speak of the dread things that had happened to me, but I saw at once that no one looked on them save as the hauntings of a dying frenzy, and so I closed my mouth and kept my own counsel.

"I must see Nils, however, and so I asked for him. My mother told me that he also had been ill with a strange fever, but that he was now quite well again. Presently they brought him in, and when we were alone I began to speak to him of the night on the mountain. I shall never forget the shock that struck me down on my pillow when the boy denied everything: denied having gone with me, ever having heard the cry, having seen the valley, or feeling the deadly chill of the ghostly fog. Nothing would shake his determined ignorance, and in spite of myself I was forced to admit that his denials came from no policy of concealment, but from blank oblivion.

"My weakened brain was in a turmoil. Was it all but the floating phantasm of delirium? Or had the horror of the real thing blotted Nils's mind into blankness so far as the events of the night in the Dead Valley were concerned? The latter explanation seemed the only one, else how explain the sudden illness which in a night had struck us both down? I said nothing more, either to Nils or to my own people, but waited, with a growing determination that, once well again, I would find that valley if it really existed.

"It was some weeks before I was really well enough to go, but finally, late in September, I chose a bright, warm, still day, the last smile of the dying summer, and started early in the morning along the path that led to Hallsberg. I was sure I knew where the trail struck off to the right, down which we had come from the valley of dead water, for a great tree grew by the Hallsberg path at the point where, with a sense of salvation, we had found the home road. Presently I saw it to the right, a little distance ahead.

"I think the bright sunlight and the clear air had worked as a tonic to me, for by the time I came to the foot of the great pine, I had quite lost faith in the verity of the vision that haunted me, believing at last that it was indeed but the nightmare of madness. Nevertheless, I turned sharply to the right, at the base of the tree, into a narrow path that led through a dense thicket. As I did so I tripped over something. A swarm of flies sung into the air around me, and looking down I saw the matted fleece, with the poor little bones thrusting through, of the dog we had bought in Hallsberg.

"Then my courage went out with a puff, and I knew that it all was true, and that now I was frightened. Pride and the desire for adventure urged me on, however, and I pressed into the close

thicket that barred my way. The path was hardly visible: merely
the worn road of some small beasts, for, though it showed in the
crisp grass, the bushes above grew thick and hardly penetrable.
The land rose slowly, and rising grew clearer, until at last I came
out on a great slope of hill, unbroken by trees or shrubs, very like
my memory of that rise of land we had topped in order that we
might find the dead valley and the icy fog. I looked at the sun; it
was bright and clear, and all around insects were humming in the
autumn air, and birds were darting to and fro. Surely there was no
danger, not until nightfall at least; so I began to whistle, and with
a rush mounted the last crest of brown hill.

"There lay the Dead Valley! A great oval basin, almost as smooth
and regular as though made by man. On all sides the grass crept
over the brink of the encircling hills, dusty green on the crests,
then fading into ashy brown, and so to a deadly white, this last
color forming a thin ring, running in a long line around the slope.
And then? Nothing. Bare, brown, hard earth, glittering with grains
of alkali, but otherwise dead and barren. Not a tuft of grass, not a
stick of brushwood, not even a stone, but only the vast expanse of
beaten clay.

"In the midst of the basin, perhaps a mile and a half away, the
level expanse was broken by a great dead tree, rising leafless and
gaunt into the air. Without a moment's hesitation I started down
into the valley and made for this goal. Every particle of fear seemed
to have left me, and even the valley itself did not look so very terrifying. At all events, I was driven by an overwhelming curiosity,
and there seemed to be but one thing in the world to do,—to get to
that Tree! As I trudged along over the hard earth, I noticed that
the multitudinous voices of birds and insects had died away. No
bee or butterfly hovered through the air, no insects leaped or crept
over the dull earth. The very air itself was stagnant.

"As I drew near the skeleton tree, I noticed the glint of sunlight on a kind of white mound around its roots, and I wondered
curiously. It was not until I had come close that I saw its nature.

"All around the roots and barkless trunk was heaped a wilderness of little bones. Tiny skulls of rodents and of birds, thousands

of them, rising about the dead tree and streaming off for several yards in all directions, until the dreadful pile ended in isolated skulls and scattered skeletons. Here and there a larger bone appeared,—the thigh of a sheep, the hoofs of a horse, and to one side, grinning slowly, a human skull.

"I stood quite still, staring with all my eyes, when suddenly the dense silence was broken by a faint, forlorn cry high over my head. I looked up and saw a great falcon turning and sailing downward just over the tree. In a moment more she fell motionless on the bleaching bones.

"Horror struck me, and I rushed for home, my brain whirling, a strange numbness growing in me. I ran steadily, on and on. At last I glanced up. Where was the rise of hill? I looked around wildly. Close before me was the dead tree with its pile of bones. I had circled it round and round, and the valley wall was still a mile and a half away.

"I stood dazed and frozen. The sun was sinking, red and dull, towards the line of hills. In the east the dark was growing fast. Was there still time? *Time!* It was not *that* I wanted, it was *will!* My feet seemed clogged as in a nightmare. I could hardly drag them over the barren earth. And then I felt the slow chill creeping through me. I looked down. Out of the earth a thin mist was rising, collecting in little pools that grew ever larger until they joined here and there, their currents swirling slowly like thin blue smoke. The western hills halved the copper sun. When it was dark I should hear that shriek again, and then I should die. I knew that, and with every remaining atom of will I staggered towards the red west through the writhing mist that crept clammily around my ankles, retarding my steps.

"And as I fought my way off from the Tree, the horror grew, until at last I thought I was going to die. The silence pursued me like dumb ghosts, the still air held my breath, the hellish fog caught at my feet like cold hands.

"But I won! though not a moment too soon. As I crawled on my hands and knees up the brown slope, I heard, far away and high in the air, the cry that already had almost bereft me of reason. It was

faint and vague, but unmistakable in its horrible intensity. I
glanced behind. The fog was dense and pallid, heaving undulously
up the brown slope. The sky was gold under the setting sun, but
below was the ashy gray of death. I stood for a moment on the brink
of this sea of hell, and then leaped down the slope. The sunset
opened before me, the night closed behind, and as I crawled home
weak and tired, darkness shut down on the Dead Valley."

Tales of the Supernatural

James Platt

The Seven Sigils

Part I

Bravo and Poisoner

The bottomless lake of our Legend was reputed an outlet of the Bottomless Pit. No creature of our world had ever swum its lethal ebb and flow, but on the nights of the great Sabbaths, when the wizardry of all Italy swept to its beetling cliffs as to their Holiest of Holies, its waters eructed to the rendezvous the retinue of Hell— the wealth of an argosy would not have tempted a Lombard to venture within eye-shot of it after nightfall. Who, then, are these two men of mortal mould that outstare the depths of the Bottomless Lake itself, and not only that but from the very horns of the Altar of the Black Mass, and not only that, but at the witching hour forsooth of night, when graveyards yawn, and the everlasting doors of Tophet open wide? Their guardian angels of good have surely turned from their right hands, and their evil guardians of the left are grinning from horn to horn. With the chime of twelve from the distant steeple dies out the last echo of admonition, and they begin to work out such unhallowed errand as alone can have brought them to so damned a spot; the elder of the two in a tone of hushed solemnity addresses a series of questions to the younger, who responds to them with an equally awful gravity, after the manner of a catechism.

"Dost know me who I am?"

"Tosca of Venice, bravo and poisoner."

"And Yourself?"

"Janko the Illyrian, bravo with a right good will, but not yet poisoner."

"My ancestry?"

"Sorcerer stock, whose secrets you would fain have inherited and their trade pursued."

"Why did I not?"

"The Council of Ten bore down upon your race, and but for your extreme youth you yourself would have crossed the Bridge of Sighs. Orphaned by the State, and retaining for sole inheritance the swashing blade that still gnaws at your scabbard, and a few recipes for poisons (which last, however, were worth a Borgia's envy), you soon found yourself compelled to use both the one and the other to buy you bed and board. Proceeding at first with hesitancy, and never sojourning long in one locality, you became by degrees the repository of so many family secrets that at the present day you may stalk assured through the length and breadth of Italy, and ruffle it in what company you will."

"And your own story?"

"I know not by what catastrophe the memory of all my earliest years was shaken loose from me. Suffice it then, that once on a visit to my native country you found me wandering an orphan like yourself, and with a mind so blank that you appropriated it instantly to write on it as it were your own ten commandments. Since that day I have never left you, and I am only repeating what you yourself tell me when I say that you have made me your equal master in every trick of fence. But of that other art of yours that rivals the Creator, my most dutiful entreaties have never availed with you to teach me anything."

"But did I not reasonably argue that you would better attend the heaviness of so terrific a responsibility, until you were of man's estate? And is not to-day the anniversary of your coming of age? And have we not pelted hither hot-foot from the confines of the land upon that very business?"

"It is true that before entrusting me with even the least of these your ancient awful secrets you have brought me here to-night—for what?"

"To enter you with fitting state upon the beadroll of that glorious mystery, that with the mere putting on of a glove, or sniffing of a flower can check the most rebellious blood with a thus far shall thou flow, but no farther!"

"Say, rather to better the assurance that you have of me already from years of fraternal familiar common life, by laying upon me in addition a binding bond ensanctified by centuries of warlock use, and now to be imposed in this very spot where the Master whom thereby we both shall serve is at this hour present, though to us invisible, the Prince of the Power of the Air."

"You are at any rate resolved to link yourself to me with fetters forged in the fire that is not quenched, and by a testament registered in the Chancery of Hell to the effect that any treachery from one of us to the other shall be resented and avenged by that common Master of ours who hears us at this moment from his postern gate, the Bottomless Lake below?"

"I am resolved to that for which I came here."

"Follow, then, with me the observance of that visible sign and token that unites us in one blood and in one flesh. This horn is from that beast whose form our Master loves to take, when from this altar where we stand he greets his liegemen and his liege-women turned backward like his prayers. This horn I charge to the half with my own blood, obtained by the biting of my arm. Now do you likewise bite and fill and then drink (to my health) the moiety of the draught so mixed."

"May you live till the Last Trump!"

"You have pledged me in it as I now pledge you, and there remains but one more ceremony. I am about to throw this emptied receptacle into the waters of the Bottomless Lake. You know already that everything that touches its surface, whether living or dead, is forfeit to that Ancient of Days that crouches in wait below. Do you agree that this will be the fate reserved for that one of us two that shall first contravene this super-sacred oath?"

"His soul be the devil's fee."

The emptied horn shot like an elf-bolt into the pathless waters of the Bottomless Lake. The benighted pair that watched it from the unhallowed shrine above could have sworn that a hand came up and caught it as it fell, but a sudden flash of lightning that snapped in their eyes and a peal of thunder that made the four corners of the earth to quake rendered that fact uncertain. The strangers would then have been only too gladly drenched to the skin that they might have hugged their wagered souls in the belief that this unweather was of Nature, and not of the Evil One. But the Heavens shed no tear. There succeeded to that single flash and single peal only the same deadly calm that had preceded them. Although their business there was over, neither of the two men cared to suggest to the other his secret persuasion that there was no need for further stay. One o'clock whispered from afar its holy amen to their accursed ritual. Other hours flitted by, and still they gazed into unplummeted waves enwrapped in gloom as in their cloaks. At last as it were by a simultaneous impulse they turned together, and with a mutual sigh descended in the direction of the dawning city. From what has been said of the superstitious awe with which the Bottomless Lake was regarded, it will be readily understood that they had to traverse a considerable distance of uninhabited country before coming in sight of the main travelled road.

When at last after the painful up and down of many hills, they perceived the highway cutting through a valley at their feet, the habitual reserve engendered by their profession moved them to await atop the passage of a carriage that appeared in sight in the distance going towards the town rather than continue their journey, and be passed by it. As it came nearer both these men who had recently drunk so deeply of forbidden founts, suddenly uttered an exclamation that sounded very like a fear. For they saw at the self-same second that the coach contained a girl of beauty beyond a sultan's dream, and that some dozen or so of foot-pads darted from both sides of the road and seized the heads of her horses. The report of a pistol was obviously connected with the fall of the driver like a log from his box. The young lady was left with no other defender than a large black dog that ran behind the carriage, but as the assailants threw the doors open and hustled her out it became apparent that he was chained to the vehicle, and in an instant they were beyond his reach. But at this critical juncture Tosca descended almost, as it seemed, to the startled abductors with one leap from the heights above, and with a howl like a wild beast.

Although they did not know it, the finest sword player in Europe was in their midst. They went down by couples before him, spitted like larks. They had scarcely grasped the miracle of his presence before the lovely vision of the coach was resting in his left arm (the right still continuing to deal destruction), and she had scarcely glanced at his face, when, with a sigh of evident content with her defender, she hid her golden head in his breast to shut out the shambles from her eyes. But the fight was already past. Half the ravishers lay stretched upon the ground, and the bravo of Venice needed no second or even first glance at them to know that they would never rise again. The remainder, appalled by a result which they were far from attributing to the purely human agency which had caused it, had only to cast a look beneath his black-a-vised brows, when with a shriek that he was signed in the corner of his eye with the devil's private mark, they precipitately fled. The bravo dropped his sword into its sheath, and now with both arms round her waist he drew the goddess (as she appeared to him) towards her carriage. In doing so he perceived that she had fainted, and printed upon her lips the fiercest as it was the chastest kiss that he had ever bestowed upon woman. By an extraordinary chance (but there was more than chance in it), after completing the foulest rite, he had stumbled upon the purest passion of his life. For no other woman would he have shut the carriage door as he did now after placing her within it, remaining himself outside. And it is needful to add in this connexion that he had entirely forgotten the very existence of that comrade just bound to him by a tie indissoluble. That comrade, nevertheless, had watched the whole from the altitude where both had first stood. Could he have followed the giddy foot-hold of his patron he would in that moment have slain him in his tracks. And that he could in no wise stir from where he stood either previously to take part in that chance

medley, or now to snatch a share in the reward of it, was due not at
all to cowardice (a thing that must of necessity be unknown to any
that followed the fortunes of Tosca), but to a kind of spell as he
fancied that froze him to his place. And of this he was indeed well
qualified to judge since he had already experienced the self-same
sensation on one (and one only) former occasion. What puzzled
him was that the obvious cause in the prior case was a certain
amulet of unknown antiquity and power, which Tosca was accustomed to wear round his neck upon a chain of gold, and which in a
moment of confidence he had shown that once to his pupil.
Whereas on the present occasion the cause of his vertigo could
scarcely be the same, the talisman being invisible. And yet the
effect was identical. If anything more than another had been the
actual moving cause of his present icy chill it must certainly be the
damsel of the coach. So unmistakeable was the hold which the mere
sight of her had taken upon him, that at the instant when Tosca
placed his lips upon hers (and they had never been touched before
by man), the surging up of jealousy burst the shackles of the spell,
and the Illyrian clattered down like an avalanche. He reached the
road at the important moment when his oblivious partner, after
shutting the door of the coach, was upon the point of mounting
the box to drive the young beauty he knew not whither. Nor did it
occur to him that he knew not. But at this precise juncture his
dream was shattered by the advent of the Illyrian flashing fires of
jealous heat from his eyes. So choked with it was he that he could
not speak, but only pointed with one hand to the carriage while he
clenched the other in Tosca's face. The Venetian was equally taken
aback by the sudden resurrection of one whose presence in the
world he had totally overlooked. How long they would have stared
at one another had nothing intervened it would be impossible to
say. They were heedless of the barking of the black dog, since that
had continued without intermission from the first irruption of the
bid-stands. But they were twitched bolt round in the direction of
the coach by a sudden crack of its wheels. Whether the coachman
had fallen from his box through a genuine belief that he was hurt;

or whether through an equally genuine desire not to be; or, lastly, through collusion did not appear, but it was sufficiently obvious that the fellow had not received a scratch. Concluding the danger to be over he had now quietly reassumed his post, and was driving off. He took no more notice of the other two than if he had not seen them (which again might really have been the case), and used his whip to such good purpose that the vehicle was lost to sight (to memory dear) before the rivals had taken a step to arrest its progress. Then burst the storm of mutual recrimination. Tosca first spoke.

"Darkness and devils! You have robbed me of that for which I would not leave whole the skin of any man alive."

"'S death, kinsman, would you draw on me? Remember you not the oath of some few hours ago? Are you already so anxious to tap at that postern we both wot of? Knock then, and it shall be opened unto you. Ho, you pale at this reminder, and suffer your hand to drop from the hilt of that ancestral spit of yours."

"You were well advised to speak before I had drawn, or you would perchance have learned ere this that there are one or two tricks of fence I never taught even to you."

"Deceit upon deceit. You have always given me to understand that there was absolutely nothing in that branch of our partnership that you had not revealed to me. Perchance I shall ere long come upon some other tit-bit churlishly rapt aside. But why do I chide you for teaching me too little, when I had rather cause to weep salt tears that you have fathered me too much? When you met me, I had, as you have told me oft, a mind so blank that you could write on it (and that was the attraction that led you to adopt me) whatever kind of script you chose. And you chose to scribble the Devil's A, B, C. It is through your corruption of my innocent youth that I am unfit to-day to even look upon such as she who has just escaped us (and there ruled her favouring star). And if you reply that you have kept me till I was of age, unspotted from the worst half of your villainies, I dare swear that I should not be far out in conjecturing that regard for the safety of your body, rather than for that of my soul, was the true reason why you have never yet suffered me to wear the glass mask in your laboratories. And, to crown all, you kissed her."

"Did I kiss her? I thought it was a dream."

Thus Tosca murmured softly to himself, his head falling upon his breast, as if in communion with some saint. It was Janko who this time broke the silence by clutching of his sword. But Tosca looked up with a glance so diabolical, that he dropped it again at once. By a motion of his hand, the Venetian, as it were, compelled him to seat himself by the side of the road; and, sitting quietly beside him, commenced in. the following strain:—

"You make me laugh apart when you speak of my corrupting your innocent youth. If you only knew the truth! Or, as you said just now (God knows whether inspired by good or evil chance), if you only knew that tit-bit rapt aside, as you thought, churlishly (when you merely guessed at it), but in reality with more generosity than you will be decently able to thank me for (when you only know the facts). Your innocent youth, indeed!! By the God above us, whom we both fear, and neither serves, you will see by the story I am about to tell you that I knew all the time, and as I say with generosity have concealed from you, the nature of that catastrophe that shook loose from you the memories of all your earliest years. You will see that before your mind became a blank, I had read upon it (tender as were your years) the lurid brand of Cain. You will see that your brain was seared by your own atrocious hand, and that my adoption of you afterwards was based on the calculation that for a bravo and poisoner there could be in the whole round world no better raw material than a matricide! Start not till you have heard me out. I was in Illyria. Reasons which your experience of ups and downs in our profession will readily enable you to appreciate had caused me to retire (rather hurriedly, I confess) from the town which I had honoured with my presence for some months. The same reasons oblige me to travel in preference by night, and to secrete myself by day. On the first occasion of my doing this latter, I settled upon an apparently deserted hut in the trackless depths of the forest. This hut consisted of a large front room (reaching to the roof tree) for the accommodation of the two-footed, and a stall at back for that of the four-footed creation. The latter did not run so high as the front room, inasmuch as it contained a loft for fodder atop, and it was in this airy apartment that I decided to take my siesta, since it had openings both upon the stables (if I may so call it) and the front chamber, and my disposition as you know is strategic. I had slept, I know not how long, when I was awakened by a noise in front, and speedily ascertained that it was caused by an altercation going on among visitors to the parlour. Do not start till you have heard me out. One of the disputants was yourself. The other, who occupied the only stool in the place, was a grey-haired, blear-eyed female of considerable antiquity. I know nothing of your accursed Illyrian jargon. But without understanding the conversation I could see the beldame hugging to her withered breast a jewel, small, but of great price, and withal slung upon a golden chain. I tell you without hesitation that it was the same amulet you have been shown by me upon a previous occasion, foolishly as it happened, since it stirred you so profoundly as to almost resurrect your buried remembrances. That it came into the hands of your precious dame by some feat of robbery I have no doubt whatever. How it came into mine you will presently see. Your excited gesture, as it seemed to me, might afford me some clue to the progress of the quarrel, which I presumed had arisen as to the fate of your booty, but I had scarcely awakened up sufficiently to pull my reasoning faculties together when the whole thing ended in an, even to me, unexpectedly horrible manner. You suddenly pushed a pail (which stood hard by) beneath the back of the unsuspecting crone, and flashing a hanger from under your rags you swept off her grey head into the bucket with the single shearing stroke of a seasoned cut-throat. Then throwing upon the floor the glittering bauble of contention, you surprised me still more by swiftly separating the hands and feet, then the arms at elbow, and the legs at knee, then the stumps from the trunk, and finally the trunk itself into smaller parcels. That moment, and to-day, are the two occasions of my life upon which I have loathed my calling. By my word and oath I was as sick as a dog upon the litter of your loft. When I looked again you had cast down the weeping steel which had been the unwilling instrument of your crime. Packing all the sections in a kind of bag or sack you rolled it up compactly. Then seizing the ensanguined pail in the hand that was not occupied by that pitiful truss of what had just been humanity, you strode with them both from the desecrated home, but how you disposed of your burdens I neither know nor care. That you had loaded your conscience with a grislier deed than it could bear, I soon had good reason to know. Perturbed at my perturbation I had scrambled to *terra firma*, and had recovered myself sufficiently only to secure that amulet (which as you know I still wear), when you re-entered empty handed in that same state of idiocy, which moved me to overcome my distaste for associates and adjoin you to myself in my profession. Besides, I could not but admit (when once more fully myself) that you had shown for it considerable vocation."

The face of the Illyrian rolled with beads of sweat. For the third time he was bound hard and fast by that same fascination which already twice before had enthralled him. And as each time before so again it was for a different cause. The first of these two prior occasions resulted, as we know, from the sighting of the amulet. The second on the sighting of the divinity of the coach. But this third time was again different from the other two, in this respect, that (although he would not have confessed it for all the riches entombed in earth) he had now fully recognised the reason and connexion of all three. He rose deliberately and spoke:—

"Now, you have told me, to suit your own purposes, a certain amount of the truth, I remember to your confusion the details you intentionally omitted. You lie in your throat when you say that when I re-entered that room I was in the vacant state already. I re-entered that room (and you know it) as sane as when I left it. I found you standing there prepared with a glib story to the effect that you were a stranger just stepped into the hut with the view of seeing whether it was inhabited or not by anyone who could serve you as a guide through the forest. Not knowing you so well as I do now, I was simple enough to believe you. It never entered my head that you could have witnessed the drama that had just been played, nor did I think of the talisman in my momentary confusion at seeing in the place a foreigner. I have now no doubt but that if I had looked for it I should not have been able to find it. You diverted my attention by inviting me to quaff from your spirit flask on the plea that I looked unwell, as in truth I might, after the ordeal I had just passed through. In my innocence (for I was innocent) I accepted the draught, and the drug which you had placed in the liquor beforehand destroyed my memory, never to return, until this eventful day. Yet I think there was, however, one former occasion which it just missed a return. That was when you showed me that ill-omened amulet, and it awakened in me sentiment inexplicable then, but which now I am no longer at a loss to understand. That jewel was wrought by the science of my kinswoman, in whose hands you surprised it—for my people, too, were of the ancient religion, like your own, and sorcerers of the Black Side."

At the commencement of this speech, Tosca seemed momentarily disconcerted, but, as it continued, this sentiment was succeeded by something very like prostration, and when he replied it was with reverence.

"What a galliard this is, and how aright I guessed when I saw in him the making of a master in my trade. I thought to dash him with my revelation of a monstrosity among crimes. I was a fool, indeed, to think that a younker would bleach over the dissection of a granny, who had anointed him from his cradle with the grease of unbaptised babes. But I failed, and there's an end on't, and now sheer steel must decide the issue, for we meet on equal ground. Equal do I say? Nay! the boy is my superior in callousness, for I dearly loved my own old people, though I never say God rest their souls."

He rose, and both men laid their hands upon their hilts. One of them had not very long to live. But before entering upon the fateful lists, the Illyrian turned to speak again.

"In case you slay me, which I believe will not be the case (for God does sometimes defend the right), I cannot forbear an answer to your last taunt. You did not understand, and you have never understood, and you never will understand the real meaning of the scene you saw enacted in that room upon that day. I am not sure whether it was a blessing or a curse upon our race that you did not catch the drift of our remarks in our native language, which you contemptuously term jargon. Had you done so the fate of all three of us would have been better or worse, but at any rate far different. The tortures of the Inquisition would not force from me the secret, which was confided to me then by that ancient lady whom you saw me slay indeed, but only after her own repeated prayers and instructions. I shudder to think what has become of her remains which she entrusted to my pious care, and which for your accursed interference I have been unwillingly prevented from attending to. I know, indeed, the fate of her other legacy (for the amulet was a legacy that you thought a theft); but it is now too late (again through your accursed interference) for me to make such use of that knowledge as she had enjoined upon me to do. But to you (who know nothing of its use and profit) it shall hang as a millstone round your neck, and whether you live or whether you die it shall infallibly sink you now or hereafter to the undiscovered bottom of that Bottomless Lake whose source we both do know. And whichever of us falls shall by the terms of that enactment (of so short a while ago) be resented and avenged by that Master of ours, who waits even at this moment for that most unhappy man."

The face of Tosca became white and red. He flashed that time-honoured blade of his from its sheath, and motioned with it to the Illyrian to take up a position opposite to him. Janko turned round for one second to do so, and in that second the sword of his faithless foe was plunged remorselessly through his back. The point protruded through his breast. The next instant the sword had been withdrawn, and the Illyrian lay upon the turf among the ragged hedge pirates, who had fallen before by the same trained hand. But this time the Venetian took the trouble to assure himself of the death of his foe before returning his sword to its bed. That was the only honour he paid to the body that had once been only less dear to him than his own. That done, he threw himself down at the road side, and took out from under his doublet that very talisman of which we have heard so much. It had gained greatly in his estimation by the mystery which had lately thickened round it. We have already mentioned that it was suspended round his neck by a gold chain; but we must now give a more particular description of the gem itself. It had undoubtedly originally been intended for a seal, or, to speak more correctly, seven seals, for it had (and this constituted its particularity) seven sides or facets, and on each of these engraved a sigil or cabalistic monogram, and each sigil was that of a different planet of the seven that rule over the seven days of the week. All this the bravo, from his early environment, was sufficiently skilled to know. He also recognised at once that the person wishing to use the stone for its original purpose of sealing, would choose on each day that facet of the gem which bore the signature of the planet that presided over the day in question. But this, though no doubt of considerable efficiency, was not by any means of so great virtue as to sufficiently explain the very enigmatical manner in which the amulet had been alluded to by the hapless boy, whose present fate he shuddered to reflect on. He endeavoured, with more or less success, to banish speculation on that point by returning to his examination of the ring, if we may apply that term to a jewel which was not pierced with sufficiently large a hole to fit even upon the smallest of fingers. Such hole as it had, and through which its chain now passed, he conjectured must have been originally intended to receive the handle of the seal, upon which, fitting loosely, the gem turning round and round could be made to present any facet desired to the paper which its owner intended to impress. At this point of his meditation the bravo was aroused by the sound of footsteps. A number of officials, both on horse and otherwise, had arrived from the neighbouring town. These he recognised at once as belonging to that inconvenient class (the guardians, let us say, of public safety) from whom he had fled on many another well remembered occasion besides the one he had just made mention of in his story to the ill-starred Illyrian. Yet at the present moment he had no fear of them. Perhaps this was because he knew that they came on account of the depositions of the lodestar of his dreams, and that he would have run any risk to be brought once more into chain with her. A less hardened adventurer might have been embarrassed by the presence of Janko's body. But to a fertility of resource such as Tosca had needs acquired, it presented no obstacle whatever. He rose, and bowed with a grace he had learned in the very highest society. The officers returned his salute. They conjectured rightly that this stranger of distinguished appearance was the beaten blade who had performed the prodigies of valour, which when told them in the city they had deemed to be fabulous, but of which they now saw the proofs before their eyes. The obliging champion was quite willing to relate his own private version of the affair. He paused only to consider whether it would be advisable to have been wounded slightly, but he decided against this fiction as liable to lead to trouble.

"Yes; as you say, I naturally wished to rest awhile after the fatigues of such a combat Besides, I guessed, of course, that I should soon see upon the field of battle you gentlemen of justice, whose promptness in these matters has become proverbial, and with whom I would not for the world have lost the chance of an interview. I might, it is true, have foisted myself into the carriage for its journey to town. But the lady, as she doubtless told you, had fainted right away, and I was therefore debarred from obtaining that permission, without which no man of breeding could venture to take such a liberty. And before I had time to achieve a seat on the box, the coachman was off; for the fellow was drunk, as your penetration must have perceived from the muddled state of his evidence. Of the valour you so kindly allude to, my modesty forbids me to speak. But I am bound in honour to temper your flattering opinion of the achievement by confessing that I am a fencing master by profession, and that a score or so of thrusts and parries is merely a matter of daily bread with me. I must add, in this connexion, that I am also a physician, and one possessed of medicaments that cure all ills. Further, I was proceeding to your town with the view of establishing a dual practice among you, when this trifle we are discussing fell athwart the even tenor of my way, and I hope still to establish myself there, and even to continue my journey in your company (which is such as I most affect) now this accident has given me, as I perceive, introduction to all the most desirable connexions in the place. You will notice yonder, by the way, a fellow of better apparal than the rest of the run-a-gates, and whom I take to be their captain. The other scaramouches gave me no trouble whatever, but I must confess that the spadassin in question was a little bit more of a customer. I had the lady on one arm (as she doubtless told you), and had the rabble been able to get on all sides of me at once, the affair would indeed have been the devil's delight. But since I kept my back, like an old campaigner, to the coach, I felt no kind of flurry; and, as I knew from the first that I should, I came at length to disarm him. The poltroon then turned to save his skin (I had thought him braver stuff); but I, as you may suppose, was far too limber for him, and skewered him through the back. You can see for yourselves how my point pro-truded through his breast. In my humble opinion he might well dance in chains here on a gibbet upon the scene of his crime, as a warning to the rest of his riff-raff that scuttled away from my in-vincible arm as soon as their leader fell."

This Tosca considered the master-stroke of his dissimulation. No suspicion could now light upon him. The lady had seen but him, and knew nothing of his companion. The coachman had either seen two men or none. If he spoke of two they would ascribe it to his drunkenness, and inquire if he did not also see two ladies. Tosca was furthest of all from suspecting that by this very suggestion he thought to be so masterly he was forging the bolt that should de-stroy him. With delight he perceived that the officers had clutched at his idea, and immediately set their underlings to work upon the gallows, after first entombing the raggeder ruffians ignominiously in a ditch. Leaving them to their congenial work Tosca proceeded with the officers to town, and gathered as he went all the particu-lars that he could of his enchantress. And her name, which he heard for the first time, seemed familiar as a household word. Vergilia had resided for months in the city, but was by birth a stranger, from what country no one knew. It was only known that she had sojourned for similar periods in other principal places. She was an orphan, she was unmarried, she was an heiress. Wherever she pleased to set her wandering feet men flocked in shoals to be trampled beneath them. And of these, Tosca shrewdly guessed, were the majority of his present companions. She consistently refused all offers, and this was the unanswerable argument of the more logical sex to their women, who hated her like poison, and who would have it that she made use of love philtres to effect her endless conquests. The only ground for this assertion seemed to be that wherever she travelled her bed chamber was always sacredly reserved to her own person, entered by no one else under any circumstances whatever, and locked when she was not within, she herself performing all domestic duties connected with it. Those admirers of hers, who had not yet put their fate to the touch, all indignantly scouted the theory advanced by the rejected that she concealed a lover in this sanctum. Nor was such an idea surely possible to any one who looked with unjaundiced eye, even once on her virginal purity. Tosca gazed on her for the second time that day, and swore within his heart of hearts (quite drowning all recollection of that prior oath) that the very first lover she should have would be none other than himself.

PART II

THE DEVIL'S CANDLE

The revolution of our legend brings us once more round to that same direful boundary hour, with which it was commenced between midnight and the first born of the day. But on the hills a gibbet stands that stood not there before, a beacon to the minions of the moon. Alas for the misguided youth that hangs there helpless and unhouseled. His brave attire the cupidity of his topsmen had appropriated to their own use. His body they had arrayed for the sake of decency in rags stripped from the verminiferous trunks of his several supposed followers, and these huddled him like the swathings of some dismantled mummy. A gorged carrion bird dozes upon each of his shoulders. The hinds, whom their business brought upon the road even so late as twilight, had run afield copiously crossing themselves. Who, then, is this—a woman, too— that comes at the awfullest hour of all, and to the very foot of the gallows? Nothing but her eyes can be seen from under her hood. Are those the eyes of Vergilia that Tosca dreams of and deems unfathomable as the Bottomless Lake itself? Is the intuition of her sex, then, unfailing after all, and she a witch, that with love philtres works her syren spell, and seeks at this dread hour for the wherewithal? And what, then, can she peer for about the foundations of a gibbet, save alone that fetid and fearsome white-flowered orange-berried Devil's Candle mandragora that is engendered in the womb of earth from a gibbeted murderer's drippings on the midnight of his death? The Illyrian bravo had been seven times a murderer (if not seventy times seven), and many a lost soul rejoiced in Hell that night over the weird that the witch woman was to work. She has found it at last, the favourable specimen, by her long sought through fruitless years. She has found the root in human form complete—two armed, two legged—the Microcosm caricaturing man. And now her low whistle brings her black hound forward out of the black night. Even she is affected as she kisses him for the last time. Iscariotical kiss! With a cord from her youthful waist she attaches animal and plant together, and flees from thence, stopping her ears as she runs. The hound (whose faith is to strike his death-knell) seeks to follow her, and finds himself held back. He wrestles with the invisible obstacle and conquers, but to die, for as the unholy mannikin root is perforce torn out of its mother earth it utters a piercing shriek that makes rattle the chains of its father above, and the hound, in an instant foaming at the mouth, in fits expires. Then, and then only, turns the murderess back on her blood-stained steps. The carcase of her sole unvenial follower she casts falteringly apart. The girdle is already attached by one end to the gruesome plant. By throwing round to it the other end she completes the circuit of her shapely throat, and held fast by this improvised necklace tucks the loathsome herb creature into her lovely bosom, which no being of its sex had ever yet been free of. Hence now to develop him, for to this is that secret chamber destined that had never seen denizen but herself before. There is her laboratory, and there shall this earth child be magically tendered and nourished, and most magically grow to more and more of man's resemblance. Since in a manner by his mystical birth he is one flesh and blood with the murderer that begot him, he is perforce of Hell, and can Hell's secrets impart to the enchantress that holds him in her power. To what her cravings tend, which by his means or any other that affords itself, she must and will by hook or crook attain, we now shall shortly see. In spite of her evident youth, Vergilia was far too accomplished an actress, of course, to reveal by word or sign her secret studies to the gilded youth that continue to throng her halls. But Tosca visited her upon a different footing. Spending his days with her in the body, and his nights with her in the spirit—spacing out with drink and dice the unutterable intervals when he could do neither one nor the other— he neglected his professional avocations altogether, and existed absolutely for her. On her part she had shown him, as we have seen, particular favour from the first moment she saw him, and this became continuously more and more after she had wormed his story from him—as much as he chose to tell, and which of course excluded entirely the existence of the Illyrian—until at length she requited him with like confidence. What the butterflies that sought their own purposes about her chose to think of her preference she cared not, but her modesty at length obliged her to account for it in private to the preferred one himself by alleging the similarity of their descent (for that she also came of old necromantic stock), and to explain her refusal of all suitors (even to coronets) on the grounds that none of them could satisfy, till Tosca came, her yearnings for the occult. To an archimage alone would she give her right hand, and his right hand she meant to be. The blessing of the Church would be a curse to such a pair. Heedless then of what, in their position, they needs must deem the degradation of any such ceremony, she had herself devised her own test piece by which a favoured suitor could be at the same time tried, and by its failure or success dismissed or indissolubly wedded. She had sworn in fact to bestow herself without reserve upon the student (his person being also to her fancy) who could call up for her substantial from the vasty deep a magical palace in which her fantastic imagination had long run riot, and in which carnal love and cabalistic lore

should wander hand in hand the livelong day without let or hin-
drance from the outer world well lost. Prone to such thoughts from
her cradle, this aerial architecture of hers had taken final shape in
the first days of her visit to that town, when disdaining the legend
of the boors, she had penetrated the precincts of the Bottomless
Lake, and quickened her brain with the idea of how suitable to a
lover and his mistress would be retreat into a never-visited seclusion such as that. Then the thing grew. She pictured and demol-
ished one after another various enchanted buildings floating upon
the waters themselves (and that was the common thread that ran
through them all) sailing to the shore upon the wish of the dwell-
ers in them, but entirely inaccessible to any outward authority,
either human or divine. Now that she had discovered the Venetian
to be the one man to whom she would accord permission to sub-
stantialise her dreams (supposing he could find the power) she
submitted to him with much shy laughter her latest ground plan
of this castle in the air. She had borrowed from the sensuous East
its key-hole arches and quadrangular bowers built round, and en-
closing court yards glowing with flowers from every region of the
earth, and never the same at two successive visits. Birds inter-
changed at every inspection in like manner were to agitate the air
with their antiphonies. And the fountains in the centres of all the
court yards (fed from the waters of the Bottomless Lake) when
lapped into the beakers of the lovers would become the rarest wine.
The outermost waters would glister with gold and silver fish, shot
through with the plungings of white aquatic birds. Within the building, the rooms kaleidoscopically should never meet them twice with
the same face. Their servants should be automata scattered through
every chamber, and ready at a touch to fly to master or mistress
like genii of the Arabian Nights, but instantly relapsing after
service into their first stony insensibility. Of much more Vergilia
whispered such as at times frenzied in Tosca the knowledge of his
impotence to win her upon her terms. Had he but inherited the
secrets of his fathers! Had he but the knowledge stored up in the
grey brain of that hairless blear-eyed Hell-sent hag of Illyria! Could
he but solve the enigma of the Seven Sigils, that at any rate might

bring him somewhat nearer to his end! And his rivals envied him. Closer and closer there seemed to flutter to him the moth they thought he had singed. But never close enough. Then came an event that led up to his climax of fruition found green in the mouth. Stated in short, it fell somewhat as follows: At the end of her daily banquet she was wont to leave her guests to their wine, while she paid one of her frequent visits to that unseen chamber. One of those disappointed suitors of hers (as it chanced, or was fated on a certain day), inspired with the valour of much wine imbibed after she had left her table, swore roundly that he would follow her, and pluck out at any hazard the heart of that mystery. Before he could be stopped by fellow guest or flunkey he had stumbled up the stairway, and burst open the door she had but lately closed behind her. The next moment a most frightful shriek resounded through every corner of the house. It was not Vergilia's. It was uttered by the foolhardy intruder. The company started from their seats. But before they could do anything he staggered into the room again with hair as white as snow, and lips that gibbered loathsomely. Amid a scene of indescribable confusion he was carried off by his friends insane and inpenetrable as to the cause of his fright, nor did he ever recover sufficiently to give an explanation of it. When all the rest of the terrified crowd of loungers and lackeys had hustled pell mell from the house, Tosca alone remained. His hour he thought had come. But it was only in a measure so. The lady of the house re-appeared, it is true, after the hurried exodus of masters and servants, and agitated as he had expected, but not to his surprise by their defection. She babbled brokenly, instead, of some one else whom she had lost through the unexpected intrusion of that venturesome drunkard, now sobered for good and all. Thus she rooted from that moment in the mind of Tosca the horrible suspicion that the story of the concealed lover might have some truth in it after all. How could he know aught of her experimental mandrake culture, for of course it was the mandrake she referred to? The only creature besides herself that had witnessed her infernal arcana had just been borne a mouthing maniac from the seat of her operations, and perhaps not even had time enough to notice the nature of the disaster, which his untimely interference had brought about. However, for the time Tosca dismissed his suspicions when she fell into his arms and telling him between laughter and tears that he was now the only hope that remained to her, she begged him at once to summon together all his scattered occult acquirements, and make an incantation that very night that should yield them both their heart's desire. He swore to do so, hardly knowing what he swore, and fled from her in a wind of excited passion and passionate resolve. For some time after this he endeavoured to put his ideas coherently together by dint of pacing madly through the streets. It was already dusk, and at first he elicited no remark. But presently he noticed that his footsteps were being dogged. He was a connoisseur in such matters. This must be a rival more fixed than the remainder of the craven herd that had so readily taken flight, and one that had watched the bravo during the time that he stayed behind. Or perchance nothing more mysterious than a dunning creditor, for Tosca had lately run out of ready money, and while exercising no trade still maintained a splendid appearance. Nor had this also been altogether without weight with him when he accepted the challenge of his bewitching mistress. Not wishing to embroil himself with the person whom he supposed to be shadowing him, he entered a tavern and called for wine. He had scarcely seated himself when a masked stranger of short stature and somewhat uncouth appearance entered the same inn, and sat down at the same table, giving the same order. The nerves of our Venetian were more shaken by the extraordinary episode of the afternoon than he would himself have cared to own. Not liking the looks of his would-be boon companion, and conjecturing some connexion between that individual and the counter of his paces, Tosca got up and left the tavern without awaiting the execution of his command. To his consternation the stranger followed him. An exciting chase ensued. The bravo entered house after house, seating himself in each case, and always closely hugged by his mysterious hanger on, who as regularly seated himself by the bravo's side, and as soon as he withdrew followed him out into the street. A kind of panic seized the fearless swordsman. A challenge to the inexplicable stranger stuck again and again in his throat. At last the houses began to close their shutters. The baffled fugitive struck desperately out of the town into the open country, and made his way in the direction of the Bottomless Lake. As the footfalls of his ghostly visitant pattered still behind him he consoled himself with the grim reflection that right up to that ill-omened shore, at any rate, the spy would not dare to venture. But he was mistaken. As he paused breathless on the brink of that Stygian sea and faced round boldly on to what he deemed to be invisibility, he found it was instead the form of his fear that stood there as before. He was seized with the boldness of desperation, and addressed the mysterious and still masked being with a voice of tolerable calm.

"Who are you, and what is your need of me?"

"I am Magloire, a necromancer of France, and it is you that have need of me."

"You are over bold to say so."

"I say what I know. Dare you deny that you entertain the intention of making an incantation here this very night, and that you lack only the means to do so? A scheme of geomancy acquainted me with your design, and being entangled in your fate, for reasons that you must not know (for you will know them if anything too soon) I sped from afar upon wings of wind to conduct your conjuration for you."

"You have a price for this?"

"I see you are a man of the world, and are aware that nothing is usually given for nothing. I ask you merely to sign this bond."

"I understand your interest in me better than you seem to think, and on no account will I barter away my immortal soul."

"Your immortal soul, do you say? By the Nine Legions of Hell, does the man think that the cross was stretched on Calvary for any such scum as he? Your immortal soul, of which you hug yourself the possessor, was lost irredeemably from your cradle up. The signature to the bond is a matter of form."

"You do not think so since you ask me to sign it. But ask of me anything else, and it shall be given to you."

"By the tie of which I spoke, that is stronger than blood as blood is thicker than water (so they say), I will help you, though you vouchsafe me a mere keepsake. Make over to me that amulet that you wear around your neck, and the bargain is firm and true. The dawn shall caress a tenement based on the shifting foundation of these waters, such as even shall satisfy the caprices of Vergilia."

The bravo had recovered himself, as we have said, but these evidences of an intimate knowledge of his affairs filled him again with apprehension. And the stranger still continued masked. After a short deliberation, however, Tosca decided not to let slip an opportunity as welcome as unexpected, and granted apparently in exchange for a trinket of no worth to him whatever, though he was not unaware that it might be of inestimable value to any one who knew (as this Frenchman presumably did) the secret of the Seven Sigils. With a parting sigh for its enigma still unsolved, so often the toy of his leisure hours, he detached it from his neck, and passed it on to the Gaul, who fastened it about his own. That he was a wizard of his word became immediately apparent. Taking up a piece of chalk he scored out rapidly a double circle, one circumference within the other, upon the shelf of rock upon which they stood. Between the two circumferences he drew a ring of symbols of purport to the Venetian unknown, but which he endeavoured to retain in his memory for possible future use. Within the innermost of these two lines of defence the sorcerer collected a quantity of brushwood, and after having ignited these materials he entrusted the bravo with sundry perfumes, some in the shape of evil smelling dried stuffs, and some sealed up in phials, with minute instructions as to the order and quantities in which (the incantation having commenced) they were to feed the fire. To Magloire would fall the duty of reciting the continuous charge which for the whole duration of the work was to hold the evil angels in thrall. Lastly, the Gaul drew his companion's attention to the fact that as soon as midnight sounded the conjuration was to commence, and before one must end. For that hour alone would signatory protectors avail him against the furies he evoked. But this Tosca already knew. He was, as we have seen, no such novice in the worship of powers retrograde as this schooling showed his colleague to believe. The distant clock now struck (how well the bravo remembered all the circumstances in which he had heard that sound from this spot before), and the sorcerer began in a thunderous voice to recite his litanies. Couched throughout in somewhat dubious Latinity they were by the bravo only partially understood, but he perceived that commencing with extravagant bead roll of the Heavenly powers with which they two had fortified themselves, and with impudent encomiums of their own matchless courage and endurance among men, Magloire proceeded to eulogise the nine princes of the lower world in terms the most complimentary, exhorting them to satisfy their good friends the exorcists in the mere trifle they demanded. As this modest request was not responded to, the reciter gradually changed his tone. The compliments became thinned by degrees and beautifully less, and were fairly well mixed with horrible threats, and approbrious epithets, which again meeting with no recognition, the theme of the chant now ceased to contain any allusion whatever of a gratifying character. All was menace piled on menace and insult piled on insult, Pelion upon Ossa till the riotous whirl of words merged into one continuous curse, in the midst of which reverberated again and again (amid the shudders of the waters and the trembling of the earth) that ineffable sacred and secret Name of Names, at which the celestials and the terrestrials and the infernals do shake together and are troubled and confused. And with that there rumbled thunders round the skirts of earth and belched forth lightnings from their midst. And the lightnings continued to lighten without pause, until they seemed all one meteor of fire that hovered over the surface of the Bottomless Lake. And the meteor burst and shot forth myriads upon myriads of shapeless forms down towards the surface, whilst upwards from the surface rose a sort of scum or mist. And this scum or mist, meeting those shapeless forms, they seemed to seize upon it—and work it—and make it build as it were walls. But all was seen as through a glass darkly, and, besides, the bravo was still employed in casting priceless balsams upon hissing flames that many a time and oft became half extinguished (to his terror) by the sweat that rained from his brow. By his side the French enchanter still swayed his arms towards on high, and on high unceasingly rolled his incomprehensible cabala. The slightest fear or the slightest hesitation, and what might not be their fate? For such a slip innumerable infernal skirmishers were hovering hard by in readiness. But now the danger is almost over. The gangs have done their grudging work, and a palace hangs between wind and water seductive and serene where nothing hung before. The last odours are burning. The weird wailing of the magus is slackening into the majestic formulae of dismissal. Without this termination to the ritual the magicians on leaving their sanctuary would have been torn limb from limb by the awaiting fiends. But being expelled as ceremoniously as they had been evoked, the filmy hosts had no choice for it but to crumble into the nothingness from which they came.

"Go in peace unto your place! Peace be between you and us! Be you ready to come when you are called."

These culminating words of the oration were uttered at the very moment that the faithful distant watchman proclaimed it the hour of one. As the two daring trespassers upon realms forbid stepped out from their double breast-work, the bravo in vain endeavoured to make out the exact architectural details of his palace in the darkness. It was pretty clear to him, however, that instructions given had been faithfully fulfilled. He considered that he had done a very good night's work How unexpected when he left Vergilia's house was this chance rencounter that fate had in store for him. He began to have some regard for Providence. He paid no attention to the wizard who was commencing to obliterate his signs. Magloire had done his work well, but he had been paid for it in advance. So much for Monsieur Magloire (of France), who, he presumed, would now be off again about his own affairs. Tosca strolled towards the city. His business was to wait upon his betrothed (for such she now surely was), and drag her off at once to the castle of her behest. A day of luxury followed by a night of love. That was his bill of fare. But he had reckoned without his host. He was ignorant that, in exchange for the palace, he had bartered the true key to the situation and most stringent claim of all upon the regard of his Vergilia. He was far from suspecting that essential clue to the labyrinth which Janko had recovered only just before his death, but which world without end would never have wrung from him to the advantage of his assassin. This essential clue consisted in the recognition of the hag of Illyria and the beautiful Vergilia as one and the same person. Now Janko had been her kinsman, and her intimate in her former existence, and had been privy and assistant (as we know) to the rite by which her youth was to be renewed. To him the inheritance was destined of the seal which she had constructed for this end, and by the existence of which alone her rejuvenescence could be effected. Upon the success of her experiment, after seven days of seeming death, it was intended that he should restore it to her; but we are already aware that, through the interference of the Venetian, that success he had never seen. The memory of his obligation being destroyed by the drug of the poisoner, the talisman that was bound up with it became the plaything of the bravo. The plaything of the bravo we repeat, and it could never be anything else to him, so long as he remained in ignorance of the peculiar power it exerted over the transfigured witch. For the amulet was the invisible load-stone that at the moment when first they met had drawn her head down irresistibly to his breast, where it lay concealed. Hold out as she might, she must nevertheless infallibly have ultimately yielded to the spell by which the Seven Sigils gave its holder power over her life. And Tosca had unwittingly exchanged it for Dead Sea fruit. The fantastical personage calling himself Magloire was, on the other hand, well aware (for reasons which, for the moment, we leave in the dark) of the power of the pawn he thus obtained. His proffer of the bond, in the first instance, was a ruse (for he knew it would not be signed), and it served very well its end of diverting suspicion from his real purpose by making that appear an after thought. Now that he had obtained the long-sought-for prize, he stopped in his work of demolishing his geometry (the bravo being no longer in sight), and stood for a long time collecting in the jewel every possible ray of light. Then he did a most extraordinary thing, even for him, whose every

deed was extraordinary. He took it off its chain, which he threw
carelessly away, and conveying the glittering heptagon to his
mouth, he swallowed it. There was method in his apparent madness. Its virtues would not suffer in the slightest from its imprisonment. The fortunes borne by its Seven Sigils for good or for evil
were henceforth indissolubly bound up with his being. In this way
he avoided any possible chance of its ever passing out of his possession. But the most urgent reason for his caution was the imminent return of his late assistant. He had gauged the character of
that individual too deeply to feel safe while in his company. And
in his company he evidently intended to remain. The sun had now
risen, and the structure he had wrought by a word out of nothing
was at last entirely visible. And he saw that it was good. The waters
around it swarmed with love and feud between fishes gold and
silver and white aquatic birds. Other feathered life hopped the
countless little streamers which adorned the shining turrets. A
broad landing stage fronted the chief gate which was the higher of
it to the extent of a magnificent flight of steps. As to the interior
the Moorish lattices were inscrutable. But curiosity need not long
remain unsatisfied. The handsome pair for whom this casket was
destined were already joyously approaching. The bravo started
when he came in sight of the secretive Gaul still masked, and as at
the moment when he left him rubbing out the traces of his circles.
Vergilia started, as if in recognition of some acquaintance perchance of her youth. The vaguely mysterious Seven Sigils had
launched their erotic work. The bravo surprised the attention which
the Frenchman had excited—remembered that he had never liked
him from the first—and began to look upon him as a possible rival.
But the desire to take French leave of him begot the bewildering
discovery that although the castle floated, complete as per contract, he was powerless himself by any exertion of wish or will to
cause it to sail to shore that they might enter in according to the
original plan sketched out by its fair young architect. In this dilem-
ma the Gaul came bowing and scraping to his aid, and showed that
by a simple signal of his hand he could attract it to him as a mag-
net attracts iron. And now Tosca began to suspect the lurking of

some design in all this. His suspicions were confirmed when Magloire stepped with them upon the threshold of their new home, and the palace immediately resumed its place in the centre of the Bottomless Lake. There was now no chance for it but to admit the unwelcome guest. Their feet were lost to the ankles in the carpet that covered the nakedness of that royal flight of stairs we have already alluded to. They passed into a banqueting hall of exquisite proportion, and sculpt with a fairy chisel. Through keyhole arches that overlooked a central court, the melodies of all kinds of singing birds were wafted contrapuntally across the strains of the equally invisible musicians inside the banqueting hall itself, while the sun-litten plashings of a fountain formed the organ point that threaded through the whole—so much as this the Venetian came, and saw, and enjoyed; but as to the laced and liveried semblances of life with which the banqueting hall was alive, they were semblances of death for all the service which the wish and will of Tosca sought to exact from them. And here again the Frenchman came to his aid, and these genii, at his command, throbbed with obsequious ichor. Tables (in a second, magnificently clothed) groaned under the newest of foods and beakers filled at the central spring (fed from the waters of the Bottomless Lake) brimmed with the oldest of wines. Vergilia and Magloire appeared infused with perfect life, but to the bravo all was bitter in the mouth. He saw by the action of the genii of the place that the contract agreed to, and possibly only too literally carried out, had not been sufficiently comprehensive. The day had dawned, it is true, upon a tenement that eminently satisfied the caprices of Vergilia. But the bravo was only in name its master and hers. The castle that mocked his efforts to move it came and went at the motion of his rival, the servants that were automata to Tosca were alive to the bidding of Magloire, and Vergilia had forsaken her old love and beamed only upon the new. Nay, she cast upon Magloire the self-same love light which had fired Tosca's blood in her defence when he snatched her from her ravishers, that never to be forgotten day when first they met. He had thought his valour saved her from a fortune worse than death, which now he feared would have affected her not at all. For he saw that all the signs of an apparently virgin love could rise up like phoenix from the ashes of a past one. And he shuddered to think how often this process might have been repeated. Had all her lovers then enjoyed her perchance save Tosca alone? And yet all the more she sank in his estimation, the fuller swelled the tide of his desire. The long luxurious banquet was a torture to him with this death's head at his feast. His rage increased steadily with the jealousy it fed upon. The long drawn courses were no sooner over than he seized upon some trifling pretext (we know not what) to leave Vergilia alone for a few moments while he drew his rival to that central court, whence perfumed zephyrs blew. The stranger still continued masked. To this Tosca first alluded laying his hand upon the hilt of that famous old sword of his.

"Unmask your face that I may know you."

"You shall know me too well ere long."

"Restore me that amulet unearned by your accursed jugglery."

"You will never see it again."

"Then let this sword of justice decide between us that has settled many a case for me before, and the Devil help his own! But first reveal to me your real style and title (and a fig for the assumed one that you go by), that I may learn with what enemy I have to deal that has cause to hunt me down as you have hunted me."

"You deal with the Resenter and Avenger of the murder of the Illyrian."

A shiver ran down the spine of the Venetian. Yet his blade nevertheless flashed from its sheath, and he motioned to the stranger to take up a position opposite to him. Magloire turned round for one second to do so, and in that second the sword of his faithless foe was plunged remorselessly through his back. The point protruded through his breast. The next instant the sword had been withdrawn, and the still unexplained Frenchman lay prone upon the ground by the self-same stratagem that had availed with the man of whom he styled himself avenger. And this time also the Venetian took the trouble to assure himself of the death of his victim before returning his sword to its scabbard. That done, he

proceeded next to ascertain the real identity of this mysterious
being whom he had supposed to be one of his numerous enemies
working out a long delayed vendetta. With a clutch the mask was
torn to ribbons, and with a shriek the bravest of the brave recoiled
from the Mandrake it revealed; and, as the shrieker heard his
shriek, he recognised its kind. It was fellow to that one he had heard
the day before from the chamber of Vergilia, never deeming that
he himself in turn would be frighted with the same basilisk face.
But it frighted him (after all) with a difference. The soul of the pot
valiant courtier had been reft from its silken frame, but the tempered ribs of the Man of War held fast their trust within. His brain
whirled and steadied itself—his blood shot forth and back again—
his eye grew dark and cleared. On to his knees he sank, indeed,
that never had bent to conquered (or unconquered) foe before, but
that was the only abatement from his pride of place. That was his
only homage to the escaped familiar of the sorceress' privacy, that
grim guardian whose gorgon glimpse had yesterday sobered the
drunkard and petrified the itching flesh of lust. And the situation
brought its panacea. Ignorant still of the effect of the Seven Sigils,
he fancied he had discovered now why the sorceress had favoured
the Mandragorean watchman with the love glance once reserved
for Tosca. It must be because that monster also had rendered service to her virtue as the bravo had rendered it before. One question still remained unanswered. Had Vergilia herself never seen
the face of this awful animated root? Or had she, by daily touch,
kept up from the very first plucking of the plant, so grown up along
with its progressing hideosity as to feel no inception of abhorrence?
At any rate, his Mandrakeship was now placed finally *hors de boudoir*. And the bravo reflected that he laughs best who laughs the
last. Take heed, though, Tosca, there rests one yet unslain till the
day of final doom, in whose danger you still stand, and whose claws
are creeping towards you from the dark places of the earth! Who
sups with the Devil had need have a very long spoon. But now there
flashes like a sunbeam through the court the golden-haired vision
of whose destiny he now hoped himself sole arbiter. Roused by that
fell shriek, her anxiety nevertheless was far from being for the

utterer of it. With a cry of agonised acute despair she flung past the outstretched arms of the bravo on to the prostrate body of the lover still bound to her in death by the magic of the talisman he had swallowed with so justified a foresight. The bravo knelt no longer to the Mandrake, but to her, and with a cry plucked up the thoughts of his deepest soul.

"Thou wanton and thing of many lovers, yet whom still I madly love! By the love you once bore me, have pity on me now and vouchsafe me but the leavings of this man or monster. A living dog is better than a dead lion, so they say. Call me your dog or what you will, so that you call me yours. For you I placed my soul in pledge, and would you now desert me in my indignity? Nay then, if your choice be irrevocably riveted to this carrion, so be it! But you shall share the fate of him whom you so fancy. The Grand Seignieur is connoisseur in the art of fittest punishing the faithless. With my own eyes I have seen his favourite odalisques sewn up in sacks, and dropped into the Bosphorus. And with my own hands I will deal with you even so. You shall have your fill of local colour ere you have done with your palace of the East."

The bravo was now crouching instead of kneeling, and gathering himself up into a spring as of a panther he plunged upon the still disconsolable mourner. Twining his fingers recklessly about the golden hair he oft had kissed, he dragged her, not without difficulty from the corpse of the Thing, whose fall she wept, jerking her spasmodically into the hall and overturning its furniture right and left. Amid the crashing of shattered bric-a-brac, he grabbed at the nearest cushion from a divan that stood hard by, and ripping out its entrails with the ferocity of an attack upon a living thing, he felled the shrieking girl to the ground with a blow that would have startled an ox, and forced his contrived receptacle somehow and anyhow over her body, she uttering never a syllable the while. Did she think that he had no heart to carry to a finish such a deed? Or was it still the eccentric influence of the Seven Sigils that made death to her preferable to life apart from the one beloved? This we cannot answer. Enough that Tosca seemed in deadly earnest as he shook together the members of his mistress, and compressing the mouth of his improvised sarcophagus, tied it up with the belt from his waist. This done he left it on the couch, and returned to the central court drowsy with incense laden flowers. He intended to yield Vergilia one more chance. Left to herself, and already wrapped in her winding sheet, the present expectation of a painful death would surely lead to second thoughts, and induce her to lavish less carelessly the future of her youth and beauty—the splash that heralded the committal of her paramour to the water would be echoed by her appeal for mercy—and he had resolved in that case to forgive her the worst she dared confess to him. But now to the work. Not entirely without spasms of fresh fear he re-entered the courtyard of the fateful duel, and where the duellist who had fallen lay. His body the bravo now conveyed down the steps to the landing stage in front of the main building. It did not fail to occur to the practical mind of the Venetian as he strained under the repulsive corpse of his quondam adversary that somewhere upon his person (as he thought) must lie concealed the talisman of the Seven Sigils. He did not know that to find it he should have to search for it within and not without. The consequence naturally was that his search was unrewarded by any trace whatever of the coveted gem. But the more he searched and pondered—and pondered and searched again—the more he became convinced of the necessity for finding it, and the clearer became to him the momentous part it had played in recent events. He remembered now too late that while he had it in his possession his suit with Vergilia had prospered, whereas Heaven had begun to frown upon him as soon as he had parted with it to Magloire. He was too shrewd a conjuror to fail to connect the one fact with the other, and with them both the anxiety of the Mandrake to possess the talisman of whose virtues he had obviously knowledge. Yet still it could not be found upon his person. With a fearful oath the Venetian at length gave up the search, and consigned the fruitless body to the Bottomless Lake. He would find the bauble yet (he swore) by all his left hand gods in whatsoever nook of earth it lay. And with that very oath upon his lips he cast it off unwittingly for ever, deep buried in the body that he spurned. Flotsam and jetsam, whatsoever touched the surface of those Stygian waves became the forfeit of the Fiend. Such was the fate of body and gem. No more to appear in substance in our story, the seal of the Seven Sigils shall, nevertheless, ride through it to the end, completing the curse of the Illyrian. The Venetian (ignorant as we have said of the loss he had inflicted upon himself) once more re-entered the banqueting hall. His purpose, before dealing with the question of his lady-love, was to order up a second collation accompanied by fresh founts of wine. This *tete-a-tete* (as he ordained it in his mind) should obliterate the memory of the previous banquet with its presence of an inconvenient third. He gave his order roundly to the servants, quite forgetting how impotent his commands. The automata remained unmoved, save for the fancy of the bravo that they leered somewhat upon him with an unmistakeable expression of contempt. Stung to sudden rage he drew his keen ancestral blade, and made a lunge at the vitals of the nearest one. In a moment he saw his mistake. The steel shivered into a thousand fragments, and shattered in its flight all the mirrors of the room. The hilt alone remained in his hand, which was jarred through and through by the shock. But the mental effect was even worse. For the first time a sense of impending Nemesis began to steal upon him. This unique companion of all his vicissitudes had been beloved of his inmost soul. From his jeopardous early days up he had been accustomed never to sleep without it, until it had become almost necessary to his slumbers that he should clap it to his breast. Slowly he recovered, and even comforted himself. What could his ancient hanger on avail him in his imprisonment on that island of enchantment? And had he not at hand metal far more attractive—damaskeened with gold—and suppler than Damascus steel? He gathered together lingeringly the shards of his faithful bedfellow, that he might cast those also into that Bottomless Lake that had just received their latest victim. But when he had them all embraced together in his arms, and had thrown aside the portal that he might descend the steps to the landing stage—he was blasted with a shock not so easy to rebound from as this matter of a broken weapon—there existed no longer a landing stage at all! Where it formerly stood the remorseless tide of the Bottomless Lake now swept the foot of the steps! The bravo reeled. For a moment the air was thick with curses loud and deep upon the day when the Seven Sigils had first flashed its baleful light athwart his path. He now saw the full significance of the fact that Magloire alone could shift the castle's site, and vivify its phlegmatic flunkeydom. The castle having been created by Magloire, for him alone existed. The handing over of his body to Beelzebub, of which the bravo himself had been the unthinking agent, had finally snapped the charm which held the building in existence. It was now slowly sinking into the waters from which it rose, and would continue to slowly sink till not a stone of it was visible above the surface of the darkling deep. Tosca reeled at this slap in the face that his fortune dealt him. He never knew how he found himself once more within the central court, a beaker in his hand, filling it to the brim with a vintage of the fountains of which we made mention before. He raised the vessel to his lips. The next moment it fell from his palsied hand and dashed into a thousand pieces. The fluid he had tried to drink slobbered over his knees as he rolled ignominiously upon the tesselated pavement. It was no longer wine that the fountain had yielded, but the fetid water of the Bottomless Lake! And this also resulted from the breaking of the charm by burial of the body of Magloire. The curse of the Illyrian was closing in upon its victim. The fate of the Venetian was written large upon his forehead. Abrupt Despair gripped upon his heartstrings. Yet still the honour of the bout remained with Tosca. For he remembered in his extremity that the bundle on the couch with all its possibilities was his. In despite of all that Doom had done he still remained the owner of a wallet that beggared Fortunatus. He sprang to his feet like an Antaeus, all the tenser for his momentary lapse to earth. He stretched out his arms towards the Bottomless Lake, and roared in tones of thunder:—

"Hell from beneath is moved for me to meet me at my coming! Now runs my sand apace, and I am ripe for my enrolment in the legions that eternally curse God and do not die! Yet still the victory of victories is mine, and eyeless Death shall not outstare me from it! Is it for this you work (you who sit in the High Places of the Pit), that I should flaunt in your faces the most fragrant hour of Life? Oh, how you have wrought your work awry! And you—you myriad victims of the dagger or the bowl that I have ushered unannealed to the account—I invite you every one to my bridal! Is this then your vengeance (oh, viperine Magloire!) that fruition should wait on my desire? And you, Illyrian Janko, is this then your revenge that you watch my wedding eve from the impotent other side of that great gulf fixed between? Here, on this side, I exact value in advance for the eternal price I pay. Here shall our ardent heat outblaze your fires, and when your ruffian waters reach our level shall the floor above receive us—and still the floor above— till on the roof itself at last we still out-laugh you! Hours must elapse or ever your icy billows reach our hearts, and wash them to the portal of Infinity! These hours shall be mine (though all Gehenna gnash its teeth), and our content shall give the lie to Hell."

Firm as a rock, he strode to his bag and cast off the belt from its mouth. A head appeared. But not a golden one. Its scanty hair was grey. Tosca recoiled. The ground reeled beneath him. His brain was furnace, and his blood arterial snow. With a mighty effort he recovered himself, and leaped like a madman into the sack, rending it seam from seam. The whole fabric parted, and disclosed, not the nonpareil that he had placed in its safe keeping, but the withered stubs of limbs and yellow disjected trunk of that ancient harridan of Illyria, whom he had seen on that never to be forgotten former occasion anatomised by the hand of Janko. And as he stared dead eyed upon that death, he was mercifully unaware that his feet were being swept by the inexorable waves of the advancing Bottomless Lake.

The Hand of Glory

Part I

Mine Host of the Four Cross Roads

The year of grace 1609. Our scene, a tavern within, and yet apart from, the bustle of a seaport town. Damned by its site upon an ill-omened juncture of crossroads, which, at a time when the town had not straggled so far, had been the burial ground of suicide and sorcerer; haunted by bones still sleepless, although centuries had gone since their last rag of flesh reeked off into the medicinal air; solitary in a crowd, except for such strangers as never learnt the local traditions. For these very reasons it attracted the attention of a class that feared men more than ghosts; and thus it came to be whispered among the neighbours as the house of call for the wizards of the Basque Provinces.

Such was the situation upon which the curtain rises. Our readers may now form a guess as to the character of the traveller that sought admittance upon the evening in question. This traveller was apparently alone—only apparently—for another sentient being suddenly makes known to us his presence on the scene. The cabalistic ring which graced the finger of our traveller shot a double-lightning from its tenant stone as the fist of its lord beat a devil's tattoo on the tavern door. The demon that was imprisoned within the ring had lifted for one second his pendulous eyelids. Foreknowledge of his approaching freedom to be wrought under that roof (as this chronicle shall in due order tell), had touched up buried fires; but patience born of immortality resumed its pride of place, and the Demon dissembling again a hope too soon revealed, there died in the instant all light from the gem, and left it fuscous as before. The fist in knocking was naturally raised above the head of the cabalist that wore the ring. The traveller consequently failed to perceive the eyebeams of his familiar. Be sure if he caught sight of that glint of evil glee he would have read in it an omen of impending disaster to the enterprise that turned him to that tavern. The future of cabalist and demon would then have hung upon his decision whether to dree the weird or 'scape it. But the significants that ruled his horoscope withheld the timely warning, and the traveller continued his endeavours to get hearing from the all too early retired household. Thus the moment of possible retreat passed irrevocably by. A wicket sunk in the stubborn thickness of the door, was thrown suddenly open. A pair of eyes appeared—luminous, terrible. They fixed those of the cabalist unflinchingly, beams to beams, lights to lights, and the cabalist recognised in the eyes of his adversary the self-same, tell-tale film through which he flashed his own. Not the film of the eagle neither, that may enable the king of birds to peruse the noonday sun, but would impotently shrivel before the venomous exhalations that stream from fiery pits that blaze under fallen angels' brows, no, the eyes of the intervisible twain were sheathed with the shard of the born exorcist—the heir of the secrets and physical gifts of a line of wizard sires. From behind these horny casements they had measured the frown of Satan's self, and danced undaunted and undulled. Sparse were the mortals whom the cabalist reckoned fellow-men; but here, at any rate, was one of them. The cabalist waxed kindly, as he proceeded to interrogate what he felt to be a kindred spirit.

"Is this the hostelry of the Four Cross Roads?"

"By some such name is it noted among the vulgar."

"And are you he of whom they whisper, under the name of Aquelarre?"

"I am the master of this house."

"You are then he to whom I am recommended by one I have good reason to trust."

"May I trouble you for his name?"

"To me he is known as Lisaldo."

"Under that name, at any rate, I do not know him; but that argues nothing. A thousand soldiers know the lieutenant whom the lieutenant does not know."

"By this token you may know him, that he gave you a name of praise and fear—that of the devil's correspondent for the viscounty of Labourt."

"And if it were so?"

"Then over and above being yourself sunk from sole to crown in the study of supernature you have traced the gigantic plan of linking yourself together with all else that tread untrodden ways. And I saw that the design was good—for in union there is strength— and if we in the far New World from which I come, are to-day unthreatened by the bigotry of the church, it would nevertheless be short sight indeed if we played the spectator, while among you runs the writ of cord and faggot. To-morrow, mayhap, we shall be persecuted in our turn, and ashes the brethren that could have bettered us. For this, then, am I travelled hither, as I may say at your bidding, since the suggestion proceeded from one who knows you, though him you may not know; that we may survey together the field of your danger, and in consort draft such measure of defiance and defence as shall eat up this persecution at the root. This evening disembarked and understanding from that same Lisaldo, that under cover of the tavern of the Four Cross Roads your pursue your devil's procuracy, I have hustled hither straight to take up my quarters beneath your kindly roof."

"Are you then alone or do I rightly see two others that linger in your rear among the shadows?"

"The one of them is this Lisaldo that I speak of, to whom I owe your name, and who has attached himself to my personal service; and in this connexion I may mention that I shall require two communicating bedrooms (or be it one with a dressing-room adjacent) to gratify my long, and now invincible, vogue of keeping my servant all night within my call. My other follower is a creole of the family Ataurresagasti; by trade an honest seaman, but not, I believe, too honest to be of possible use to our cause. Told off to do us service during the long and perilous passage he has been only too anxious to be of comfort to us, and we are indebted to him for countless little offices. Arrived at your wharves we could satisfy him with nothing less than the porterage of half our effects, and since the whole were too heavy for Lisaldo, 'twas but policy to accept his friendly offer, rather than initiate a stranger into our destination. Accommodated with a bed in this same house, he will be under our united ken—should you consider him metal that may be moulded to our purpose he need never return to his ship."

"Nor for the matter of that in the contrary case either, since it were unsafe for him to have even touched the skirts of our common secret. 'Tis child's play for such as you and I to rot the thread of life with an oblivious gruel."

"We will confer upon that matter in the bedroom which you allot me, while Lisaldo and the sailor are refreshing themselves below. You are satisfied with my credentials, and will admit us without delay, since the night is wasting shrewdly?"

"There is one thing wanting—your name."

"My name I have never syllabled since my birth, nor would it be possible to deceive you with a false one, you being what you are and I wearing this ring by whose fame you and all of life occult may know me."

The cabalist jerked his slender hand from out of the folds of his cloak, where he had thrust it after the opening of the wicket. Its crouching prisoner (wiser than before) allowed never a wink to escape him. But that it was in sooth the very ring that contained the familiar (renowned among the sorcerers of the whole round world) Aquelarre well could see. An insane impulse to strike down the insolent owner, and incontinently seize the matchless gem, contracted every fibre of his body. Had the door not stood between them, he would have made the rash attempt, only to remember, when too late, that the allegiance of the Demon could never by violence transfer from man to man. He ground the wicket into its place to hide the distortion of his features, and busied himself with bolts and bars that they might clatter above the gnashing of his teeth. By the time he had undone the fastenings the impulse had passed.

Recollecting all the restrictions that fenced the ring around, he had become once more himself. Meanwhile the nameless cabalist had summoned with a whistle his two attendants forward. Youths of about an equal age, the one was white as a cosset page, and the other tanned like a galley-slave.

The massive portal swung a-side with a suddenness that even drew a start from the seasoned nerves of the cabalist, though it must be evident that one who had put together such a ring must be steeped in no ordinary course of sciences and surprises. A blaze of light shot through the widening passage into the dark deserted street. A host of obsequious hands stretched out of the blinding drift and relieved the two bearers of their luggage. Before the three newcomers had acquired the proper focus to even perceive who had thus helped them, the helpers were out of sight. Viands and vintages which had appeared with startling rapidity alone remained to prove to their eyes which the travellers rubbed, the substantiality of the just present bodies. Also the master of the house stood there, unbonneted, and bowing his welcome. The cabalist refused to break a fast which was integral to some experiment in hand; leaving this, then, to the more congenial age of Lisaldo and the sailor, he withdrew with Aquelarre to his apartments. Thus the youths so like, and yet so unlike, at last were left alone together.

The footfalls of the brothers of the black art had hardly died away above stairs when the sailor turned to Lisaldo abruptly and whispered in a tone attuned to every sweetness—

"Lisalda!"

The page started as if stung to death, at thus hearing an address in the feminine form of the name, instead of in the masculine. His face at first blanched with sudden terror, and then flooded with rosy red. He made a confused attempt at correction.

"You mean Lisaldo."

"Lisalda, and Lisalda, and Lisalda."

The sailor persisted—this apparent error seemed to water in his mouth—then remembering himself he became sheepish as a chidden child, and sank presently on to his knees. The page eyed him guiltily, then the sailor took courage in his hands and made sensible his inmost heart.

"I love you, Lisalda, and love has keener sight than many that call it blind. I felt your sex from the first hour you stepped aboard. I kindled to it with an instinct that strangled reason. It possessed every fibre of me through all our days becalmed on Sargasso seas that to me seemed flower shotten meads. I clenched my teeth on it our tropic nights when hand in hand you walked my watch with me, and learnt from me the blazonry of heaven. Months ago I should have given throat to the heart that hungered within me. But in my surly sailor fashion I only tightened my belt around it. I am no saint, Lisalda, I have served apprentice to buccaneers on Caribbean seas—men that never set a hand to honest tool save when they planted chests of gold in the earth, I have swam o' days in blood and o' nights in wine. But the hand that scattered the brains of Don and Dutchman was an aspen held in yours. Terror tremendously overruled me, when I would fain have slipped the cable of my desire, and it is a marvel to me now that I kneel at your feet, though I know full well that my revealment is wrung from me by the parting asunder of our ways. Here must I speak or ever after hold my peace, here you may infuse yourself with a heart no less honest than rough, that has beat for naught nor will beat for aught save you; or here you may rule me unworthy of more that has already enjoyed overmuch. It bodes me ill I fear, Lisalda, that you never read a heart so confounded with your own; but, whatever you say will be for me the voice of oracle that is worshipped whether good or ill."

"The oracle is dumb to-night, Ataurresagasti, though you have taught me that I knew your love from the first. I cannot decide at once whether I have done you irreparable wrong, or added to your fulness of life. To-morrow, friend (if that title does not jar upon you) shall learn you all your heart's desire. And (whatever that morrow's disillusion) to-night at any rate, your image will disturb my no longer virgin sleep."

"Your sleep, Lisalda, there's the rub that galls my jealous loin. To-night that I have a share in you (though it be but for to-night) I

shudder at the thought of your retiring to the ante-room of the
bedchamber of that other man. Throughout the voyage every lip
before the mast has shriven him with curses (not loud, but deep)
for the wayward winds his Jonah presence fetched athwart our
course. The bated breath of the forecastle credited him with the
wearing of a familiar spirit imprisoned in the setting of that ring
upon his hand. How did such as you come to foregather with one
so unkindly, and withal so far from this your birthplace? And what
is his need of you that one so powerful should claim you close at
heel?"

"Ataurresagasti, it were too long to tell you how I came to be
orphaned, and at buffet with the world. Too long again to recount
the chances that transferred me from here to the Indies. Enough
that I must have been in desperate straits when I donned the disguise I still wear, and entered the vacant service of my present lord
and master. That he lived in evil odour had come to my ears, and
that he never kept his servants long, but that they either went mad
or died was more than gossip to me that first attended my master
to the funeral of my predecessor. I was situated so sorely that I
would have worn Satan's livery to earn me bed and board. Now the
secret of the wants of my master and the wastage amongst his
servants is this: his nerves are completely shattered by terrible
experiments, the nature of which I never dare to know. He sees
through the veil that round us wraps impenetrably. He is haunted
day and night by hosts of beings incorporately awful. Over these,
indeed, some sway of his extends (else were he long since torn to
shreds), but only by the continual strain of every resource of his
science. The demon that is familiar of the ring you speak of—the
loathsome creepiness that writhes within a crystal cell and impotently spits at such as dare to see—is on the one hand the crowning glory of his labours, and the envy of the wizard world—and on
the other hand an anxious horror that makes cheap the mere rou-
tine of Hell. Day it turns to night, night to nightmare, and still the
worst of all remains—the hour between midnight and cockcrow
when the heavenly patrols are relieving guard and the nether
gates swing open and all the rout of Hell are free to seek their own

devilish devices. Now you can guess, can you not, Ataurresagasti, why the cabalist never remains alone in the dark?"

"By the God I never praised till I met you, Lisalda, this passes the worst I had imagined. But do you still think so ill of me (after the centuries of mingled life we have crushed into so curt an orbit), do you still so little value my self esteem as to believe me capable (now I know what your service is) of allowing you to continue it for even yet one grain of the hour glass? To the devil with this enemy and friend of his, and let the poor prisoner of the ring have his day! I, too, am a prisoner and feel for all in bonds."

"You are the best of men, Ataurresagasti, and fittest to be free. But for this night at any rate (however your reasons may touch me) I must fulfil my contract, as of use and wont. Whatever new combination to-morrow's sun may bring, it is too late to-night, at any rate, to find a substitute to comrade the broken slumbers of the cabalist."

"It is never too late, Lisalda, to crown my broad shoulders with the lightness of a burden saved from yours. I beseech you, as a lover whom you may yet reject, not to refuse me this (as it may be) last sad privilege—chance itself (if all be not fated from the first) plays patron to my innocent stratagem. The landlord of this tavern of the Four Cross Roads (and may I die the day I see a more ill-favoured fellow) has heard our names, it is true, but can have no means of telling which is which. Do you call yourself the cabin-boy, Ataurresagasti, and vouchsafe me for one brief snatch, to be bone of the bone, and flesh of the flesh with Lisalda (or Lisaldo). The certainty that you are bolted and barred once more in a room alone, will bear me up through all that teems from Tophet. The cabalist is the only eye that could detect the substitution, and he keeps (or you would never have remained his) respectfully on his own side the partition until morning. The dawn may see him damned, so far as his hold on either of us is concerned, and we will set forth (together I trust) about our own peace and pleasure."

"As to that I can give you no promise, Ataurresagasti, save to remember you in any case until the last sigh of life. But this, as you say, is all the more reason why I should let you be my proxy, if it will give you any unfeigned satisfaction. And here comes back our host on the heels of our accord, and the curtain rises on our play."

The sailor rose to his feet. It was as Lisalda said, for such (her secret once revealed) we may as well henceforth style her, Aquelarre having finished his business with the cabalist come to summon the page to his attendance. But he first drew a bottle and three goblets from a press and placed the latter on one of the tables. Filling them to the overflow, he appointed one to each to drink a parting cup. All three raised on high and touched together their goblets in token of sentiment, somewhat hollow. Ataurresagasti had scarcely put his lips to the liquid, when memory started armed from his brain. It was hocussed. There was no doubt about it. He had been drugged once before by the pressgang of the pirate, with whom he had served out his buccaneer articles. Once bit, twice shy. He replaced the goblet on the table, the other two mechanically followed his example. The good fellowship that shone upon his weather-beaten face was in inverse ratio to the ready subtlety that scanned every loophole from within; and presently he swooped down with unerring instinct upon the only possible coign of vantage. The meaning eyes of the landlord had turned upon the innocent eyes of Lisalda. He was staring out her inmost soul. Taking advantage of this absorption of the two, Ataurresagasti reversed the positions of the drugged goblet and that of the landlord. So smartly did he execute this manoeuvre that it would most certainly have escaped the notice of an ordinary observer. But had it escaped the lynx-eyed Aquelarre? The sailor breathed more freely when, upon all three once more raising their goblets, the whole of the hocussed stuff disappeared without question down the landlord's corded throat. All having drained to the dregs, Aquelarre turned and addressed himself to the quondam buccaneer:—

"May I be burnt by the Parliament of Bordeaux if my customer upstairs let me into the secret as to which of you two he mastered. Now I'll be bound 'tis you, my jolly Roger (and not this queasy cabin-boy) that has chaffered for gold his rest o' nights to the wandering Jew up aloft there."

"Your guess does honour to your penetration, Monsieur Four Cross Roads, though you did overshoot your bolt a bit when you called me Jolly Roger."

"Ho, ho, Monsieur Lisaldo, so you turned your skin then with your livery, and no longer acknowledge the Black Flag?"

"How do you know that I had ever anything in common with the Black Flag?"

"Easy as lying, Monsieur Lisaldo, easy as lying. Your face, my friend (and for the matter of that, everyone's face), is as an open book whereon I read. Nay, your hand alone, my friend, shouts your past, your present, and your future to such as I that have ears to hear."

"Of the past and of the present I am already sick at heart, but I am open to receive any index (what it may befit me to know) as to how the future shall shape itself before me."

"A good wish upon you! I am permitted to tell you, at any rate, that you chose your vocation under a healthy star, for you were never born to be drowned!"

The sailor hardly knew whether to be amused or annoyed at the tone adopted by the chiromantist. He continued to balance the matter in a confused sort of way, after he had taken shy leave of Lisalda. Arrived in his room, he barred and bolted the outer door with a thoroughness born of much adventuring. He loosened a hanger that he wore at his side, and tied it by its belt as with a sword knot to his wrist. That had been the *toilet de rigueur* for the night among his former messmates, the pirates of the Antilles. In this array then, supine upon the bed, he confidently awaited developments. To keep himself awake he continued to agitate the mysterious character and conduct of Aquelarre. The events of the evening, since the ill-assorted three had left their ship together, all forced themselves into the question. This opened the road to a review of the whole voyage and the change it had wrought in his life. And that life—what turn would it take on the morrow? What result from the heart-probing of Lisalda? The singularity was that the more plausible he painted the future, the darker shaded the present, and the past, of his sweetheart. He felt it was an insult to

her to question her about that past of which she had denied the
recital. And yet he longed—and how he longed—to rise to her from
his very bed to question her. And her relations with the cabalist—
how long before the voyage she had served him Ataurresagasti
never knew, but apart from that it was gall and wormwood to him
that she should even have shared his state room at sea. The fancy
forced itself upon the sailor that the cabalist—who saw through all
things—had seen through her disguise. The more he turned over
the reasons assigned by Lisalda for the cabalist never sleeping
alone, the more unlikely it appeared that a prince of all the Magi,
and tamer of the Demon of the Ring, should show a side so puny.
In spite of his better self there forced itself upon him another, and
quite opposite, picture of the nights that these two had passed together. Yet why (and here for a moment he threw off that thraldom)
yet why had Lisalda, this particular evening, apparently willingly
exchanged with him the place, which by that hateful theory she
should have found a pleasance. Again wider issues loomed in every
direction, until he returned again bewildered to what seemed willy-
nilly his keynote for that night. He tossed from side to side. Picture after picture stood out before his mind's eye, until he even
reached the length of fancying Lisalda at that moment on the other
side with the cabalist, while Ataurresagasti on his side lay befooled.
That she could not have got there by any human means was a difficulty which did not even occur to him for solution. The sweat
stood out thick upon his brow. He positively saw Lisalda twined
about the body of his rival. His hair (he felt it) was turning grey.
He saw the cabalist (a wonder of satiety) remove that ring of rings
from his finger and fit it jestingly upon hers. At this precise juncture of his nightmare, Ataurresagasti suddenly started broad awake
to his feet. Dream or no dream—whatever the rest of the night had
been—there was certainly now something awful in progress in
the adjoining apartment. Something (which he instinctively felt
was not human) was struggling for life and death with the luckless
cabalist. The hair of the sailor stood on end. There was no mistake
about it this time. Time had been when he fancied he felt fear, but

he knew now that only at this moment had he learnt its kind. All at once a most terrible shriek rang out through every corner of the house. Ataurresagasti dashed the partition into splinters with a blow that would have shattered steel. He leaped into the room just in time to arrest the escape of some huge incredible beast, that stood sullenly at bay, in the straggling streak of dawn. The mystery was solved. Down came the hanger with an impulse so irresistible that it sheared off a whole limb of the accursed one. The point of the hanger actually penetrated so deeply into the flooring that it was a moment of anxiety (during which his quarry, although maimed, might have bested him) before Ataurresagasti succeeded in getting it out again. But when he had recovered it, the animal had disappeared, impossible to find out how or where. This alone he saw in the imperfect light (or rather in the imperfect darkness) that the whole room was scattered from end to end with blood and bones and brain, which was all that was left of that most unhappy man.

A sickness came upon the victor. He mopped his dripping forehead. He turned to leave the presence-chamber of death and doom; he picked up as he did so the severed limb, a casual glance at which confirmed his general impression that the gaunt game had been but a particularly large and loathly wolf, such as occasionally penetrated the precincts of towns in the neighbourhood of the Pyrenees. Ataurresagasti walked down straight into the reception room of the night before. For the moment the possible alarm of Lisalda at that terrible shriek of dissolution of the cabalist had not even entered his mind. His object was to summon Aquelarre. To his surprise he found him crouching there already white as a ghost apparently with fear; He sprang to his feet at sight of the sailor, and barely suppressed a cry. This time it was the sailor that read, and the landlord's face that provided reading matter. Amazement was writ legibly in every line of it, and his eyes were opened to the size of saucers. And Ataurresagasti asked himself, without finding answer, what connexion all this had with the attempt to drug him, which he had discovered the preceding evening. The two men stared at one another for some minutes without finding speech, of which indeed the innkeeper, at any rate, seemed incapable. The word when taken up was taken up by Ataurresagasti.

"My pharmaceutical friend seems somewhat upset by my early appearance after draining the drowsy cup which he compounded for me overnight."

"And it is not natural that a landlord should be fearful for his slate when he sees an uncancelled score slinking downstairs to the outlet at such unearthly hour?"

"Alas, for your slate (if that touch you so nearly) a fiscal fleeter than yourself has attended here this night, and collected your other lodger's scot."

"What means this matin pleasantry? How goes it with the ca-balist?"

"Well, I hope, although I dare not think it well. His reckoning, I fear, will overreach him."

"Is he dead?"

"As much of him as can still be traced is unquestionably dead."

"That then undid my beauty sleep. I thought I dreamed an unforgetful shriek."

"'Twas murder mouthed it. God rest his soul, that died in such a case as he was overtaken in."

"He died, you say, by the hand of God?"

"I say by the limb of a wolf, rather, which I arriving overdue did incontinently lop from its trunk. The felon then evading by exit to me invisible, I descended hither by what impulse I scarcely know save that my intentions tended justiceward."

"You meant perchance to summon authority to certify to cause of death. But this must be looked to by myself before anyone else is admitted. What became of the piece of conviction?"

"Behold it!"

"Out upon you! What providence have we here! O perjured windpipe you are most miraculously self-accused by this mischosen joint! Limb of a wolf did you dare to say? Nay, behold assassin, to your confusion, 'tis the disjointed member of your master that you have brought away with you from the presence chamber."

A cry of horror burst from the palsied lips of the sailor. It was as Aquelarre stated. Not the hacked-off trophy of his prowess had he carried in his hand; by some inexplicable equivocation it was the sundered fist of the cabalist still bearing the ring of the familiar. Chilled to the marrow by the ghastly riddle Ataurresagasti stammered some broken phrase of explanation; but the landlord cut him short.

"Hold your peace, rogue (and fool as much as rogue), you have miscast your account if you think to cope in a game of brag with a man of the world like Aquelarre. You do but squander breath which you may want ere long when the hangman ties your cravat. 'Twas then the bauble on yonder finger whose fatuous fire lured you into slippery sin—I misfancied even yesternight your gallows visage, that will ere long grin through a halter: 'twill dog my conscience till the day I die that I whispered no warning to that gentle sage. But by these five bones! I will lay no second blood to my debit. Rather than see a gallant (if misguided) boy turn rope-dancer I will hold the nose of correction from your trail. But think not that I shall also permit you to lay that flattering booty to your soul—you must make over to me the gaud that cozened you to crime. Indeed, if I left it in your possession, you would never dare to look a clothesline in the face. Whereas, never doubt but that I shall make the best possible use of it, such as I have no time to bethink myself of at the moment. Masses (perchance) for the soul of its late owner done to death unofficed by Holy Church. Whatever he would have liked to do for me had I been slain, and he Aquelarre. Oh, I can promise you a binding promise of that. But we palter out the time of opportunity. Your safety lies in instant flight. The Bidassoa lies within easy avail. Take the bridge that throws over it at Behobia. Once on the Spanish side of the river, the hemp is not sown that shall throttle you. For this crime at any rate, I remaining shall run the risk, if risk there be to run. Quick then with the gewgaw— 'tis a dull stone at best—why do you hesitate when the path divides before you? One way leads to length of life, the other is a short cut to cordage."

"You son of a burnt witch! The broom-ridden hag that taught you to spell out the Devil's books, and to find fortunes in hands—past, present, and future forsooth—she taught you all askew. I have done no such deeds as your second sight credits me with. The matter squared precisely with my account of it, but I am fortune's fool, and in change for my own handiwork I took hold (I know not how) of this Hand of Glory. In view of the public opinion that whispers you a wizard I should not exclaim over and above if it turned out to be your own hocus pocus that brought about the barter. Nay, it is possible and even probable that the wolf was but a go-between, guided by a hand not a hundred miles from here (and I spit upon mine that grasped it in friendship yester-even) but you are seemingly only an understrapper in the Devil's workshop since you cut only yourself with your unnecessary tool. We did not do these things by deputy upon the Spanish Main. Viewed in the light of your press for the possession of the ring (of whose virtues you apparently believe me to be ignorant) the riddle of last night's sleeping draught need not long remain unread. That after stripping you to this nakedness I should clothe you with the purple and fine linen of the ring would be too much for any but yourself to expect."

"Cry you mercy! You have signed your own death-warrant. What you cast in my teeth is guesswork. But you are rivetted hand and foot to the matter of fact. Pass me the ring and you go free—refuse, and you shall play the pendulum."

"And would you play the gatesman? Odds my life, and do you think I dare not go free until Aquelarre lifts the latch? Deputy devil, look to yourself!"

Aquelarre placed his back to the door. The buccaneer swooped down upon him with a yell that split the throat of echo. With all his force he struck him in the face with the abominable relic of the cabalist. The effect was electric. Aquelarre threw up his arms, and fell like a log dumb and blind to the ground. The buccaneer wrenched open the door and disappeared down one of the Four Cross Roads.

PART II
THE DEVIL'S ATTORNEY

The dial had sweat twelve hours of day ere we resume the broken thread of our story. At the sign of the Four Cross Roads (whether accident or design) matters stood in some such case as when we opened our first part. The cabalist having paid the debt which he had owed so lightly and so long, the ring now graced the little finger of the sailor. The inscrutable door strained under his muscular fist, that this time summoned passage. It opened, and again, with startling abruptness, Ataurresagasti crossed the fateful lintel. The door (which apparently worked of itself) flew back with a horrid, ominous jar. Aquelarre stood with his arms crossed in an attitude of expectation. Sailor and sorcerer took stock of one another from head to foot. But when the latter caught sight of the ring, he burst (as if inspired) into speech.

"So you have returned upon your tracks; I foresaw you would, and have awaited you. You remembered, when in safely yonder side of the frontier, that you had left a jewel in danger behind, outweighing that you wear. Desire came uppermost in the throw with fear."

"You man of second sight, is she still here,—since you know it is a she I seek?"

"You set me a painful task (my friend and admirer), if you are so ignorant of all that has happened during your somewhat protracted constitutional as to require the rigmarole of it from me. However, since you already doubtless know (and at any rate I care not to conceal from you) that I am the official representative in Labourt of a certain proud and damned Prince, you doubtless look to me as to the fountain head. So be it then, and to the task. But you did a black day's work as ever you did under the Black Flag, when you saved your hide this morning at the expense of your mistress's skin. Nay, hear me out. I know that you were shaken out of all self. But you had scarcely kicked my dust from off your feet, when the officers of justice, whom you so churlishly evaded had plucked me by the beard. The swan song of him from whom you filched that ring had pierced the universal ear. That murder had deflowered the bed you wot of, the constables had no room to doubt. Indeed, your Carib fashion of piece-mealing a victim put them to the unsavoury task of making out an inventory of the deceased. My own good fame being above suspicion, it fell from the first upon Lisalda, unearthed and laid willy-nilly by the heels. Her sex (another item of distrust about her) was of necessity discovered in the Torture Chamber."

"The Torture Chamber!"

"Aye, the Torture Chamber. You saved your four limbs. She will never use again one of her arms, that was crippled in their grips of hellish engines. The surgeon (save the mark) pronounced that she could bear no more to-day. To-morrow they practice upon the other arm. And after that there will be enough of her sweet body to feed their tools a week."

"But she is innocent—my God, how innocent—and I, who begin almost to believe that I am guilty, will surrender at once in her place."

"Small good (my untutored friend), save the melancholy satisfaction of pressing the same rack with her. The Parliament of Bordeaux never let slip a single victim, nor is it any longer merely the indictment for the murder of the Cabalist that piles the faggots for her. You are a babe and suckling in these horrors. I am prematurely grey with them. Had you but seen (as I have) the mother burnt with the child at her breast—the loving pair chilled at the same stake—the friendship of years dissolved in smoke, but enough—to get out of the Torture Chamber (as you should readily guess) the corpus vile reduced to a crushed craze will sign any depositions that may be held out as a bait. The consequence is that your girl has already avowed her identity with a desperate, long-sought-for witch and sacristan to one of the most noted of our Black Priests. So much for the wringing of one set of nerves. To what may they not confess her before they have writhed her into a bag of quivering pulp?"

"Enough, enough, enough, can nothing be done to save her? O, you whom all this persecution has left upright (and a refuge as

men whisper to the threatened) from whatever source your com-
mission comes, I wrap about me the hem of your mantle. Be your
aid of God, or Devil, I invoke it!"

"Do you know what you ask? The Indians of Darian are charity, compared to me and mine. Be my aid of God, or Devil do you
say? You shall rest in no doubt upon that head. The bare mention
of the name of God is a source of danger among us of the opposition, save when we take it (for our own purposes) in vain. And of
the opposition I have been, am, and shall be. That with which sur-
mise is rife be here with certainty known to you! You treat with
one having authority deputed from the Most High, the Prince of
this World and of Hell."

"I have never shrunk from any, save one woman, and I do not
shrink from you. In all this storm you are my sheet anchor."

"Then in my character of the Devil's proxy I offer you your
heart's ease in tender for your soul!"

"In the event of my agreeing to your proposition how do you
set to work to save her?"

"By the substitution for her of a golem, a device that I learnt
from a Rabbi of Provence that was my teacher in the art of cabala.
It is a doll of wax (or indeed of any substance), no matter how uncouth, and upon the forehead of which in angelical letters one
writes a chosen name—in your case the name Lisalda—I shall then
conjure for you in a strong circle. You will clinch the bargain with
my master in person by striking hands with him. And his claw will
leave you for your lifetime branded with his private brand. This
done he will breathe upon the golem. Obedient to the breath of
life it starts (to all outward appearance) into a perfect double of
the person in whose name it may have been inscribed. In your case
the name Lisalda. Nor will you yourself be able to tell whether
Lisalda or the devil's coin stands before you. You will forgive my
suggesting that in some respects you might be better off with the
ideal than the real, since it starts in life (like a child) with a clear
slate and you may teach it in what sort you will."

"How now! Do you libel my love?"

"I speak but as a man of the world and to some extent of the next world also. However, to resume our ways and means. My Prince having bestowed upon the golem such life as it is only his and God's to give, I then smuggle the innocent know-nothing into the prison of your Lisalda and carry off Lisalda in exchange. Then to horse and hey for love and leisure—on the further side of the Bidassoa; but the cheat will never be discovered, and in fine and in finish the golem will run to ash like so many of her betters."

"Is there no other way?"

"There is no other way. Bethink yourself. The offer is there to take it or leave it. Shake hands with my Master or shake your fist at him. Be one of us or one of her executioners."

"I cannot boggle long at that. Death of my soul! Have with you then Aquelarre and let fruition crowd the heels of haste."

"There is yet one thing that you may boggle at. You have ratified the bargain with my Master but not the fee of my procuracy. You cannot do anything without me and I cannot do anything without that Ring which you wear upon your finger as my handsel."

"Your fee is a fleabite to your Master's. The ring I wear is yours but not as earnest money. I pass it over to you only after service rendered. And now lead on to this golem you speak of."

"Be it as you say. The preliminaries being all settled between the high contracting parties, I usher you to the actual presence of my principal."

As he thus concluded the negotiation a covetous light (like to nothing in heaven or earth) shot through the lashes of the devil's attorney. He stood at last upon the brink of attainment of that Ring so thirstily craved. With an imperious gesture he summoned the sailor to follow him and turned off behind the staircase. Directly the sorcerer's back was turned Ataurresagasti could not forbear a broad grin. He had outwitted (at any rate he thought so) both the infernal furious spirit and his attorney. And first as to the latter. The fact was that the only ring worn by the sailor himself, and pledged to Aquelarre by the letter of the bond, was a tawdry hoop of silver. The Ring that contained the familiar had never left the

dead man's hand. How then had the inn-keeper imagined otherwise? Simply because the sailor, with a view to better protection,
had drawn up his right arm within his sleeve and held the Hand of
Glory by the wrist in such a position as to appear his own. The
Ring which thus appeared to adorn the sailor's little finger was in
reality still upon that of its architect. And, therefore, it was still
unpawned to Aquelarre. But this was not the only or even the first
fruits of the trick which Ataurresagasti (or his good angel) had set
in motion. As he gathered from the sorcerer that the devil would
imprint his private mark upon him by means of a grip of hands,
Ataurresagasti (or, again, his good angel) jumped at once to the
obvious deduction that by going through with the same sleight of
hand, Beelzebub would come claw to claw with only the dead
Cabalist and earn no soul but his. Earn no soul but his, which was
undoubtedly already long-earned and already in heats of hell. Thus,
by a single piece of hugger-mugger, the buccaneer hoped to go free
with his sweetheart and do no harm to anyone. Or, at any rate, to
anyone that stood within the reach of harm, the only sufferers
being the devil and his lost. How the whirligig of time brought
round its revenges the sequel of this story will show. Now that the
reader is conversant with what was passing through the mind of
the sailor we must return to where we left him at the back of the
staircase. Aquelarre, stooping down, by some device which the
sailor did not fathom, raised one of the stone slabs of the flooring
from its place. This impromptu trap-door disclosed a flight of steps
that fell down into absolute darkness. A motion from the landlord
and Ataurresagasti fearlessly stalked down them to some distance,
where he stopped until he had seen his confederate also enter.
Aquelarre drew down the trap-door after him. This last action was
fatal, of course, to such light as had previously washed the upper
part of the stairs. All was now equal night. Yet the buccaneer
continued his descent. The steps seemed endless. At last he
stopped. He listened. To his surprise and horror no footfall
sounded above. What had become of Aquelarre? The sailor suspected some deception put upon him. He retraced his steps as
quickly as was possible under the difficult circumstances of the

ascent. That he reached the top was made apparent to him by the crash of his head against the stone. He reeled and all but fell. What had become of Aquelarre? Recovering himself he tried with all his might to obtain egress but not unnaturally without avail. He mopped his brow and tried to think. Escape being impossible in this direction he decided to recommence the descent; come what might he could be no worse off than where he was even if he went down, down, down to the earth's centre. He tried to persuade himself that worse things happen at sea, but his heart of hearts nailed the lie. Down, down, down! He counted (as he thought) a thousand steps but not without dizzy doubts. And then he lost all count—all doubt—all but damned certainty. He had never been sick at sea but now—and then suddenly he staggered against some obstacle. It yielded. It was a door. Firelight danced in his eyes. He rolled into a corner and stood up against a wall. He was in an underground chamber and before him was Aquelarre. How the devil's advocate had got there before him who can tell? Doubtless in some devil's way. Aquelarre made no remark upon the sailor's entrance nor ceased from his work of drawing (on the ground) circle within circle, distant from one another about a hand's-breadth. The sailor rubbed his eyes and looked about him. The space (at one end of the vault) reserved for the circles was scrupulously clean, as well it might be, since one speck of pollution would have nullified their every virtue. The rest of the subterrane was a hotchpotch of horrors—the *disjecta membra* of a magical laboratory scattered broadcast over every inch of the floor. Here were receptacles of unsightly shapes, crucible and cucurbit, alembic and aludel. Here were the spoils of charnel-house and churchyard, ear and eye excrement and entrail. Here squat phials bore charges of price, poison and philtre, *lac virginis*, and *elixir vitae*. In one corner gibbered a gigantic skeleton. In another lay a Jacob's Staff and a Pentacle of Solomon. In a third heaped up musty vellums, presumably occult; and of these last Ataurresagasti picked up one, and was about to open it at random, when Aquelarre turned suddenly white, and fetched a roar so sudden that the startled sailor dropped it as if it burnt him.

The magician (who had just finished inscribing his series of circles) came forward with a brow of night. His fist was clenched as if to strike. But after glaring some moments at the buccaneer, he twisted his nails out of his palm again where they left four bleeding scars. He calmed down still farther before he could speak.

"Madman let this teach you never more to tamper with such wild-fire as a magic book. There are spells on every page of that volume which (had you exposed even one of them to the air) would have dissolved us both into death and hell. It is easy to see that this is your maiden bout as sidesman to an exorcist. Were you an ordinary neophyte, even your failure to play Paul Pry, would have quenched you the light of day. But take heart of grace and fear nothing mortal, for on your life great issues hang. But lest you should make another slip (and perchance to perdition) mark well what I am now about to teach you. And firstly to instal our golem— yonder it hangs in the fourth corner of the vault, suspended and swinging above our heads. You ask me why it so suspends and swings. I will tell you. Look at its forehead and you will see a name, which if you could read our angelical letters you would find to be the name of De Lancre, of the Parliament of Bordeaux. De Lancre, that is the torturer of our wizardry and of your bride, and the touch-wood of a thousand fires that depopulate Labourt. But his turn shall yet be served. By the sympathy which I have established between this mannikin and him (by only the sealing of it with his name) I have got into my hands more power over his body than your untortured fancy would conceive. I could even bring his life to a close at this very second, by piercing his heart with a pin. But at the moment I am content by this swinging between earth and sky (as they say swings Mahomet's coffin) to afflict him with horrors, to which death were meat and drink,—to afflict him with dizziness, vertigo, and whirlpool, with falling sickness and ceaseless belch-ing, yea, to the innermost membrane of his soul. But that your need of this lay figure is greater than his, he should sleep never a wink to-night. Nay, not all the drowsy drinks of the Herbal should gum his eyelids up. But behold I release him and lean him against this wall, and erase his name with my finger. 'Tis done, and De Lancre at the very instant far away is restored to perfect health. Some charlatan will doubtless get the credit for a cure."

He broke into a peal of horrible laughter. But the sailor scarcely heeded. He was gazing at the figure which he understood was to be transformed with a blasphemous breath into an exact simulacrum of his betrothed. A greater difference than at present existed between the two could scarcely be imagined. Lisalda was—well we will not attempt the impossible task of reproducing a lover's raptures. The golem was a rude lump of modelling wax with five projections, occupying respectively such parts of the main body as suggested that they were meant for its legs, arms, and head. The last distinguished itself from the four limbs by several additional clues to its identity. It had eyes indicated by a couple of stones. It had ears, or, at any rate, handles, on either side, and a third in front for nose. It had a mouth which left even more to the imagination, since its hieroglyphic was a herring bone. Lastly, it was thatched (somewhat scantily, it must be confessed), with what appeared to be the bristles of a hog. With a view no doubt to decency, the devil's attorney tied a rag about its middle. Another about its right arm he explained as representing the prison bandages which swathed the tortured limb of the real Lisalda. Finally, he inscribed upon its brow a name, and declared it to be complete. And now for a lesson in ceremonial magic. Seven circles Aquelarre had compassed, waxing smaller and smaller within each other. In the innermost (which is where the two daring exorcists should stand) the devil's advocate placed a pan of coals, the same that had hitherto only given light to the room, but of which the real use and purpose was suffumigation. This suffumigation was that part of the work which was to fall to the lot of Ataurresagasti. For this the landlord placed beside the pan various packets of perfumes each numbered in the order with which they were to feed the flames. And woe unto the exorcists, if in the flurry of even one second Ataurresagasti changed the order of succession. They had better have never been born! And now Aquelarre girt him with his magic sword and hung a pentacle about his neck. The time had come to pass the series of circles.

"Put off thy shoes from off thy feet, for the place whereon thou standest is holy ground."

Ataurresagasti assimilated himself to the guise of his companion. He entered the inmost circle. Aquelarre took once more his crayon and inserted within each circle (one and all being yet in blank) a symbol illegible to the sailor, but which the devil's advocate translated as he proceeded somewhat as follows:

"The name of the hour wherein you do the work, the name of the angel of the hour, the seal of the angel of the hour, the name of the angel that rules the day in which you work and the names of his ministers, the name of the present time, the names of the spirits ruling in that part of time and their presidents, the name of the head of the sign ruling in that time."

This done all appeared to be in order and the exorcism forthwith commenced. Aquelarre commanded the sailor to cast the first packet upon the flames ("and unwrap it not lest it skin thy hand"); the which being done the former brightness of the light burns directly a hideous red of leaping blood and every object in the room tinges to match. The magician draws his sword and makes passes with it in his right hand. He places his left upon the pentacle on his breast and commences in the following strain:—

"In the name of the holy, blessed, and glorious Trinity proceed we to work in these mysteries to accomplish that which we desire. We, therefore, in the name aforesaid, consecrate this piece of ground for our defence, so that no spirit whatsoever shall be able to break these boundaries, neither be able to cause injury, nor detriment to either of us here assembled. But that he may be compelled to stand before this circle and answer truly on demand, so far as it pleaseth Him who liveth for ever and ever, and who says I am Alpha and Omega, the beginning and the end, which is and which was, and which is to come—the Almighty. I am the first and the last who am living and was dead, and, behold! I live for ever and ever, and I have the keys of death and hell. Bless, O Lord, this creature of earth wherein we stand. Confirm, O God, thy strength in us so that neither the adversary nor any evil thing may cause us to fail."

The chant of the magus grows shriller and shriller, till it thins into a final continuous shriek. And there mingles with it thunder, and the re-echoed echo of shriek and thunder, to the splitting of ear and brain. And the earth rocks until there remains no longer floor nor roof, but sometimes one was uppermost and sometimes the other, and only the rapidity of the motion makes it possible to keep place in the circle. Thus, alternately, the venturous pair stood erect or head downwards. In this part of the ordeal, however, the sailor's professional habit stands his friend in need; but his teeth were twisted out of rank by clenching, to avoid a cry. The fire (now yellow) burns foul in the nose and hangs upon the hair in folds of smoke. Ceaseless lightnings lash the streaming eye. Clothed as it were, in those folds of smoke, there gradually appears to incorporate itself a large, full, and gross body—sanguine and gross—in a gold colour, with the tincture of blood; its motion is like the lightnings of heaven; the sign of its becoming visible is that it moves the person to sweat that calls it; the sorcerer becomes mute before the majesty of that presence and the thunder is hushed in its breath. There creeps a claw from out the draping clouds and steals towards the right hand of the sailor—say the right hand of the Cabalist rather, for it is that which the sailor clasps fearlessly to the arch fiend's itching grip. A second's compress—a grit of bone against bone—a hiss, as of a branding iron, and the talon is withdrawn. The sailor gazes appalled for a moment at the blackening, indelible sign manual, now seared upon the palm of the Cabalist. His heart of hearts sings a pean of victory over a lie palmed off upon even the Father of lies. The blowing of the Fiend now falls upon the golem and a gradual inflation swells out that pitiful suggestion into full and female form. Eyes like orbs of night light the vault and outburn the yellow jealousy of the brazier. Ears like seashells, and teeth like pearls of the sea, hair that paragons Godiva. O God, and is this but a counterfeit that can so kindle our sailor's senses? But he is recalled to gruff reality by the sight of her prison dress and bleeding bandaged arm. He is about to step out of the circle when a buffet from his companion fells him like an ox to the ground, scattering splashes of yellow flame in his fall. The magician indicates by signs rather than words, that the devil called up has yet to be laid before either of the callers can venture forth with safety. And then Aquelarre proceeds with full strength of lung (lest haply further risk betide) to recite the accepted form of dismissal.

"Go in peace unto your place. Peace be between us and you. Be you ready to come when you are called."

Ataurresagasti awakened to his sense of duty, sacrifices yet another packet of incense. Blue of heaven burns the flame, and sweet the savour that (after a struggle) overpowers its predecessor. The Prince of fallen pride dissolves into fulgurant reek. Earth recovers its footing. The fire at last resumes its work-a-day tone. Nothing but a grateful suspicion of the incense still about the convalescent air remains to betray what manner of work has been done. And now with assurance the exorcists may leave their circle. Aquelarre cannot forbear to bring home to his sidesman the gravity of that false step he nearly made.

"Should your stars ever fate you again to dally with infernal fire, be never tempted to leave your circle until the spirit is dismissed; nay, even when the spirit refuses to appear at your call you must still formally dismiss him according to the rules of art, lest haply he be actually present (though to you invisible) with intent to pluck your soul."

"'Tis a lesson I shall never need to learn again."

"But now to the next step in our progress. From the opposite end of this vault to that by which you entered there is a subway to the condemned cell. Many a time and oft has this been useful to me before, for you need not plume yourself the first that has self-sacrificed upon the altar of his love. Parent or child—lover or spouse—have employed me as middleman over and over again. My memory teems triumphant with case after case where the burners, unknowingly have burnt but the shadow of a witch. And so shall it be again. I take the golem with me and rejoin you with your prize."

He touched a spring in the opposite wall which threw open the indicated door. The bottom of a flight of steps appeared, the pendant of that which the sailor had descended. Aquelarre took the

apparently bewildered golem by the hand and with her disappeared. The door closed with a vicious snap. The sailor was left
alone in a chamber hermetically sealed and Heaven knows how far
beneath the foundation of the tavern of the Four Cross Roads.
There were none of mortal kind around save bones of unshriven
suicides who dreamed of judgment and woke up shrieking that they
made the blood of youth run cold to hear them. These were his
brothers in exile. He was fain to shout aloud, that corner to re-
echoing corner of the vault might make him colloquy. But was this
jangled terror his that they groaned into his ears? Was this the
note to which the lung of storm gave precedence in happier days
upon the sea? How long this weird conversation lasted the sailor
never knew. At length his straining ear caught the footfall which
he had dared so much to hear again. To snatch Lisalda into his
arms as she entered, to feel that she yielded to his embrace was
breath and blood to our hero. But the devil's attorney touched him
on the shoulder. He pointed sternly to the other door that led again
to the inn. In Indian file (there was room for but one on a step) all
three commenced the ascent. How quickly it sped compared with
that well remembered descent. But the sailor found time to hide in
his waistband the Cabalist's branded hand. When they reached
their wonted level Aquelarre closed the trap, and throwing open
the door of the street disclosed (he did not do things by halves) a
fully caparisoned horse waiting outside. His whole face brightened
into a smile of supreme content with himself and (for the nonce)
all the world. His work was done. He held out his hand for the
payment. The sailor did not smile. He took the silver ring ostenta-
tiously from his little finger and placed it upon that of the devil's
attorney. The face of Aquelarre underwent a very sudden change.

"Gates and gulfs of Hell! Do you realise with whom it is you
jest?"

"Jest do you say? It is sober, serious, earnest."

"What the devil's name! You pledged me the ring you wear on
your finger."

"I pledged it to you and I have passed it you—the only ring I
ever wore—but if you refer to the Ring of the demon, that has never
left the dead man's hand since for its sake you left him dead."

Before Aquelarre could recover from his stupefaction at this thunderbolt, Ataurresagasti swept Lisalda into the crupper and sprang to the saddle in front of her. And then loose rein and bloody heel, they dashed down one of the cross roads from which the tavern derived its name. Ride, ride, ride. Dark though the way and cold the wind, Ataurresagasti rolls a name upon his tongue that lights the path and warms the ambient air. Lisalda! Lisalda! Lisalda! Shock snowy polls of Pyrenean hills start up behind the haze. The lights of Behobia star the drift. Its cobbles fly to sparks beneath the horse's hoofs. The river cuts athwart the highway; the bridge is reached. Another stride and the *fleur de lys* is left behind for good. A customs officer leaps out of his box and seizes the horse's head; he is dragged several yards along the track. A torrent of imprecations in Basque, French and Spanish. Ataurresagasti pulls his mount back on to its haunches. The officer is ultimately convinced that he is no smuggler, and relinquishes somewhat charily his prey. Ataurresagasti winds gently along the bank. When beyond the range of pry or spy he dismounted and swung Lisalda to the ground. Once in his arms he did not readily let her go but showered kiss after kiss. The horse unheeded proceeded to explore on his own account and soon was lost to sight. Ataurresagasti showered kiss after kiss upon her wounded arm, her neck, her mouth, her eyes, her brow; but what is this—his lips are blistered in contact with the hair that shades that brow; he pushes the hair aside. A name in fiery angelical characters is flaring there. Horror of horrors, 'tis the golem! In his far off tavern Aquelarre is laughing in his sleeve. Ataurresagasti stands aghast. The creature regards him with puzzled eyes. She does not understand this sudden change; her mouth smiles and the first word she has ever uttered crosses her lips. It is her own name picked up, parrot-like from the iteration of the sailor. It had a different effect from what the poor thing expected.

"Lisalda!"

His cry of agony jarred her dulcet note. Every cord of his body was strung in an instant to one thought. To destroy this soulless creature—to annihilate—to erase her—to have her from God's earth.

He pounced upon her. But the poor pretty monster seemed to feel by instinct that this was another guess embrace from the first ardent one. And instinctively she wrestled with him. It was an awful unheard-of bout. Not a syllable was spoken, nor a cry. The blood now streamed like rain from her wounded arm. They slipped in the puddling soil. And Ataurresagasti could not get rid of the horrible idea that it was, after all, the real Lisalda that he was wiping out of life. Bit by bit, and one by one he obliterated the cursed characters. And bit by bit as the execution proceeded a horrible change came over her. Her limbs grew lean and spidery that she twisted about him. Her eyes grew dull and fishy. Her hair fell out by handfuls. She was dying letter meal. At length he forced her to his feet still clinging to his knees. The last figure of the angelical name disappeared beneath his thumb. Before him there lay no longer She but It. No longer a Lisalda, but a battered waxen doll with two pebbles and a herring-bone clapped on to one side of its head to distinguish front from back. Laughable—yes, perhaps—but Ataurresagasti did not laugh. He fell upon his face and wept. Something like an hour passed before he rose. Then drawing his hanger, and selecting the greenest spot, he proceeded to dig a grave. This he lined with masses of such wild flowers as he could find, and then reverently disposed the golem upon them. He shovelled back the earth upon the body, as he could not help but call it. He stamped it down obliterating all traces of his handiwork. He had said no prayer, but prayers crowded into his mind. He seemed in his tangled consciousness to have buried the real Lisalda, and with her all his love. He drew towards the river and stared into its inscrutable depths, turning over in his mind the *pro* and *con* as touching suicide. But after mature deliberation he decided, in preference, to return to that officer at Behobia, and give himself up for wife murder. He took a gloomy pleasure in this idea, and might even have carried it through. But suddenly a mocking peal of laughter—fiendish laughter—struck, as he thought, familiarly on his ears. He rubbed his eyes and looked across the river. On the French side of the boundary stream, there stood facing him the devil's attorney, hand in hand with what the now crazed sailor took

for a golem. The existence in the world of a real Lisalda never occurred to his wandering wits. Aquelarre knew full well what had
transpired. The sight of the discomfiture of his rival seemed balsam to his wounded self-esteem. Nor did he evidently as yet despair of making all things square. He addressed Ataurresagasti at
first with real or assumed jocularity.

"Hola? master gaff topsail, and have you found the truth of what
I once told you, that two can play in a game of brag? Come, we are
surely quits by this time. Let bygones be bygones, and let us adjust our contra accounts. You hold on your side what is of value to
me, and I on my side what is of value to you. Exchange is no robbery. Cast me the Ring across the stream, and Lisalda shall join
you at Behobia."

"Lisalda, do you say? And do you really think to befool me with
a golem, in the making of which I myself had a hand? Lisalda, I
know, is dead. By this hand she died, and I would cut it from me
were it not that the bloody crust on it is the only relic of her that
remains to me."

"Madman, you rave! Oh this I never dreamed of, that his reason should wander so untimely. Pull yourself together, man, 'Tis
no golem that stands beside me. 'Tis your own Lisalda,—your cutest medicine—could I but get you to take it. Oh, be but for an hour
sane, and then put eternity out of joint if you will! Again I say, the
Ring across the stream, and take Lisalda in exchange; that turns
the scale against your immortal soul!"

"Never waste your lies on me, man! 'Tis nothing but a golem
that you seek to palm off upon me. Lisalda, I know too well, is
dead,—by the token that these same impious hands that snatched
her into darkness have just smothered her into a heathen grave. I
had thought to have bedded her in other guise, but it seems my
fondest star had never appraised me as so worthy. Take away your
golem, and I shall keep the devil's autograph."

"Perdition be your speed! This passes patience. All is indeed at
an end between us. All save my vengeance. For I will tell you now
a secret that shall open your eyes to the imminent deadly breach
between us. This Lisalda (whose name you would add to the long

list already tattooed upon your hairy bosom) has not, does not, nor will ever love any other but myself. Sacristan at my Sabbaths from her earliest years—my living altar at the Black Mass—she is more to me than all your Ring. Nay the very plot and plan for conveying that Ring from its rightful owner was conceived and carried out by her. For that she undertook a special trip to the New World; for that she donned the disguise in which she wormed herself into the confidence of the Cabalist, and ultimately persuaded him to visit me at the Four Cross Roads. Unfortunately (you gentleman swab) you took it into your cursed costard to see further into a millstone than other people. We tried to make account of your sea-dogged persistency by drugging your nightcap with a view to palm you off upon justice (save the mark) as the murderer of the Cabalist. But again, through your ferreting foresight (darkened be your eyes), you tripped upon the tragedy in the worst possible moment (trust you for that), and even blundered into possession of the Ring. And now keep your ill-gotten gear, and Aquelarre for the first time in life is content to be bought and sold."

He broke off abruptly as if unable to contain himself, and throwing himself upon the girl with ferocious ardour he covered all her face with kisses. Kisses that absolutely foamed at the mouth. Kisses which she with even greater abandonment returned. Ataurresagasti caught fire at the sight (as mayhap it was intended with devilish cunning that he should) and cried out across the stream, every muscle of his face quivering with jealousy.

"This is the stroke that beggars fate! All is indeed at an end between us! Bought and sold! Ataurresagasti is bought and sold! But I can touch you in what (in spite of all you say) I know is still a raw. The devil bless you, and thus to the devil with demon and ring!"

"Stop, stop, stop! 'Tis no hand of the Cabalist upon which the ring sparkles but the hand of his murderess whom you love! Through you in your ignorance it was branded with the brand of Beelzebub, and if you relinquish it her soul will be struck from her!"

He crowded the words together incredibly in his eagerness, but yet he was too late. The Hand of Glory now acknowledged to be hand of Lisalda, had already left the sailor's touch. It flew through the air and as it flew, shot a double lightning of great joy. For the Demon (so long imprisoned within the crystal) knew at length that his appointed hour was come. Too late, the sailor grasped the stupendous revelation of Aquelarre. Too late, he recognised Lisalda in the supposed golem, and in Lisalda the murderess, whose shorn hand he had so long carried about him. The moment that he hurled it violently from him a startling change took place in the girl. Her garments became shaggy hair. Her glorious eyes narrow and slanting. Her teeth protruded at great length and yellow. Name of Mercy! This was then that large and loathly wolf (a werewolf as he now astounded saw) that had scattered the life of the Cabalist. The huge incredible beast (with a mournful howl that curdled the sailor to the marrow) sprang desperately after the brand which bound her soul. But being short of one paw she failed to arrest it. The Hand of Glory crashed down upon the water with an impact that shivered its crystal setting. It burst with a flame and smoke, and a hellish explosion with which mingled the dying shriek of the werewolf. With a roar that made rock the whole Pyrenean chain, the demon thus set free had darted upon her! He shot up as it seemed through her very body in a column like a waterspout that seemed to pierce the skies. She was instantly riven into a million shreds and sprinkled in a red rain as far as eye could reach over the length and breadth of the stream.

The Rabbi Lion

The clock of the Jewish quarter of Prague moves in the opposite direction to its brethren of the Christian town, yet each in its own way arrives second by second at the same inexorable facts of time. It was an hour short of midnight by both baptised and unbaptised reckoning—a misty rain was falling and mingled with the mist that rose from the river. Black obscure clouds veiled the face of the moon. Thunder roared at intervals. A flash of lightning that lifted momentarily the edge of the darkness revealed nothing kindlier than a gibbet. Dead bones that once had lived were creaking in its chains. The flesh had taken wing, the fowls of the air knew whither. Another flash showed a living man who crouched smothered up in a cloak at the foot of the unsightly tree. This unhappy outlaw if he dared seek no choicer shelter was, perhaps, even more to be pitied than his brother above. Whatever his reason, he made no motion in the direction of a light that shone afar and presaged warmth and shelter.

It was an inn. Its occupants concern us. They consisted of a company of half-a-dozen youths that had palpably imbibed both long and deep. Their carouse, however, was drawing to an end. The landlord hovered near cogitating over his bill, and yet with an ear to the conversation of his guests, lest haply he might catch some word. In this he was unsuccessful, and no wonder. The language they spoke was not only foreign to the landlord, but was that one of all others of which the angels themselves are traditionally supposed to be ignorant. In a word, it was Chaldee. But how did these youngsters come to speak in the secret language of Cabala? The reason is not far to seek. They were students of the Cabala and of magic under a Rabbi—one of the most esteemed of his time. The occasion they were celebrating with the flowing bowl was, indeed, no other than the conclusion of their seven years' apprenticeship. So far so good. But there was more in it than that. There was a death's head at their feast. Something that necessitated for its discussion their gift of tongues, something that took the heat from food and made the red wine show white through their skins. Upon entering their course they had set their hands in blood to the customary indentures of the magical schools of that period. After seven years (so the bond provided) only five of the pupils were to leave their Alma Mater their occult education complete; the sixth was forfeit to the devil, his due for acquiescence and assistance in their studies. A point on which the academies differed was the method of selecting among the apprentices which was to suffer as damned soul. Some held a kind of glorified race in which the runner that last attained the winning-post was torn asunder by the fiend. But the Rabbi who conducted the reading party in which we are interested had laughed at a decision made on physical grounds. The graduates should be chosen (he thought) not for fleetness of foot, but for the foremost quality of their sorcery. The scapegoat should similarly be thrown out not for unsoundness of wind or limb, but for the inadequate result of Black Art cramming. Logical enough all this. There remained but to discriminate between the competitors. To do this the Rabbi had decided that on the morrow of the night when our story opens he would hold a solemn incantation. It would be the first serious function of which the neophytes could boast. Their seven years' candidacy had been occupied with theory and had never ventured on practice. They would now find out the difference between knowing how to raise the devil and doing it. A difference which is even greater in this particular case than between word and deed in other arts and sciences. The idea of the Rabbi was that beginning gradually the terror should be accumulated ever thicker and faster until it reached a point where one of the men would break. This then would be the victim to be forced instantly from his circle and snatched soul from body by the enemy.

The reader is now cognizant of the mysterious business that fluttered these young hearts. We may add that their use of a dead language had another source besides the need for secrecy. No two of these ill-fated ones were natives of the same country, no two of them spoke a common speech. Such was the cosmopolitan fame of the Rabbi at whose feet they sat that he could pick his lads from Arctica to Cancer.

We have already remarked that the supper drew to an end. The six had tried their manfullest to drown care, but they had found it impossible to get rightly drunk in the shadow of Death and of Hell. With despair for their toastmaster they drank every time the health of five, and thought the more that they spoke no word of the eternal ruin of the sixth. The roofless wretch outside was less to be pitied than these. They had discussed without hope every loophole of escape and hopeless rejected all. There was nothing for it now but to return home. The Rabbi would never have allowed them out so late on any less momentous eve, but he had no fear of losing them now they had run out their course of lessons. He had done his part, they had received their consideration, trust him to look after his own that keeps the tally of the damned.

The reckoning had been adjusted to the satisfaction of the landlord, by the chairman of the feast. That youth (who was apparently a Bohemian by birth) now led his companions out of the house which some one of them was never to re-enter. And each turned back to look at it uncertain to what tune beggarly Fortune next might dance. They proceeded in the direction of the gallows we have already alluded to. Rain was still falling. The outlaw had disappeared, but will turn up later in our path. As they approached the grisly standard even the seasoned nerves of the sorcerers were troubled at the sight of its charge. They would have turned aside but for the Bohemian, who sturdily harangued them on their cowardice.

"The Devil walk arm in arm with you! Is this the way you stand to your guns at the sight of a gutted envelope—of a cast peascod— you that are due in but a few hours' space to outfront the root of all evil! I tell you the pit is digging deep for him that shows such favour then. But my liver is of another colour. What, fear a sloughed garment, and more rags than ribbons at that! Why I have only to set my hand to it"—

The incident ended in a manner entirely unforeseen. The Bohemian had barely touched the corpse when it dropped upon his shoulders. At this the other sorcerers shod with fear incontinently fled. The Bohemian stood his ground for only a moment. It had been in his mind that the thing would fall to pieces, but when he felt a burning breath, and the bony arms closing round his throat his brave soul shrunk like the kernel of a nut, and rattled against his sides. With the horrible revenant ever tightening its grasp the Bohemian started to flee. In doing this he followed in the footsteps of his companions, who had made their way back to the tavern. The landlord was in the act of putting up his shutters when his late guests tumultuously helter-skeltered to his door, and shrieked for immediate rations of strong waters. Nothing loath he planted them again at his tables and exchanged their solids for his fluids. At this juncture the Bohemian appeared, alone, but sweating to the very palms. He steadied himself against the wall and drank off the landlord's proffer at a gulp.

"Your health!" cried out a mocking voice from the very midst of the convives.

The Bohemian dropped his glass with a crash that sowed its fragments wide. There was a stranger sitting in the midst of their company, and drinking as if one of themselves; no one had seen him enter. The host appeared as much at a loss as they were. But the unknown being obviously man of mortal mould the Bohemian soon recovered his wits. He challenged the unbidden guest.

"Who are you? And why do you drink to me?"

The stranger rose to his full height, which was more than common tall. We repeat that none of those present knew him; but to continue our practice of dealing fairly with the reader we identify him with the outlaw with whom we commenced our story huddled up at the feet of justice. This understood, we record the stranger's speech:—

"Walls have ears, and if you would know me you must breathe the outer air. As to my drinking of your health, between man and man, do you not look as if you needed it?"

The obvious truth of this remark was only fuel to the Bohemian's fire. The more anxious on that account to know who the mysterious one was, he signed to his companions to come outside. The rain had now ceased. As they retraced—not without trepidation—the path they had so hastily left, they noticed that the gibbet was again occupied, but no one dared to ask the Bohemian how he had got rid of his unwelcome visitant. It was the stranger who renewed the conversation by abruptly mentioning his name.

"I am Iron Haquin!"

His hearers started. They had expected nothing like this. It was a name proscribed, and upon which a heavy price was set. It was the name of the comrade (still at large)—of him that shook a leg on the gallows. But Iron Haquin knew that these men were nothing to be feared. The affair of the dead bandit had given them their fill—of thief-taking, at any rate—for that one night. The living might safely laugh them out of countenance about that exploit. He addressed himself accordingly to the Bohemian.

"What! frightened with the rattling of bones that ride the gale? Would have me believe that the unrepentant thief descended from the cross? A sorrow on your fears! Take such tales to your confessor, for I'll have none of them, be sure! You had looked too long upon the jewelled wine, and that's the long and the short of it. I'll even touch hands with my dead mate myself, just to show you how unfounded your stampede. You will see no windfall vouchsafed to me, shake I never so shrewdly the tree."

He suited the action to the word and the event proved him right. The sorcerers would have turned tail at half a suspicion. But never a miracle occurred this time. The corpse continued to hug its chains. The Bohemian waxed wilder and still more wild, but he did not cease to listen to Iron Haquin.

"Fear has no share in life of mine—death has been all too long my fellow—familiarity breeds contempt. I believe I could make the Devil's pulse jump could I only obtain an interview. That, at any rate, is the one thing left that might fathom the resources of my heart. I saved the life of a Hebrew once, who, in return, gave me lessons in magic. I never worked so hard in my life. I looked to shortly kiss the mouth of hell, but, as ill luck would have it, I quarrelled with my Rabbi, and never found a chance."

The Bohemian could scarcely help showing his incredulity, nor did he care much for the stranger's feelings.

"What possible cause of quarrel could you have with a man whose life you saved?"

"Cause enough for anything and everything since he introduced me to his betrothed and I fell in love with her. He poisoned her mind against me, and on a chance cast me into a well. The water, however, was sufficient to break my fall, and I escaped after starving many days. It was twenty years ago, but I have never been able to forget it. He shall yet curse the mother that bore him. I tell you all this frankly as I told you my name, because I know that you are not what you seem!"

The Bohemian followed this relation, and chewed the cud of it. An idea had occurred to him fraught with unholy joy. He saw (as he thought) how he could achieve his own salvation at one stroke with the death of the intruder. How it worked out we shall see in the sequel. This is how the Bohemian set it going.

"What do you mean by saying that we are not what we seem?"

"Because, although your outer man is clad in this world's uniform, your hearts are of the livery colours of hell; you are students of sorcery, and no later than to-morrow you are to conjure in your strength. Do I not read you rightly?"

The Bohemian stared in something very much like stupor. Where on earth could the man have got his information? It sealed his death warrant, in any event. He knew too much for sure! The Bohemian, by this time, had matured his plans, which he now expressed in words.

"Whatever your source of knowledge you have hit us off correctly, I admit; nor can we deny hospitality to such a man. We are within (as you say) a few hours of a magical ceremony. If you are so anxious as you pretend to face such odds I will go so far as to yield my place to you."

For the life of him the Bohemian could not help something of a smile as he made this handsome offer. He was ignorant still whether the bandit was aware of the exceptional nature of this incantation. His reply would decide that point. If he knew the rules of the approaching contest he would certainly refuse. If he did not, he could hardly maintain his fame without becoming a substitute for the Bohemian. To do him justice, Iron Haquin did not hesitate for a moment.

"Your hand upon the bargain, man, and never fear but I shall do you credit. Since the beginning of recorded time there shall have been no such conjuration. We will quench the light of adverse stars. Hell's idiom has no word for what we shall do."

Still wearing the same sardonic grin, the Bohemian broke in upon this enthusiasm. His department was the practical.

"Permit me to draw your attention to the fact that we have been drifting slowly on and shall soon have reached the Rabbi's house. It befits us, therefore, to arrange our order of business. It may not have occurred to you that the Rabbi must know nothing about this. If he did he might possibly veto the affair. But there will be no difficulty in circumventing him. The house is built square around a central court where the conjuration will take place in open air. You will enter with us muffled in your cloak, and your presence will not be detected among so many; you will conceal yourself under the staircase while the Rabbi takes us to our bedrooms, which are the topmost of the house. The old gentleman locks us in all night, for we are strictly looked after, I can assure you. When we are released (after a brief slumber) it will still be dark, and if I slip into your hiding-place and you assume my authority I do not see why the Rabbi should be the wiser. As to the risk you run that is, of course, more your affair than mine. I shall pray for you from my coign of vantage if I can remember any but backward prayers. But now, confess, are you not moved at length with fear?"

"Nay, by horn and hoof! I shall weather the devil as I have got the weather of death, and be hail-fellow-well-met with both! At the worst a man can die but once—I had rather thus than a prod and a sod like so many that I have sent to their account. And, to end all, is this your destination? Why, it is the house of Rabbi Lion!"

"The Rabbi Lion is our teacher."

The Bohemian was only too glad that the matter was thus settled. His fears for himself, and of the other, were disposed of in one ingenious coup. The remaining five sorcerers had followed the negotiations with mixed admiration and envy. From them no remonstrance was to be expected, quite the contrary, since they believed and hoped that the bandit as a novice in magical matters would be the one to pay penalty to the fiend. They had yet to find out that their dupe had more knowledge than they bargained for. Meanwhile the Bohemian has knocked at the door. From within there comes a clangour of bolt and bars. The door is opened, and the Rabbi appears. His pupils enter in as much of a hustle as possible, allowing Iron Haquin to conceal himself as arranged. The students file upstairs to be disposed of by their tutor, who will presently return alone.

During this absence of the Rabbi, Iron Haquin took by the forelock the opportunity of looking around. The courtyard itself was bare, the lofty walls of the house built it in on all four sides. Under the roof half-a-dozen windows seemed to indicate the garrets of as many students. On the level of the ground there was nothing but two doors to break the monotonous courses of stone. One of these massive portals was that of the street through which Iron Haquin had entered. The other, which faced it on the opposite side, had been left ajar by the Rabbi. It was of a certainty the passage way to his sanctum. The bandit approached it and looked through. A mighty chamber lay behind. The light which streamed from it into the courtyard was engendered by a central lamp, one of that sort which are traditionally reputed to burn with an everlasting flame; from the ceiling hung stuffed reptiles and other grotesques that seemed to shiver in the current of fresh air. Tables conveniently disposed for work were loaded with books and manuscripts; every available niche and nook was piled with tools of necromancy that the bandit had no time to identify. Hearing the steps of the Rabbi

descending, he slipped to his covert just in time. The ancient Isra-
elite re-entered his studio and slammed the door behind him. The
wondrous light was thus extinguished, and the courtyard plunged
in darkness. But not for long. The outlaw had scarcely disposed
himself for sleep—better quarters this than the gibbet's foot—when
the door was again thrown wide. He looked in the expectation of
seeing once more the Rabbi's work-room; but to his utter surprise
and consternation it was a different room altogether, though in-
disputably the self-same door. This time it was a lady's boudoir
that was revealed, of immense size, imperially furnished—a thousand mirrors flashing back its chandeliers. There was no trace of
the Rabbi who had just entered that very door, instead, a beautiful
girl of about twenty summers glided out to the cooling breeze. Had
it not been for her Iron Haquin would have been dumbfounded at
the inexplicable shift of rooms. But the moment he set eyes on her
so much greater a surprise beset him that it drove all other out of
mind.

It was the woman of whom he had spoken to the Bohemian—
the woman who had cut friendship, and all but wrought his death—
the woman whom still he loved. He strode forth without a second
thought.

"It is her very self!" he cried. The girl smiled at him as in recognition. Not the least surprise did she show at this strange meeting. She called him by his name.

"Iron Haquin!"

"You know me after all these years?"

"Who better among men should I know after all that passed
between us? And did you not first know me?"

"That is not the same thing. I am twenty years older, but you—
I can hardly believe my eyes—are the girl of twenty years ago. Has
time, too, been fooled by those eyes of yours which I have often
said would split a lover's coffin?"

"Believe me, my friend, Time's ravages are here as surely as
that you will never see them. It is your love now, as ever, that blinds
your eyes and drapes a faded woman in your poetry. When I am
dead, and my body an ordinary for worms, you will see me still in

fancy's eye just the girl you see me now. And by the same token you, that speak of being twenty years older, are in my eyes the brave and innocent boy whose lips were once my food."

"Then you loved me all the time, after all?"

"At that age, what did I know of love—or loathing?"

"But the Rabbi?"

"He is old," she cried, "past passion. Ah, Haquin, you would not know him now!"

"I cannot make it out that you are still sweet and twenty. Here is a waist would warm the arm of death! You are, if anything, lovelier, transfigured, haloed. You would hurry the pace of a star! Tell me true now, is it not some elixir of the Rabbi's that has pinnacled you beyond the teeth of Time?"

She laughed.

"Elixir of his! Why he would swallow it himself! And to prove how little I lean on him you may kill him if you will!"

"An assassination!" gasped the bandit, "the man knows no sword play."

He was thinking, as he spoke, of the primitive device by which his rival had once tried to get rid of him.

"A duel!" returned the Jewess, "for if he knows no sword play he can measure swords with steel they forge below. You are a tall man of your hands when knives are stripping, but at his trade you are the Rabbi's fool. You will need all you know to join issue with him in ceremonial of magic. No later than this morning must you pit your strength against him, for to that you were decoyed hither."

"Decoyed! I came of my own free will, for an adventure to my mind. The story is worth telling. I was dying for a sensation, so I decided to cut down a comrade and give him more decent sepulchre than a gizzard. I had just got his corpse in safety to the ground when I heard a confusion of coming footsteps. Fearing it might be noticed that the gibbet was naked I swung myself into the chains. I knew from their conversation they were magical students that passed. I had a yearning to foregather with such once more, as I did in the days of my youth. A practical joke gave me the opportunity, and Heaven be praised for the good hap!"

Iron Haquin was about to improve the occasion, but, at this
interesting juncture, a howl of rage discharged through the upper
air. It came from the head of the Bohemian thrust out of his window. The Jewess snatched up the two hands of her lover and
pressed them to her fervid lips. Almost before he was aware of it
she had retreated to her bower, and closed the door behind her. At
the same moment the Bohemian, having wriggled through his
window, leaped headlong into the courtyard. He came down
unskilfully. Iron Haquin thought he heard his leg go. He lay there
groaning, and then burst into invective against the outlaw.

"The devil rough-ride you that have seen, so close, a dream I
only sighted from afar. Bestride me the succubus, if I would have
brought you hither had I known she would come out to-night. The
skies are dark as a wolf's throat, and I believed she only walked in
the moon. Full many a night I watched it shine on her silken hair—
silken as the touch of sin—long, so that when she unbound it she
stumbled in her locks. Her silver body was fragrant as the boundaries of hell. Death and dissolvement! Let me get you in my grips,
and you shall never see her twice! Help me to my feet and unfold
your blade, and then bite on what prayers you know!"

The bandit surveyed this unexpected rival with something very
much like fellow-feeling. Then he voiced the question that was
uppermost in him.

"How old did you suppose her?"

"How old? What do I care how old? Old enough to be loved and
to love."

"How old did you suppose her?"

"If you insist on it, I suppose she wears some twenty years, and
a queenly garment they!"

"What! Twenty years in your sight also! Why I tell you this very
girl is the one of whom I spoke to you that I loved twenty years ago."

"You lie, by the Father of Lies!"

The bandit clapped his hand to hilt, and as instantly snatched
it away.

"I fight with no cripple," he hissed in his teeth, "but you shall
hear from herself God's truth!"

So saying he ran his great strength against that door. Twice and thrice he rammed it. It did not flinch. He went back a few steps to acquire a fresh impetus. But before he could return to the attack it flew abruptly open, as if moved by some hidden spring. Iron Haquin uttered an astonished cry. The boudoir was no longer there!

The mysterious chamber had undergone another Protean change. To speak more by the book, there was no longer any chamber. The door framed nothing but blackest darkness. Neither ceiling, nor walls, nor floor could be distinguished. By this time the Bohemian had struggled to his feet, and now hobbled in the direction of the door.

"Back, back," cried the bandit, "this is no place for you, nor for any christened man. The foundations of this house are laid in hell. Back, back, as you value your infinite soul!"

"To heel," shrieked the Bohemian, and he whipped our his sword, "lest I strike you in the place where you live! This is my hour, and you shall not be the only one to take her between your hands."

Before Haquin could forestall him, he had leaped the grinning door, and disappeared in enigmatical gloom. He was scarcely lost to sight, when a shriek rang out, beyond conception awful. It was his death-note. The whole air curdled. Iron Haquin fell upon his knees. What grimmest of riddles the victim solved no man shall ever know. His body—even as his soul—was lost in that abysmal horror. For a while Haquin gazed at it, and saw no sign, nor heard what could be called a sound. It was a grave that gave up no dead.

At last the outlaw rose and crossed himself, and closed the door upon its secret. Withdrawn to his corner, he set himself to think what monstrous enigma couched behind there. The worst of it was that it threw still more suspicion on the woman. But was she a woman at all? In his wanderings across Europe, from sea to sea, he had never lost the Jewess out of mind. Whenever it was possible to acquire later news of her, he spared no pains to do so. But the gossip, through which alone at such a distance he could keep himself in touch with her circumstances, was always vague, and often contradictory. He had been circumstantially assured of her death, and as circumstantially undeceived. But now he began to wonder if that report might have had foundation. To assume that upon losing her the Rabbi had supplied her place with a familiar culled from the females of the pit, would explain nearly all that he had seen. Was it woman or nightmare that couched behind there? He had arrived at no decision when the door again flew open, and he stretched out his head for the next development. But the panoramic capacity of the door seemed, for the time being, to have played itself out. The view was only the old one of the laboratory out of which the Rabbi stepped.

He was loaded with apparatus of ceremonial magic; he deposited it upon the ground; he closed the wonder-working door. His next step was to trace out two enormous circles, one within the other. The outer one embraced the whole area of the courtyard, the other one ran inside it at a distance of about a yard all round. Between the circumferences of these two circles he inscribed seven smaller ones, at equal distances apart. The outlaw, who, though disappointed at the drying-up of the resources of the door, watched all these proceedings with attention, perceived that the seven circles were intended—one each—for the Rabbi and his six attendants. He concluded that the ill-starred Bohemian, as having been undoubtedly cock of the school, would be assigned one of the two circles next the master, which was precisely the post Iron Haquin would have chosen. He was in some doubt, however, as to whether there might, or might not, be a miscarriage when the bedroom was found to be unaccountably empty. Fortunately, the Rabbi (after placing a pan of living coal in each circle) went upstairs to unlock each door, and came down again at once, without opening any. This may have been intended to allow time for his disciples to dress, but he bore as well the air of one having forgotten something, and ran as fast as his years would permit him to that door of doors. The outlaw noted as the Rabbi passed through that it was the boudoir this time visible. Apparently the thing worked round in a cycle. The Rabbi emerged again almost at once with a look of considerable relief. All this was Greek to the onlooker. The five candidates now appeared and took up the circles pointed out to them. The outlaw pulled his hat well over his features, and (as it was still dark) hoped to pass muster. He saw, as he had expected, one of the places of honour was left for the Bohemian. He boldly took his stand there; he had now burnt his boats, and must go through. The Rabbi had not yet syllabled a word, reserving his strength for the strain to come. He silently divided among his assistants the remainder of what he had brought out of his store room. This consisted of civet, amber and musk, of benzoin, camphor and myrrh, of every fragrance that wizards burn.

The Rabbi then stepped into his own circle and commenced a preliminary prayer. The supreme moment had come.

A sudden glow invaded the veins of the amateur exorcist (late Iron Haquin) as he heard that well-known voice. Bit by bit, as he warmed to the work, he remembered the ritual which this very man had once been at pains to teach him. From time to time the other five chimed in with the responses. Iron Haquin dared not risk the recognition of his voice. As the ceremony proceeded the air seemed to grow more dense until it became a matter of difficulty to breathe. It was thickening with, as yet, invisible elementals. Anon the outlaw's attention was drawn to the glances of his fellows, which timorously sought the empty space enclosed by the inmost of the two circles. He was somewhat dashed—even he—to see that this empty space had sunk below the level of the courtyard. Worse, it continued to sink until it disappeared altogether. The magicians now stood in their seven circles, around the circumference of a well. Even this was not the worst, as the bottom, though out of sight, must still be sinking, and would sink to the very confines of the underworld. Connexion was to be opened with the bottomless pit by means of this bottomless shaft. Having arrived at this by no means engaging conclusion, Iron Haquin had only to wait for the end. It came with a sudden smother and smoke that belched from the mouth of the chimney. The Rabbi threw instantly perfumes upon his fire, and his acolytes did likewise. Essence and quintessence fought desperately with the evil odours of this smoke that came straight from eternal fires. And there was borne up with the smoke a weird hubbub of voices, that blasphemed in every tongue.

Cracked lips of the damned shrieked execrations in languages long dead, whose accents unintelligible made heart stand still. In vain the Rabbi raised his voice that had never ceased from the first onset. His exorcisms were drowned in oaths both loud and deep, and with the rush and roar of furnaces stoked with blood. And now the thick air showed faces that peered in their eyes, and gibberings that were not faces, creeping and crawling things. The outlaw's skin had long ago wrung out its last drop of sweat. The Rabbi's white hair stood all on end. The moment for the trial had come.

Iron Haquin threw his hat out of the circle where it was instantly torn into a million shreds. His face thrust abruptly into the Rabbi's line of sight, he roared in tones of thunder:—

"Rabbi Lion, I am Iron Haquin!"

The effect upon the Rabbi was electric. His eyes started out of his head. The chant died away upon his lips. He dropped like a stone into the pit. One long low moan reverberated from side to side, broken up by peals of hellish jubilee. A terrible voice that hushed all else cried out three times—

"Lost! Lost! Lost!"

This was the climax, and Iron Haquin the man to bear the brunt of it. No help was to be expected from the five sucking sorcerers. They were ridden to rags. The last events had crowded so quickly together that the outlaw practically took up the litany where the Rabbi dropped it. He gave it such voice as would have been a surprise to the others, were they in a state to make the observation. The fact is, Iron Haquin was drunk with the cup of revenge. For two pins he would have bearded the fiend. The infernals shrunk from the lash and lather of such magnificent rage expressed in the highest terms of art. They of the pit sucked in their smoke and hushed the outlet of despair. The centre of the courtyard reappeared, air refined itself, victorious sweet scents flung wide their banners.

"Go in peace unto your place. Peace be between us and you. Be you ready to come when you are called."

This final, formal leave-taking of the spirits, without which no magician worth his salt would ever abandon his circle, wound up what had once looked a serious business. The six could now quit in safety the circles which a moment before had been their only bulwark against perdition. The students were too limp to pay any attention to the giant that had taken their world upon his shoulders. Their little remaining sanity was all bent to the desire to get away from an accursed house. They stumbled out of the front gate, which the outlaw had to open for them, and scattered to the four winds of heaven.

The coast being now clear the bandit made for that other door which had played so many parts. On what would the curtain now arise? He opened and discovered the boudoir. A repetition of its last role. The cycle theory was thus effectually disposed of. There was nothing for it but that the door obeyed some arbitrary will. Scarcely its own, The Rabbi was dead, and worse. There remained then only the Jewess. But where was she? The chamber had no outlet. She could in no wise have left it. Our hero ransacked every corner, he upset, and set up, and upset again every priceless piece of furniture, tore down silk and satin, and threw jewels under foot, ground beneath his heel the command of armies, and the price of the honour of queens. At last his eye was arrested by a common glass bottle, he was fascinated by it, he held it to the light, he all but dropped it. It contained the object of his search.

Yes, there was no doubt now of the death of his former love. No doubt but that the Rabbi's diabolical art and craft had replaced her by a familiar spirit. This was the receptacle in which he confined the familiar at seasons when he was not in need of her. This was the familiar herself within the bottle, reduced most delicately small. She still wore the guise of his long lost wife with which her master had endowed her. She still caused a pang to the iron heart of Haquin to see her down to such poor prison. And she knew her power over him. She knew that he would find a way. She smiled at him divinely, she clasped her tiny hands in prayer to him. But he was aware that he must needs release her. He neither thought nor would have cared that, now her master was dead, once released there was no controlling her. It just had to be done. But how to set about it? The stopper was sealed down and with a talismanic character on the seal. It was the uttermost secret of the Rabbi. Iron Haquin could not read it, and without reading it could never open the bottle. There remained but one avenue of escape—the bottle must be broken. With all the strength of his iron arm he dashed it to the ground. There was a tremendous, explosion, a roar like thunder, a flash before his eyes. Not a mirror in the chamber but was shattered and scattered. A rapidly enlarging female form escaped from the shards of the broken bottle. It lost as it enlarged all resemblance to the well-remembered Jewess. It became indefinite, it thinned into little more than a mist. It gradually disappeared, yet, as the last waft of it brushed his face the passionate lover thought he felt once more his sweetheart's lips. But he looked around and saw himself alone with solitude, and wreckage, and desire of death.

The Evil Eye

Our story opens upon a gloomy function; the burning of a gang of wizards and witches.

The bells were ringing, but it was a muffled peal, and the hammers were subdued that wrought the scaffolding in the market place. The steps of the citizens were as those that seek pleasure or plunder by night, and the very soldier trailed a pike most unsoldierly silent. A stranger, who, from the singularity of his appearance, would have attracted notice on any other occasion, to-day threaded unchallenged this German town.

Tall he was, worn down to the bone, gaunt and prematurely grey, hollow-cheeked and hollow-eyed. His dress might be described, with no great stretch of language, as little but nakedness visible. But it was sweet with the scent of the sea, and the roll of the sea was in his long legs, as he wound his way to the central square. He looked neither to the right nor to the left. Arrived at his destination he took no heed of the ominous carpenters, nor of the wood-work to which they were putting the finishing touch. He walked straight—and as if by instinct rather than by eye—into a certain tavern of those that debouched upon that place. He might have been supposed to be dumb as well as blind, since he merely made a pantomime expressive of hunger as he sank into one of the scats. The landlord looked with doubt at his visible assets. A sad thing of the nature of a smile flickered upon the burnt and blistered visage of the sailor. He evolved a coin from some miraculous hiding-place in the cobweb that was his apology for raiment. The landlord bit it, rang it, and bit it again. Ultimately he appeared satisfied, and placed food before his customer. The speed with which it vanished would have justified an observer in antedating considerably the stranger's previous meal. Leaving a clean plate he threw himself back in his chair and steadily regarded the landlord.

Then he asked, not without emotion,

"Don't you know me, old comrade?"

The landlord started as if shot.

"By all the saints and saintesses! *Marquard!*"

"Aye, Marquard it is; but not the Marquard you knew of old. It was an evil hour I ran away to sea."

"But why have you not returned these years?"

"Returned! He asks me why I did not return! I that—before I had been long enough aboard to be on good terms with my inner man—was captured by the Algerine! I that have been chained to an oar in the galley of Barbarossa every day of these years of which you speak! But pay no heed to what I say. There is news for which I burn. You that have lived humdrum can tell me of *her*, for whose coquetries I lost patience and exiled myself."

"She lives," murmured the landlord, in a half-hearted way, and he looked upon the floor.

"She lives! And what of my rival that I thought she preferred to me?"

"*He* lives, if you mean the Hungarian, whose name we could never pronounce, and whom we used to call Teremtette from his favourite oath."

"Come, tell more about them both."

The landlord cast a troubled eye upon him, and again looked down. He spoke with distinct embarrassment.

"Prepare yourself for the worst, my friend. Remember that he of whom we speak was always a hobnobber with sorcerers, and a sorcerer suspect. After your departure he became a sorcerer confessed."

"And *she*, man! What of her?"

"Alas! She followed wherever he led, though the devil's shadow was all his light. She lived with him for a time after you abandoned the field to him."

"I knew it! In my dreams they were husband and wife, the while I hugged a bare board to my aching heart."

"Husband and wife! They were never that, save at some witches' sabbath, mated by priests unfrocked and anathematised, but not in the sight of gods or men."

"Then she is free, and I shall steal her from him yet. I will marry her, but I will kill him first."

"You know not what you say. He is swollen in power until he is acknowledged the master magician of all Germany. It is *whispered* that he made a pact with Satan, and in pledge thereof exchanged one of his eyes for an eye of the fiend's. It is *known* that he walks abroad with one eye shut until he wishes to perform some evil. Then he lifts the eyelid and shoots forth a spear of light from that eye which is not his own. And it blasts wherever it falls. For this reason we call him the Evil Eye."

"His backbone shall be limp for me, his front abased, his star is set, his grave is dug, his flesh already rots! I will bury him in a church that he may hug false hopes of salvation, and then I will set my feet on his gravestone when I stand with *her* before the priest. He shall shriek curses from his coffin while I knit her life to mine, until the scandalised sacred earth shall spit him forth to those that lie in wait."

"Unhappy man, you are still dreaming of the girl you left behind! Do you not realise that, now years have rolled over her, she is a mother witch? Nay, there is worse that I had hoped to spare you. Did you not notice the stakes erected outside in the market place? To-day a host of women, and not a few evil men, are to wipe out their crimes with the last payment. At this very moment the sad procession is entering the square. Do you recognise no prisoner among them?"

He threw open the door. It was even as he said. The sailor sprang to his feet and scanned the accused.

"I do not see him there!"

"Not *he*, he flies too high for judge or jury, the devil's true knight, hell sublimate! But look again. Do you not recognise one of the women?"

With a terrible foreboding Marquard strained his eyes, but saw no face that corresponded to his memories. They were, without exception, abominable hags that were to suffer. But one of them had at once recognised *him*. Recognised him, in spite of the awful change wrought by his captivity. The foulest beldame of them all stretched her skinny arms to him. Her cracked voice called his name.

"Marquard!"

An icy hand gripped the galley-slave's heartstrings. In that second he lived all the years since last he had seen her. He saw (in his mind's eye) golden hair shade to grey, skin become parchment, roses and lilies scatter in dust. He recognised her, and he leaped forward to her like an arrow from a bow. The spectators parted in amaze, to right and left. Guards and executioners fell back from his foot and hand. He caught the outstretched hands of the witch in his. He devoured her with his looks, and she him. He was as one in a dream. He scarcely felt her press something round into one of his palms. She whispered so that he alone heard her:—

"Marquard! It is a charm I am giving you that has cost me dear. It will protect you from all evil, and especially from *him*. As you love me, never part with it while you live. I dare not wish you well lest my prayer should blast you. Good-bye, and think sometimes kindly of me."

He would have retained her, but she drew her fingers away, leaving with him that globular something to which he paid no attention. She kissed him with her eyes. He tried to speak, but words were choked in sobs. And now the soldiers, both horse and foot, bore down upon him. A cry of rescue was raised by some of the crowd that were interested in the prisoners. Others shouted them down, and shook their fists in Marquard's face. The wildest confusion reigned. His rags were torn from his back. A hundred blades were thrust into his flesh. Those that had taken his part pulled him one way, the more law-abiding citizens pulled him another. His head swam, he lost his footing, he fell, and was trampled alike by friend and foe, in the pitched battle that was fought over his body. He lost consciousness, and knew no more.

When he recovered his painful identity, it was some time before he could remember what had passed. He was sick, as he fancied, from the rollings of the galley, and sore from the laying-on of the taskmaster's whip. It was the possession of a certain ball, which he still clutched in his palm, which, after he had stared at it for a while, led him back to truth. When, by degrees, he had recovered his memory, he tried to make out of what substance it was formed, but without arriving at any conclusion, he carefully stowed it away. He was most puzzled by the fact that he was in a room. It was dark, so that a considerable time must have elapsed. He rose, and felt all round the walls. There was no doubt about it. Presently he came upon the door. He tried it. It opened. He was evidently not a prisoner. He stepped into a passage, and up to another door. This one was locked, but the key was in it. He turned it, and opening the door disclosed the square. The mystery was now solved. He was in the precincts of the tavern. He had been saved, perhaps from death, by his good friend, the inn-keeper.

The night was magnificently clear. A single star hung low in the ear of the moon. He looked all around the deserted place that during his swoon must have been the scene of butcherly justice. The remnants of the stakes were evidence that the decrees of the law had really been executed. A few fragments of charred bone were now all that remained of the girl he had loved. He seemed to scent the odour of burnt flesh in the air. Suddenly, he became aware that he was not alone in his contemplation of this field of blood. Some man was ferreting about the bases of the stakes, and sifting the human dust that paved the square. It needed no second look to tell the galley-slave who this was, so much keener than love is hate. It was the man—or more than man—of whom Marquard had conferred with the inn-keeper. It was the Hungarian—Teremtette—the Evil Eye.

For what then was he a-search among this life that had ceased to live? Marquard thought that he could answer this question. The ball of so much mystery had been given to him by the witch, as a charm that would protect from this very man The association of the Hungarian with her made it probable that he was acquainted with her possession of it, and with its powers. Such being the case, it was a property that he must itch to lay his fingers upon. Perhaps he had even attempted, and failed, to obtain it from her while she was alive. At any rate it was this, presumably, which he was agog for on the scene of her death. As a charm it would be unconsumable by fire, and had Marquard not been before him the Hungarian might have attained his end. The one weak point in the theory was that it supposed the wizard ignorant of Marquard's return. Yet this was not impossible, since surely even wizards have their limitations. Having decided upon this explanation of his rival's presence, Marquard burned to confront him face to face. He strode boldly out of his protecting doorway. The Hungarian heard his step, looked up, and sprang to his feet. The galley-slave noted with a thrill that one of his eyes was closed. It was the Evil Eye against which he was soon to test his powers of endurance. For the wizard had evidently recognised him at once. His whole face was writhen with diabolical glee. Slowly he raised the lid that covered the Evil Eye. There was a gush of blinding light from under that veil. The square was lit up as by noonday sun. The ray struck remorselessly upon the sailor. He stood erect unshaken. Astonishment was legible upon the magician's features at this evident failure of his trusted weapon. He raised the lid to its fullest extent, and put all he was worth into the uncanny stare. But the sailor stood erect, unscathed. The charm was doing the work which its donor had foreseen, and doing that work right well. The galley-slave registered a vow never to part with it. Suddenly the magician dropped his eyelid, and the market-place once more was dark. He had apparently arrived at some decision, for now—for the first time—he spoke.

"Antlers of Belial! Do I see before me my old friend Marquard?"

"Your enemy to the hilts you see."

"You must pardon my defective sight which obliged me to call in the aid of science before I recognised you. Who would have thought of seeing you here? But now I know you I shall not readily part with you. You shall sleep under no other roof than mine this night of your home-coming."

"Dare you speak thus to me, knowing that this day the woman we both loved has died a horrible death at hangman's hands, and all for following the course *you* set and staked for her?"

"Nonsense, my friend. You have been deceived by a chance resemblance, if indeed any could exist between such wrinkles as were smoothed out to-day and a face that made the stars ashamed. I regret to say that I have lost sight of her for many a year—that maiden we both knew and loved; I would give all I have left to give to see her before me as she was. Her waist was slender as the waist of death—I cannot conceive her as blue flame and grey ash. Again I say you have deceived yourself, my friend."

"Friend me no friends! What I feel for you is unscabbarded, naked hate."

"Death and the judgment! If you do not love me, you *fear* me, coward that you are!"

"Were I the crowning coward—the bye-word and mock of cowards—there would be one man beneath my fear."

"And do you mean that I am that man? I challenge you then to accompany me to my castle. It is worth the seeing."

"You need not press me. I ask nothing better than your company. You shall tire of me ere I tire of you. Lead, and I will follow you to the fringes of the Pit."

"We'll needs ride sabbatical post."

He plucked up two charred logs that lay near at hand. He thrust one between the knees of the galley-slave and the other between his own. He uttered a magic word, sharp, pungent, and obeyed. The logs became two stallions, black as grief and fleet as joy. Before Marquard had grasped the fact that he was mounted, they were out of the town.

The weather, as we have said, was of the clearest. A train of obscene hags, bound for some witches' frolic, was the only thing that rode the night. They passed it and left it easily in their rear. Their pace, in fact, was a pace to kill. They shook off a mile with every sweat drop. It took them a second to shoot through a forest. They cleared, not one river, but twos and threes at a time; the wind, striving to keep up with them, fell breathless. Huge mountains tossed their grandsire heads and deemed themselves impassable. These also the chargers crossed, and left them shrugging their fat shoulders far behind. But now a peak of peaks appeared—a Babel that overlooked earth, and peered into heaven—would they double that? They reached its summit, but at the instant, with a word from the sorcerer, they were logs again.

Marquard reeled as his feet touched ground. He steadied himself with an effort, and took a step forward. The Hungarian seized him by the collar, just in time to save him from a fall. They were standing upon the edge of a precipice. The sailor looked down and saw no bottom—a gulf that staggered reason. He shuddered at his escape, and reeled again. When he had somewhat recovered, he rubbed his eyes, and took a careful survey of the position.

They had been deposited at the extreme altitude of the mountain. But it was not a single peak, it formed a ring like the crater of a volcano, but of a diameter so stupendous that its further side-was barely visible to the naked eye. Of its depth we have already given some idea, but the most singular feature of the whole strange place—the feature which made it impossible to regard it as a mere giant volcano—was a slender spire of rock that shot up from its unknown floor to about the same height as the surrounding rim. It might be compared to a Cleopatra's Needle set in a well, or else to the stamen of some egregious petrified flower. Or from the sailor's point of view (considering the spot where he stood as mainland) it was an islet left bare by a dried-up sea. Nor was it a desert island. It was inhabited, or at any rate it was built upon. There was a castle on it which it was just large enough to hold. The outer walls merged straight down as if one piece with the wall of rock upon which they were founded. From the front entrance, a bridge of marble, with rails of gold, spanned the abyss that separated the castle from the mountain.

While Marquard was making these observations, the Hungarian took stock of him with his single eye. When the sailor had apparently sucked in all his environment, Teremtette asked him, what seemed on the face of it, a needless question.

"What do you see?"

"I see a castle, whiter than a bride, uplift upon yon mast of stone."

"What else do you see?"

"I see a bridge across the airy moat that parts us from that fantastic crow's nest."

"That castle and that bridge are of my architecture. If you consider as child's play all that you *have* dared—if you are willing to *begin* to show high courage—you can follow me within its gates."

He walked towards the bridge, crossed it, and disappeared within the castle walls. The galley slave sat down, and gazed at the fairy fabric in something very much like indecision. He felt among his garments to see if he still possessed the talisman, the witch's parting gift. It was there. He drew it forth and looked at it. A little shrivelled pellet, of some unknown dried substance, it was as much of an enigma to him as ever. He laid it upon the rock on which he sat, and turned again towards the castle. To his horror and astonishment it was losing its clearness of outline. It became—along with the bridge—semi-transparent. He could see through them both. They grew thinner, and thinner. They faded into little more than mist. Ultimately nothing of either was any more visible. Only the bare pillar stood up in the midst of the chasm. But no—there was a figure upon the now tonsured rock—it was the figure of the Hungarian. A moment's thought explained this. The castle alone was unsubstantial. In disappearing it left revealed the man that had been within it. He was too far off for the sailor to be sure of what he was engaged on. There ran through all Marquard's veins a current of fear. He felt helpless in the presence of all this glamour that he did not understand. He looked round for his only friend—the amulet—thank God! it was still there. He snatched it up, resolved never more to let it away from him. And then another wonderful thing occurred. The castle and its bridge again gradually appeared in sight. The sailor began to suspect the rules of the game. He could not forbear to put the talisman down again for a moment. The outlines of the magical buildings grew immediately dim. He took up the ball. Their solidity was immediately restored. He now knew his bearings. There could be no longer any doubt. Apart from their creator—the Hungarian—the castle and bridge were only visible to the holder of that wizened trifle. Marquard packed it away, with heightened respect, and deliberately walked up to, and across, the bridge. It rang substantial enough under his feet, for him to almost doubt the truth of what he had just seen. He was too near his enemy to hazard any more experiments. He found him in a goodly, square, and most singularly wall-papered room, inasmuch as each of its walls—where not pierced for a door—was one vast mirror. In the centre stood a table loaded with every delicacy in and out of season. At each side of the table was placed a luxurious chair. The Hungarian pointed to one of these and spoke.

"I bid you to this last supper, in the name of those that hold this house, if you dare sit down and feast."

"I dare do anything in *your* company."

"Then eat, drink, and be merry, for to-morrow one of us two dies. That, I believe, was the intention with which you accompanied me hither?"

"You are right therein, as always."

"Then for an hour we will proclaim a truce to all our differences. We will pledge the survivor in flowing bowls from vintages of a thousand years. Wine you shall have creating thirst and woman creating desire. That is if you can call *her* woman that tempted Adam out of Paradise."

"To whom do you refer?"

"To Lilith, Eve's rival, queen of all damnations!"

"Was it for *her*, then, that you sold your soul and swopped an eye with Satan?"

"Ha-ha, you have heard that story. It is true that I left my eye in pawn, but it is false that I received one in exchange. This is not an eye at all—this Evil Eye as they call it—whose beam is supposed to blight wherever it falls. In your own person you have tested its perfect harmlessness."

He paused, as if to see whether the sailor had swallowed this more than doubtful statement. The latter made no sign. The wizard then proceeded to lift his sinister eyelid, until the fiery stab of the Evil Eye was a second time unveiled. As before it had no effect whatever on Marquard. The magician then lifted his finger to it, and with a twist turned the apparent eye-ball out of its socket. It slipped over the finger that had released it, and in so doing shewed what it really was. It was a *ring*, set with an enormous blazing stone!

Yes, this was the fabled Evil Eye, this innocent circlet of gold with its flashing stone. The magician obligingly extended the hand that now wore it, to the end that Marquard might examine it more minutely. As he got accustomed to its baleful glare, he perceived that this was not generated by the gem itself. The gem was hollow, and served merely as a receptacle for something *alive* that crouched within. From the eyes of this living weevil—or devil—or whatever it was—streamed the poison of ill-effect which the public had thought to proceed from an Evil Eye. Nor were they wrong after all, only that there were *two* evil eyes, and their owner to boot—instead of one. But even this was only the beginning of the Hungarian's surprises. Having allowed the sailor to gaze long enough upon the ring, he rested the hand that wore it upon a chair. Then with the other hand he just touched the gem at his side. It flew open and the creature that lived in it came forth. She increased in size—the sailor saw that it was a woman—a woman, whose beauty would have blinded the severest eye. She would have seduced an anchorite to dimpled sin.

"You see," laughed the Hungarian, "that, if I got no eye from the devil, he gave me a rib out of his side."

When she had reached the height of her companion Lilith stopped growing, and sat down upon her chair. The magician seated himself at one hand of her, the sailor at the other, and looked inquiringly towards the vacant place that fronted her. The Hungarian intercepted his glance, and grinned.

"Look at the mirror, man," he cried, "there are more guests here—and more august—than you imagine."

The galley-slave looked at the mirror behind the vacant side of the table, and started from his seat in sudden terror. The mirror reflected the *back* of someone as if occupying that chair, which nevertheless still stood in front of it, empty. The sailor looked from chair to mirror—from mirror to chair again—but there was no mistaking that weird fact. His hair stood up. He sank into his seat. He snatched to his white lips the first goblet that came to hand. The magician at once took up his own glass and cried out, mockingly,

"I second your toast! To the health of our guest—the Orb and Sceptre of all the hells!"

From that the orgie waxed fast and furious. They swam in music. The room was grey with incense. Their lights were balls of coloured fire that flashed in the air, and ever and anon dropping into their cups hissed like snapdragons. Songs were sung that fallen angels had brought from paradise. Tales were told of doings done before the world was planned. But *who* sung, and *who* narrated was beyond the sailor's ken, a-swim as he was with wine and witchery. He grew more and more bemused. The table whirled round and round. The viands slipped away from his hands, when he turned to look at his fair neighbour he could only find the one eye of the Hungarian. The mirrors gave back distortions. All was confusion and delusion, and mocking laughter in his ears. After a brave attempt to keep his head, he rolled upon the floor. The vintages of a thousand years had done their work.

When he awoke, with a splitting headache, the room was clear. The Hungarian paced up and down at one end. A glance at him sufficed to show that the matchless ring had been restored to its socket.

"Ha-ha," laughed the sorcerer, "are you looking for the girl you were so sweet on last night? Behold her!" He lifted his eyelid, and there flashed forth coquettish lights from the prisoner of the gem.

The sailor sprang to his feet.

"Arch and unheard-of juggler," he cried, "your play is played, and your curtain is nigh to ringing down. You have done the devil's work—beshrew the like!—and you shall get the devil's wages. You shall rue the day you brought me here."

"The nightmare be your bride! Were you not girt with an adverse fate you had dawned in a fiercer place than this! And now, if you are bent upon a duel—and the laws of hospitality do not protect me—I will even let you take the lead."

"Then look to yourself, witch-master!" cried the sailor, drawing a rusty pistol from his long sea-boot. He took aim, and fired;
the bullet struck the Hungarian, and *rebounded*. A peal of laughter shook the hall.

"The devil kiss your lips!" cried the sorcerer; "you have no reach
for me! But try again if you like before I set my foot on the neck of
your revenge."

The sailor considered. It was no use wasting another leaden
bullet on a man who was evidently impregnable to such. He remembered that a silver button cut from one's coat was considered
sovereign against a wizard when all else failed. But, unfortunately,
Marquard wore no silver buttons, and very few buttons of any kind.
An idea struck him, there was the magic ball that the witch had
given him. It was true that, if it flew wide of its mark, he would
have staked, and lost, his all; since he would ho longer boast any
influence to protect him. On the other hand, he felt a presenti-
ment that it would not fail him. In any case the sorcerer, who was
aware by this time of his possession of the talisman, seemed, from
his good humour, to have forged some device by which he could
counteract it. Marquard threw his scruples to the wind, and
rammed the amulet into the pistol.

"I will bring your royal insolence a-dust," he cried, "in hack-
neyed, unoriginal death for all that you are the devil's fetch and
carry!"

He fired. Thunder shook the furthest stars. The room was full
of foetid smoke. As it partially cleared away, the galley-slave saw
his enemy lying supine upon the ground. He crept up to him, still
misdoubting, and touched him gingerly. He was dead. But when
Marquard came to look upon his face, he started back surprised,
all trace of the ring had entirely disappeared. Both the sorcerer's
eyes were open, and both were now a match. But whence had come
back this long-lost eye? It was the ball which the witch had handed
over to Marquard—the ball which Marquard had loaded into his
pistol—the ball which had steered unerring to its ancient seat, and
ousted the usurper which it found there. Marquard reverently lifted
the fallen pride of wizardry and carried him gently to the outer

gate. This man upon whom he had served the warrant of that bow-elless catch-poll—Death, this clay, after all was said and done, had once been boyhood like himself. Lovers of one girl the tunes of their two lives were built upon the same bottom note. It was with tenderness that Marquard tossed the body into the abyss. He did not know how soon he was to follow it. It had scarcely disappeared when he became aware from the thinning of the castle that he had unwittingly got rid of the power which enabled him to cross the bridge. The golden railing had already vanished. He started to run, but the marble under his feet was softening, and he sank in it to the ankles at every step. A little further and his legs went through to the knee. With incredible exertions he reached the centre, but could go no further. He floundered in the fast ebbing material, hopelessly, to the waist. Then he sank to his armpits—spread out his arms so as to hold yet a second to life—but finally the last remnants of the bridge evaporated, and he fell plumb into the gulf, turning over and over in his fall.

THE WITCHES' SABBATH

Our scene is one of those terrific peaks set apart by tradition as the trysting place of wizards and witches, and of every kind of folk that prefers dark to day.

It might have been Mount Elias, or the Brocken, associated with Doctor Faustus. It might have been the Horsel or Venusberg of Tannhaeuser, or the Black Forest. Enou9gh that it was one of these.

Not a star wrinkled the brow of night. Only in the distance the twinkling lights of some town could be seen. Low down in the skirts of the mountain rode a knight, followed closely by his page. We say a knight, because he had once owned that distinction. But a wild and bloody youth had tarnished his ancient shield, the while it kept bright and busy his ancestral sword. Behold him now, little better than a highwayman. Latterly he had wandered from border to border, without finding where to rest his faithful steed. All authority was in arms against him; Hageck, the wild knight, was posted throughout Germany. More money was set upon his head than had ever been put into his pocket. Pikemen and pistoliers had dispersed his following. None remained to him whom he could call his own, save this stripling who still rode sturdily at the tail of his horse. Him also, the outlaw had besought, even with tears, to abandon one so ostensibly cursed by stars and men. But in vain. The boy protested that he would have no home, save in his master's shadow.

They were an ill-assorted pair. The leader was all war-worn and weather-worn. Sin had marked him for its own and for the wages of sin. The page was young and slight, and marble pale. He would have looked more at home at the silken train of some great lady, than following at these heels from which the gilded spurs had long been hacked. Nevertheless, the music of the spheres themselves sings not more sweetly in accord than did these two hearts.

The wild knight, Hageck, had ascended the mountain as far as was possible to four-legged roadsters. Therefore he reined in his horse and dismounted, and addressed his companion. His voice was now quite gentle, which on occasion could quench mutiny, and in due season dry up the taste of blood in the mouths of desperate men.

"Time is that we must part, Enno."

"Master, you told me we need never part."

"Let be, child, do you not understand me? I hope with your own heart's hope that we shall meet again to-morrow in this same tarrying place. But I have not brought you to so cursed a place without some object. When I say that we must part, I mean that you must take charge of our horses while I go further up the mountain upon business, which for your own sake you must never share."

"And is this your reading of the oath of our brotherhood which we swore together?"

"The oath of our brotherhood, I fear, was writ in water. You are, in fact, the only one of all my company that has kept faith with me. For that very reason I would not spare your neck from the halter, nor your limbs from the wheel. But also for that very reason I will not set your immortal soul in jeopardy."

"My immortal soul! Is this business then unhallowed that you go upon? Now I remember me that this mountain at certain seasons is said to be haunted by evil spirits. Master, you also are bound by our oath to tell me all."

"You shall know all, Enno, were oaths even cheaper than they are. You have deserved by your devotion to be the confessor of your friend."

"Friend is no name for companionship such as ours. I am sure you would die for me. I believe I could die for you, Hageck."

"Enough, you have been more than brother to me. I had a brother once, after the fashion of this world, and it is his envious hand which has placed me where I stand. That was before I knew you, Enno, and it is some sweets in my cup at any rate, that had he not betrayed me I should never have known you. Nevertheless, you will admit that since he robbed me of the girl I loved, even your loyal heart is a poor set off for what fate and fraternity took from me. In fine, we both loved the same girl, but she loved me, and would have none of my brother. She was beautiful, Enno—how beautiful you can never guess that have not yet loved."

"I have never conceived any other love than that I bear you."

"Tush, boy, you know not what you say. But to return to my story. One day that I was walking with her my brother would have stabbed me. She threw herself between and was killed upon my breast."

He tore open his clothes at the throat and showed a great faded stain upon his skin.

"The hangman's brand shall fade," he cried, "ere that wash out. Accursed be the mother that bore me seeing that she also first bore him! The devil squat down with him in his resting, lie with him in his sleeping, as the devil has sat and slept with me every noon and night since that deed was done. Never give way to love of woman, Enno, lest you lose the one you love, and with her lose the balance of your life."

"Alas! Hageck, I fear I never shall."

"Since that miscalled day, blacker than any night, you know as well as any one the sort of death in life I led. I had the good or evil luck to fall in with some broken men like myself, fortune's foes and foes of all whom fortune cherishes, you among them. Red blood, red gold for a while ran through our fingers. Then a turn of the wheel, and, presto, my men are squandered to every wind that blows—I am a fugitive with a price upon my head!"

"And with one comrade whom, believe me, wealth is too poor to buy."

"A heart above rubies. Even so. To such alone would I confide my present purpose. You must know that my brother was a student of magic of no mean repute, and before we quarrelled had given me some insight into its mysteries. Now that I near the end

of my tether I have summed up all the little I knew, and am resolved to make a desperate cast in this mountain of despair. In a
word, I intend to hold converse with my dead sweetheart before I
die. The devil shall help me to it for the love he bears me."

"You would invoke the enemy of all mankind?"

"Him and none other. Aye, shudder not, nor seek to turn me
from it. I have gone over it again and again. The gates of Hell are
set no firmer than this resolve."

"God keep Hell far from you when you call it!"

"I had feared my science was of too elementary an order to conduct an exorcism under any but the most favourable circumstances.
Hence our journey hither. This place is one of those where parlia-
ments of evil are held, where dead and living meet on equal ground.
To-night is the appointed night of one of these great Sabbaths. I
propose to leave you here with the horses. I shall climb to the topmost peak, draw a circle that I may stand in for my defence, and
with all the vehemence of love deferred, pray for my desire."

"May all good angels speed you!"

"Nay, I have broken with such. Your good wish, Enno, is
enough."

"But did we not hear talk in the town about a hermit that spent
his life upon the mountain top, atoning for some sin in day-long
prayer and mortification? Can this evil fellowship of which you
speak still hold its meetings upon a spot which has been attached
in the name of Heaven by one good man?"

"Of this hermit I knew nothing until we reached the town. It
was then too late to seek another workshop. Should what you say
be correct, and this holy man have purged this plague spot, I can
do no worse than pass the night with him, and return to you. But
should the practices of witch and wizard continue as of yore, then
the powers of evil shall draw my love to me, be she where she may.
Aye, be it in that most secret nook of heaven where God retires
when He would weep, and where even archangels are never suffered to tread."

"O all good go with you!"

"Farewell, Enno, and if I never return count my soul not so lost but what you may say a prayer for it now and again, when you have leisure."

"I will not outlive you!"

The passionate words were lost on Hageck, who had already climbed so far as to be out of hearing. He only knew vaguely that something was shouted to him, and waved his hand above his head for a reply. On and on he climbed. Time passed. The way grew harder. At last exhausted, but fed with inward exaltation, he reached the summit. It was of considerable extent and extremely uneven. The first thing our hero noticed was the cave of the hermit. It could be nothing else, although it was closed with an iron door. A new departure, thought Hageck to himself, as he hammered upon it with the pommel of his sword, for a hermit's cell to be locked in like a fortress.

"Open, friend," he cried, "in heaven's name, or in that of the other place if you like it better."

The noise came from within of a bar being removed. The door opened. It revealed a mere hole in the rock, though large enough, it is true, to hold a considerable number of persons. Furniture was conspicuous by its absence. There was no sign even of a bed, unless a coffin that grinned in one corner served the occupant's needs. A skull, a scourge, a crucifix, a knife for his food, what more does such a hermit want? His feet were bare, his head was tonsured, but his eyebrows were long and matted, and fell like a screen over burning maniacal eyes. A fanatic, every inch of him, He scrutinised the invader from top to toe. Apparently the result was unsatisfactory. He frowned.

"A traveller," said he, "and at this unholy hour. Back, back, do you not know the sinister reputation of this time and place?"

"I know your reputation to be of the highest, reverend father; I could not credit what rumour circulates about this mountain top when I understood that one of such sanctity had taken up a perpetual abode here."

"My abode is fixed here for the very reason that it is a realm of untold horror. My task is to win back, if I can, to the dominion of the church this corner, which has been so long unloved that it cries aloud to God and man. This position of my own choice is no sine-cure. Hither at stated times the full brunt of the Sabbath sweeps to its rendezvous. Here I defy the Sabbath. You see that mighty door?"

"I had wondered, but feared to ask, what purpose such a bar-rier could serve in such a miserable place."

"You may be glad to crouch behind it if you stay here much longer. At midnight, Legion, with all the swirl of all the hells at his back, will sweep this summit like a tornado. Were you of the stuff that never trembles, yet you shall hear such sounds as shall melt your backbone. Avoid hence while there is yet time."

"But you, if you remain here, why not I?"

"I remain here as a penance for a crime I did, a crime which almost takes prisoner my reason, so different was it from the crime I set out to do, so deadly death to all my hopes. I am on my knees throughout the whole duration of this pandemonium that I tell you of, and count thick and fast my beads during the whole time. Did I cease for one second to pray, that second would be my last. The roof of my cavern would descend and efface body and soul. But you, what would you do here?"

"I seek my own ends, for which I am fully prepared. To confer with a shade from the other world I place my own soul in jeop-ardy. For the short time that must elapse, before the hour arrives when I can work, I ask but a trifle of your light and fire."

"The will-o'-the-wisp be your light, Saint Anthony's your fire! Do you not recognise me?"

The wild knight bent forward and gazed into the hermit's in-most eye, then started back, and would have fallen had his head not struck the iron door. This recalled him to his senses, and after a moment he stood firm again, and murmured between his teeth, "My brother!"

"Your brother," repeated the holy man, "your brother, whose sweetheart you stole and drove me to madness and crime."

"I drove you to no madness, I drove you to no crime. The mad-ness, the crime you expiate here, were all of your own making. She

loved me, and me alone—you shed her blood, by accident I confess, yet you shed it, and not all the prayers of your lifetime can
gather up one drop of it. What soaked into my own brain remains
there for ever, though I have sought to wash it out with an ocean
of other men's blood."

"And I," replied the hermit, and he tore his coarse frock off his
shoulders, "I have sought to drown it with an ocean of my own."

He spoke truth. Blood still oozed from his naked flesh, ploughed
into furrows by the scourge.

"You, that have committed so many murders," he continued,
"and who have reproached me so bitterly for one, all the curses of
your dying victims, all the curses I showered upon you before I
became reformed have not availed to send you yet to the gibbet or
to the wheel. You are one that, like the basil plant, grows ever the
rifer for cursing. I remember I tried to lame you, after you left
home, by driving a rusty nail into one of your footsteps, but the
charm refused to work. You were never the worse for it that I could
hear. They say the devil's children have the devil's luck. Yet some
day shall death trip up your heels."

"Peace, peace," cried the wild horseman, "let ill-will be dead
between us, and the bitterness of death be passed, as befits your
sacred calling. Even if I see her for one moment to-night, by the
aid of the science you once taught me, will you not see her for eternity in heaven some near day?"

"In heaven," cried the hermit, "do I want to see her in heaven?
On earth would I gladly see her again and account that moment
cheap if weighed against my newly discovered soul! But that can
never be. Not the art you speak of, not all the dark powers which
move men to sin, can restore her to either of us as she was that
day. And she loved you. She died to save you. You have nothing to
complain of. But to me she was like some chaste impossible star."

"I loved her most," muttered the outlaw.

"You loved her most," screamed the hermit. "Hell sit upon your
eyes! Put it to the test. Look around. Do you see anything of her
here?"

The other Hageck gazed eagerly round the cave, but without fixing upon anything.

"I see nothing," he was forced to confess.

The hermit seized the skull and held it in front of his eyes.

"This is her dear head," he cried, "fairer far than living red and white to me!"

The wild knight recoiled with a gasp of horror, snatched the ghastly relic from the hand of his brother, and hurled it over the precipice. He put his fingers over his eyes and fell to shaking like an aspen. For a moment the hermit scarcely seemed to grasp his loss. Then with a howl of rage he seized his brother by the throat.

"You have murdered her," he shrieked in tones scarcely recognisable, "she will be dashed to a hundred pieces by such a fall!"

He threw the outlaw to the ground and, retreating to his cave, slammed the door behind him, but his heart-broken sobs could still be heard distinctly. It was very evident that he was no longer in his right mind. The wild knight rose somewhat painfully and limped to a little distance where he perceived a favourable spot for erecting his circle. The sobbing of the crazed hermit presently ceased. He was aware that his rival had entered upon his operations. The hermit re-opened his door that he might more clearly catch the sound of what his foe was engaged upon. Every step was of an absorbing interest to the solitary as to the man who made it. Anon the hermit started to his feet. He fancied he heard another voice replying to his brother. Yes, it was a voice he seemed to know. He rushed out of the cave. A girlish figure clad in a stained dress was clasped in his brother's arms. Kiss after kiss the wild knight was showering upon brow, and eye, and cheek, and lip. The girl responded as the hermit had surely seen her do once before. He flew to his cave. He grasped the knife he used for his food. He darted like an arrow upon the startled pair. The woman tried to throw herself in front of her lover, but the hermit with a coarse laugh, "Not twice the dagger seeks the same breast," plunged it into the heart of her companion. The wild knight threw up his arms and without a cry fell to the ground. The girl uttered a shriek that seemed to rive the skies and flung herself across her dead. The hermit gazed at it stupidly and rubbed his eyes. He seemed like one dazed, but slowly recovering his senses. Suddenly he started, came as it were to himself, and pulled the girl by the shoulder.

"We have not a minute to lose," he cried, "the great Sabbath is all but due. If his body remains out here one second after the stroke of twelve, his soul will be lost to all eternity. It will be snatched by the fiends who even now are bound to it. Do you not see yon shadowy hosts—but I forget, you are not a witch."

"I see nothing," she replied, sullenly, rising up and peering round. The night was clear, but starless.

"I have been a wizard," he answered, "and once a wizard always a wizard, though I now fight upon the other side. Take my hand and you will see."

She took his hand, and screamed as she did so. For at the instant there became visible to her these clouds of loathsome beings that were speeding thither from every point of the compass. Warlock, and witch, and wizard rode post on every conceivable graceless mount. Their motion was like the lightning of heaven, and their varied cries—owlet hoot, caterwaul, dragon-shout—the horn of the Wild Hunter, and the hurly of risen dead—vied with the bay of Cerberus to the seldseen moon. A forest of whips was flourished aloft. The whirr of wings raised dozing echoes. The accustomed mountain shook and shivered like a jelly, with the fear of their onset.

The girl dropped his hand and immediately lost the power of seeing them. She had learned at any rate that what he said was true.

"Help me to carry the body to the cave," cried he, and in a moment it was done. The corpse was placed in the coffin of his murderer. Then the hermit crashed his door to its place. Up went bolts and bars. Some loose rocks that were probably the hermit's chairs and tables were rolled up to afford additional security.

"And now," demanded the man, "now that we have a moment of breathing space, tell me what woman-kind are you whom I find here with my brother? That you are not her I know (woe is me that

I have good reason to know) yet you are as like her as any flower that blows. I loved her, and I murdered her, and I have the right to ask, who and what are you that come to disturb my peace?"

"I am her sister."

"Her sister! Yes, I remember you. You were a child in those days. Neither I nor my brother (God rest his soul!), neither of us noticed you."

"No, he never took much notice of me. Yet I loved him as well as she did."

"You, too, loved him," whispered the hermit, as if to himself; "what did he do to be loved by two such women?"

"Yes, I loved him, though he never knew it, but I may confess it now, for you are a priest of a sort, are you not, you that shrive with steel?"

"You are bitter, like your sister. She was always so with me."

"I owe you my story," she replied more gently; "when she died and he fell into evil courses and went adrift with bad companions, I found I could not live without him, nor with anyone else, and I determined to become one of them. I dressed in boy's clothes and sought enlistment into his company of free lances. He would have driven me from him, saying it was no work for such as I, yet at last I wheedled it from him. I think there was something in my face (all undeveloped as it was and stained with walnut juice) that reminded him of her he had lost. I followed him faithfully through good and evil, cringing for a look or word from him. We were at last broken up (as you know) and I alone of all his sworn riders remained to staunch his wounds. He brought me hither that he might wager all the soul that was left to him on the chance of evoking her spirit. I had with me the dress my sister died in, that I had cherished through all my wanderings, as my sole reminder of her life and death. I put it on after he had left me, and followed him as fast as my strength would allow me. My object was to beguile him with what sorry pleasure I could, while at the same time saving him from committing the sin of disturbing the dead. God forgive me if there was mixed with it the wholly selfish yearning to be kissed by him once, only once, in my true character as loving woman, rid of my hated disguise! I have had my desire, and it has turned to apples of Sodom on my lips. You are right. All we can do now is to preserve his soul alive."

She fell on her knees beside the coffin. The hermit pressed his crucifix into her hands.

"Pray!" he cried, and at the same moment the distant clock struck twelve. There came a rush of feet, a thunder at the iron door, the cave rocked like a ship's cabin abruptly launched into the trough of a storm. An infernal whooping and hallooing filled the air outside, mixed with it imprecations that made the strong man blanch. The banner of Destruction was unfurled. All the horned heads were upon them. Thrones and Dominions, Virtues, Princes, Powers. All hell was loose that night, and the outskirts of Hell.

The siege had begun. The hermit told his beads with feverish rapidity. One Latin prayer after another rolled off his tongue in drops of sweat. The girl, to whom these were unintelligible, tried in vain to think of prayers. All she could say, as she pressed the Christ to her lips, was "Lord of my life! My Love." She scarcely heard the hurly-burly that raged outside. Crash after crash resounded against the door, but good steel tempered with holy water is bad to beat. Showers of small pieces of rock fell from the ceiling and the cave was soon filled with dust. Peals of hellish cachinnation resounded after each unsuccessful attempt to break down that defence. Living battering rams pressed it hard, dragon's spur, serpent's coil, cloven hoof, foot of clay. Tall Iniquities set their backs to it, names of terror, girt with earthquake. All the swart crew dashed their huge bulk against it, rakehelly riders, humans and superhumans, sin and its paymasters. The winds well nigh split their sides with hounding of them on. Evil stars in their courses fought against it. The seas threw up their dead. Haunted houses were no more haunted that night. Graveyards steamed. Gibbets were empty. The ghoul left his half-gnawn corpse, the vampire his victim's throat. Buried treasures rose to earth's surface that their ghostly guardians might swell the fray. Yet the hermit prayed on, and the woman wept, and the door kept its face to the foe. Will the hour of release never strike? Crested Satans now lead the van. Even steel cannot hold out for ever against those in whose veins instead of blood, runs fire. At last it bends ever so little, and the devilish hubbub is increased tenfold.

"Should they break open the door—" yelled the hermit, making a trumpet of his hands, yet she could not hear what he shouted above the abominable din, nor had he time to complete his instructions. For the door did give, and that suddenly, with a clang that was heard from far off in the town, and made many a burgher think the last trump had come. The rocks that had been rolled against the door flew off in every direction, and a surging host—and the horror of it was that they were invisible to the girl—swept in.

The hermit tore his rosary asunder, and scattered the loose beads in the faces of the fiends.

"Hold fast the corpse!" he yelled, as he was trampled under foot, and this time he made himself heard. The girl seized the long hair of her lover, pressed it convulsively, and swooned.

Years afterwards (as it seemed to her) she awakened and found the chamber still as death, and—yes—this was the hair of death which she still clutched in her dead hand. She kissed it a hundred times before it brought back to her where she was and what had passed. She looked round then for the hermit. He, poor man, was lying as if also dead. But when she could bring herself to release her hoarded treasure, she speedily brought him to some sort of consciousness. He sat up, not without difficulty, and looked around. But his mind, already half way to madness, had been totally overturned by what had occurred that woeful night.

"We have saved his soul between us," she cried. "What do I not owe you for standing by me in that fell hour?"

He regarded her in evident perplexity. "I cannot think how you come to be wearing that blood-stained dress of hers," was all he replied.

"I have told you," she said, gently, "but you have forgotten that I cherished it through all my wanderings as my sole memento of her glorious death. She laid down the last drop of her blood for him. She chose the better part. But I! my God! what in the world is to become of me?"

"I had a memento of her once," he muttered. "I had her beautiful head, but I have lost it."

"That settles it," she said, "you shall cut off mine."

"The Devil's Debt"

Somewhere about the Middle Ages—somewhere in a mediae-val town—there lived a man who walked always on the shady side of the way. None of his neighbours could have assigned a reason why he should only tread where the lapse of time leaves no trace on the dial, yet so it was. None had ever seen him in sunshine.

This man was known by the name of Porphyro, though we may reasonably doubt if it was given to him in baptism. For he belonged to a class that baptised toads by night at their Sabbaths in mock-ery of the baptism of babes by day. In a word, Porphyro was a wiz-ard, and for one circumstance (which will presently be mentioned) was perhaps better known among his like than any practiser of the Black Art before or since.

There was, and likely enough still is, in Europe a University of the occult sciences, buried underground, carved out of the roots of mountains, far from the hum of men. Here taught weird profes-sors—eerie, eldritch, elflocked. Here came weird students to tread the intoxicating wine-press of magical study. Your true wizard is set apart from birth by some particularity which bespeaks his vocation. To the University came representatives of every class which felt this call Here was the demoniac and the stigmatic, the abortion and the albino, the hermaphrodite and the changeling, the hag-ridden and the pixy-led, sleep-walker, Cesarean, Sunday-child, seventh son, and he that is born with the caul. This motley crew was of as many hues as there are ends of the earth. Many tongued as Mithridates, all wrote their notes by common consent in the *lingua angelorum.*

The University boasted a laboratory of at least a hundred paces in length and proportionately broad and high. A mock sun gave it cold light by day, and a mock moon by night. Here experiments in exorcism were conducted, of course under the strictest supervision of the principals. Here the students learned that the ghosts of dead men (having, always some of the old Adam that was unpurged from them), are easier to call back to us than elemental spirits can be wrenched from their eternal spheres. The most trivial task (and therefore that of the junior classes), was to re-incarnate some suicide, set in four cross roads, whose soul still hovered like a noxious gas about the only body where it could hope to find toleration. The pupils were very properly forbidden to incur the danger of repeating these experiments in private. Nevertheless something of the kind went on under the rose. As a rule the novices (and these were after all the lucky ones), ignominiously failed in their attempts to storm the outworks of hell. They knew how to call spirits from the vasty deep, but the spirits refused to come when they did call them. One youth, however, boasted that he had raised the devil, or at any rate, a devil. He described him to his bosom friends nearly as follows:—

"A great and full stature, soft and phlegmatic, of colour like a black obscure cloud, having a swollen countenance, with eyes red and full of water, a bald head, and teeth like a wild boar."

One of the listeners, doubtless jealous, attempted to cheapen this success of his companion, by remarking that an exorcist, if worth his salt, should be able to make the spirit appear in what guise he chose.

"Then, by the belt of Venus," swore a third, "I would command it to appear as a lovely girl with longer hair and smaller feet than any on this top which the Almighty set spinning and dubbed earth."

Another poor fellow appears to have been so inflamed with the suggestion of this rustler, that he tried to bring it into the sphere of practical politics. He was never seen alive again. Not answering to his name at the roll-call next morning, his bedroom was visited, and a thin trickle of blood found oozing under the door. One of the search party put a pistol to the lock and fired. The door flew open. A cry burst from all present, and some of the youngest, covering their faces with their hands, fled. The body of the devoted wretch who had played with unholy fire was scattered parcel meal about the room. The lopped limbs were twisted round into spirals as if boneless. One of stronger stomach than the rest of the onlookers, and who examined them more closely, declared that the bone had melted and run out under some incredible heat. One of the teachers opined that if the demon had only breathed upon the bone, it would have been enough to fuse it. There were no more experiments in students' rooms.

Apart from such accidental deaths, the Academy paid a regular yearly rent of one living soul to hell, and woe unto teachers and taught had they lapsed into arrear one day. The victim who was to suffer, that the rest might live and learn, was selected in the following traditional manner. The whole of the pupils toed a line at one extreme end of the hall, and, at a given signal raced to the opposite door. There was, as may be imagined, a terrible struggle to pass through the hangings. The last to cross the threshold was hugged to hell by the awaiting fiend. It was on such an occasion that Porphyro earned the unique distinction, alluded to above, of having successfully cozened the Prince of Darkness himself. Strain as he might, he was the last to touch the winning post. His competitors, who now breathed themselves in safety in the lobby, had given him up for lost. But no piercing shriek of dissolution stabbed the air, no fiendish laughter made horrible the echoes. Instead, voices were heard, until presently their comrade rejoined those who had already mourned him. Amid a scene of the wildest excitement, he was dragged into the light. Something unprecedented must obviously have occurred. His hair had turned snowy white. Those fell back who looked first into his eyes, for they saw in them reflected the face of Hell himself. The tale which Porphyro told them was in substance this, that when he arrived last at the curtains, and already felt the breath of punishment upon his cheek, there occurred to him one loophole of escape. He turned desperately at bay, like hunted quarry; and roundly told the scrutineer that all he could claim by the letter of his bond was Porphyro's shadow. That was the last living thing which passed out of the lists; and not Porphyro, who preceded it. Strange as it may seem, after a few heated words, the justice of this quibble was acknowledged by the father of all such juggleries. He bore off the shadow with a sort of smile, that was more terrible than men's frown, and lo and behold! when the schoolfellows, with one accord, looked down at the feet of him who had so miraculously escaped the infernal maw, they saw that Porphyro was, as he ever afterwards remained, shadowless. And now our readers can guess why our hero walked always on the shady side of the way.

Nothing had ever been known (even in circles like this) so successfully daring as this piece of evasion: Round and round the whole round globe, by means only known to wizards, the news sped fast to all the wizard world. It was proclaimed at every Sabbath, from Blockula to the Brocken. The Lapland witch whispered it to the Finland witch, as they sat tying up wind after wind in knots for their seafaring customers. The Druids of Carnac knew it, and the Persian devil worshippers. The Shamans of Siberia made a song of it and beat their magic drums thereto. The magicians of Egypt pictured it in their mirrors of ink. The African Obi men washed their great fetish in the blood of a thousand virgins, and sent it as a present, over the desert sands, to Porphyro. Even the medicine men heard of it in the heart of an undiscovered continent, and emblazoned it upon the walls of their medicine lodge. Everyone foresaw a brilliant career for Porphyro. They fully expected him to disembowel Hell. The reverse was what really happened. Instead of swinging himself at once to the top round of the ladder, he showed no disposition to trouble himself at all. He opened a private office in the town referred to at the beginning of our story, and carried on a private business in magic of the whitest kind. For him no monster evocations, with a million demons at his beck and

call, like the Sicilian whom Benvenuto Cellini employed to conjure for him in the Coliseum. Porphyro refused in the most stiff-
necked manner to exorcise on any terms for anyone. He confined
himself solely to pettyfogging business, such as writing talismans,
and reckoning magic squares, drawing horoscopes, and casting
schemes of geomancy, poisoning rivals for lovers, or close-fisted
relatives for spendthrift heirs. Need we state in black and white
the reason (concealed from everyone else), why he held his hand
from higher things? Oh, the humiliation of it! He was afraid! Yes,
Porphyro was afraid, even he, who had plucked a hair from the
devil's beard, for that very reason he was afraid. He had saved his
soul alive, losing only a shadow of little moment to him, but in
return, he had incurred the eternal enmity of one whose grudge
had once shaken the high heavens. The general adversary of all
mankind was first and beyond all things most ferociously
Porphyro's adversary. Unhappy Porphyro, who had already given
seisin to hell, Porphyro with one half of him already in the living
devil's clutch, who never slept but he dreamed of the tortures his
poor shadow suffered at the hands of those that lovingly work evil!
Tortures, which were but foreshadowings of his own! No wonder
Porphyro dared not invoke even the least of spirits. He knew too
well that the mightiest of them would appear with no greater calling than a word.

But there was one antidote which wrestled with the nightshade
in his cup, one star of the right colour appeared above his horizon.
There was a woman in his town (one only for him) a princess and
the ward of a king, an exquisite beauty. From the first time he saw
her, he loved her with a passion which reproached his meaner self.
She fed upon his sighs, without knowing that the air she breathed
was full of them. In any case, he would never have dared to speak
to her. It was sufficient daily bread to him to see her move. He
hung upon her footsteps. He kept pace with her in her rides, running ever in the shadow because he himself had no shadow to call
his own. Yet he forgot while looking at her this one great fact of
his life. Even in his dreams she presently held his hand while he
suffered. And he dreamed of her thus till he set his teeth in his

pillow. Gradually her little mouth sucked up all the breath of his body. He wrote poems about his princess and swallowed them. Often he took no other food for days. He made philtres which would infallibly have caused her to love him, had he not ruthlessly thrown them all away as soon as made. He constructed an image of her in wax, and worshipped it five times daily. It was this which wrought his downfall. Certain of his clients (they had not paid him) denounced him as a sorcerer. Without notice he received a domiciliary visit from the authorities. Apart from other evidence which the house contained, the wax image of the princess was discovered and he was at once charged with intending to make away with her life. Oh, the irony of fate, he who would have cheerfully laid down his own for her! Being forcibly removed from his house, the secret he had so long kept was discovered, and this shadowlessness, though accounted for in a hundred ways, all wide of the truth, was added at once to the long list of crimes in his indictment. At the preliminary examination, he would confess nothing. He was accordingly imprisoned pending the preparation of tortures to shake his resolution. With the aid of these refinements, he might be made to confess anything, even that he had attempted the life of his best beloved. The scaffold loomed before him. And oh, that her name should be bandied about in such context.

Meanwhile Porphyro sat, body and soul in darkness. He saw none but the jailer, who brought him food once daily, with a finger ever on his lips. Rats there were, and such small deer, but with these he could hold no converse, although in his youth he had met with men who professed to teach their languages. Porphyro was fain to chatter constantly to himself that he might have no time to think. He played his school games over again, rehearsed his school tasks to imaginary masters, held imaginary conversations with clients and with his parents long dead, and with his princess who was more than parent, and more than dead to him. He wooed her in a thousand ways, now as an emperor, raising her to his level, now as the meanest of her grooms, to whom she sweetly condescended, now he was a soldier, better used to red lips of wounds than red lips which wound, now he was a scholar, who forgot all wisdom save hers, now he was a miser, who came like Jupiter in a shower of gold. Thus riotous reigned carnival before his coming Lent.

And now comes the strangest part of all this strange eventful history. He fancied once or twice that he was replied to as he spoke. Again and again he groped all over the blind prison, and felt no one. Yet there was of a surety a tongue which answered him. And the weirdness of it was that, turn though he might, it always spoke from behind him. Again he searched the litter of the dungeon, and again without result. The voice was at first unintelligible, like the murmur of the sea, yet with a cadence which soon struck his ear as strangely familiar. He had heard it only once before, but it had been in that cock-pit underground where he had fought a main which had coloured his whole life. He was bound up with the memory of it like a poor prisoner whom men fetter to a corpse. It was the still small voice which dominates the brawl of Hell.

His hair could grow no whiter, else it had done so. He listened with all his ears and began to catch syllables and afterwards words, till at last he made out that the Tempter was proposing terms of peace with him.

Right well knew Porphyro (none better), the price that must be paid for such a truce. His soul must feed the quick of Hell. It seemed hard to yield up at last that immortal henchman which he had once so gloriously saved from these same talons. Yet what chance had he? On the one hand, if he maintained his feud with the Evil One, the halter was weaving which must strangle love and life. On the other part, if he surrendered his soul to the Exile, he could at any rate make what terms he pleased. And there were terms he pictured himself exacting which made ultimate payment of the highest price seem easy to the blood which had once stood face to face with Satan, and given him better than he gave. Porphyro still continued to argue *pro* and *con*, though his decision was a foregone conclusion. At last he formulated his demands to the spirit. He must marry the Princess. He must be her husband, were it but for a single night.

The walls of the dungeon suddenly became bright with a kind of phosphorescent glow. Porphyro (still alone, or, at any rate, he seemed so) saw a table standing in front of him, bearing a bond already drawn and the materials for signing it. The terms set forth were those he had himself proposed. He signed, sealed, and delivered it, and was plunged into darkness again as his finger left the parchment. A sense of infernal laughter pervaded the air, though nothing was to be heard. Porphyro fell full length to the ground in a fainting fit.

When he recovered his jailer was standing over him, come (as he thought) to bring him food, but he was soon disabused of any such notion by the man himself. He, who had refused on all prior occasions to hold converse with his prisoner, now spoke voluntarily to tell him the sands of his captivity had run out. At first the dazed cage bird (who had forgotten for the moment his compact) believed that he was on the point of expiating his crimes, real and imaginary, upon the scaffold. But the jailer, not without difficulty, made it clear to him that all captives received pardon on the joyous occasion of the marriage of their Princess, which was fixed for that day. Then Porphyro remembered all, and swooned again.

When he revived, our hero was sitting in the open air upon the steps which led from the jail. He caught the smell of oxen roasting whole in the market-place. The sky was red with the fires. The streets as far as he could see them, were paved with flowers and decorated with triumphal arches. The citizens were bustling about in holiday attire. Music seemed to be playing everywhere. Occasionally some exuberant person fired off a gun. Porphyro rubbed his eyes and wondered whether this could really be his wedding day. He had faith in the boundless powers of the banner under which he had enrolled himself. And yet was it possible? But his faith was amply justified. An equerry suddenly rode up, parting the spectators to right and left, leading a spare horse magnificently caparisoned, and followed in the distance by a brilliant retinue. He doffed his cap to Porphyro and sprang to the ground, and with a profound obeisance, said in tones of deep respect:—

"I trust your Highness has recovered from your indisposition. I have brought the horse as your Highness commanded."

Porphyro dimly understood that some potent influence was at work on his behalf. With the assistance of his squire he took to the saddle. The latter then, with another bow, remounted his own horse, scattered a handful of gold to each side to break up the crowd, and with the rest of the train (which had caught up with them) they galloped to the Cathedral. Porphyro noted with stupid surprise that all the fountains spouted wine, whereto certain of the citizens, judging by the hiccups which mingled with their cheers, had already applied themselves, not wisely but too well. But our hero was in a state of so great fog himself as to feel his heart warm more towards these than to the soberer ones, whose salutations he clumsily returned. By the time the Cathedral was reached, he was rolling in his saddle. He could not have dismounted without help. The incense made him dizzy. He could not get the ringing of the bells out of his ears. The candles danced before his eyes; of all the service he heard one word, and that was uttered by one who stood beside him, and whom alone he saw (and that through a mist) of all that gay assembly. It was the Princess. He pressed her hand as if he would never part with it.

The service over, he had no idea how, or in what order they reached the castle, and the banquet which followed was more or less of a blank to him. The wines of which he partook liberally, could make him no more drunk, nor all the compliments of all the fulsome speeches (had he heard them) raise by one degree his pride. He soared empyrean high in the thought that he had won the right to crush into one cup, one moment, all the eternal delirium of all the heavens.

That moment of fruition had come at last. Porphyro stood in that holy of holies, his princess's chamber. A guard of soldiers was ranged along the lour walls of this dainty nest. Each leaned with one arm upon a pike, while with the other hand he held aloft a blazing torch. Great personages were also present, both courtiers and noble dames, and at last the bride herself was brought in by her women. While complimentary discourse passed from mouth to mouth, Porphyro longed with his whole bartered soul to be alone with her. He was burning with internal fire which he could hold in little longer. At last he approached one that appeared to act as master of the ceremonies.

"When is this rigmarole going to end?" he muttered between his teeth.

"Whenever your Highness pleases to draw your sword and lay it in the middle of the bed, the princess will take up her place upon one side of it, while you occupy the other," was the reply.

Porphyro started. He surely recognised that voice. The official kept his face averted, but it was undoubtedly the demon.

"What mean you by this gabble of naked swords between me and her?" thundered Porphyro, unheeding who might hear. "Damned posture master, is she not my wife?"

"Your wife, yes, but only by letters of procuration," and there was a note of triumph in that voice.

"God of the Judgment! What is that you say?"

"I say you must be dreaming not to remember that you are only temporarily united to the princess in your character of proxy for his Imperial Majesty, the Holy Roman Emperor."

"Alas the while! Then I am dreaming, indeed!"

"These soldiers," continued the demon, "will remain here all night. These ladies and gentlemen will also attend here till morning, to entertain you and your bride of an hour through your somewhat tedious spell of lying fully dressed together."

"Death and the Pit! Is this true?"

"True as death, assured as the pit. To-morrow you will sheathe your sword, and depart from her for ever."

Porphyro pressed his hands to his temples. He thought his brain would burst. He saw it all now. He was the dupe of the fiend who had once been his dupe. His place in this pageant had been contrived with infernal subtlety, only to wring the uttermost pang from his heart strings. He who sups with the devil (they say) must needs have a very long spoon. No help was possible. The Evil One was reaping his revenge. And now he was assured his victim had at last grasped the situation, he threw off the mask, and showed himself in his true colours. He raised his eyes for the first time from the ground, those brimming lakes of bottomless hate which Porphyro had fronted once before in the underground hall. It was his turn now to quail.

"Ha! ha!" laughed the fallen angel. "By mine ancient seat in heaven (and that is an oath I never lightly take as you may guess), confess, have I not bested you, friend Porphyro? He laughs best who laughs the last; is it not so?"

"But what about that bond registered between us in Hell's chancery?" cried Porphyro, in a voice which would have melted triple brass.

"Your bond," shrieked Beelzebub. "Do you remind me of your bond; you who once outfaced me that a bond should be read by the letter, and not by the spirit? I have come round to your views, and I now fling that word back in your teeth. You have had your bond to the letter, and now go and kill yourself, for there is nothing more for you to do."

Porphyro bent like a broken reed. He had found his over-mastering fate. His hopes were ash. He breathed in gasps. He staggered to the window, and threw open the casement. A great pitiful star looked in, but to his eyes it appeared red and bloodshot. He turned round again to the room. He wished to see once more before he died that mistress of his soul for whose sake he had flung it away. But the figure of his master had swelled, and was swelling so rapidly in size that it seemed to fill every available corner of the room. Porphyro raised his hands to heaven, and called upon his lady's name. Three times he called it, and then sprang out of the window. The princess, who had grasped nothing of what had passed, ran to the shutter, and looked out just in time to hear the splash of his body as it fell into the moat. It was the first sign of interest in him which she had shown.

COACHWHIP PUBLICATIONS

COACHWHIPBOOKS.COM

COACHWHIP PUBLICATIONS

ALSO AVAILABLE

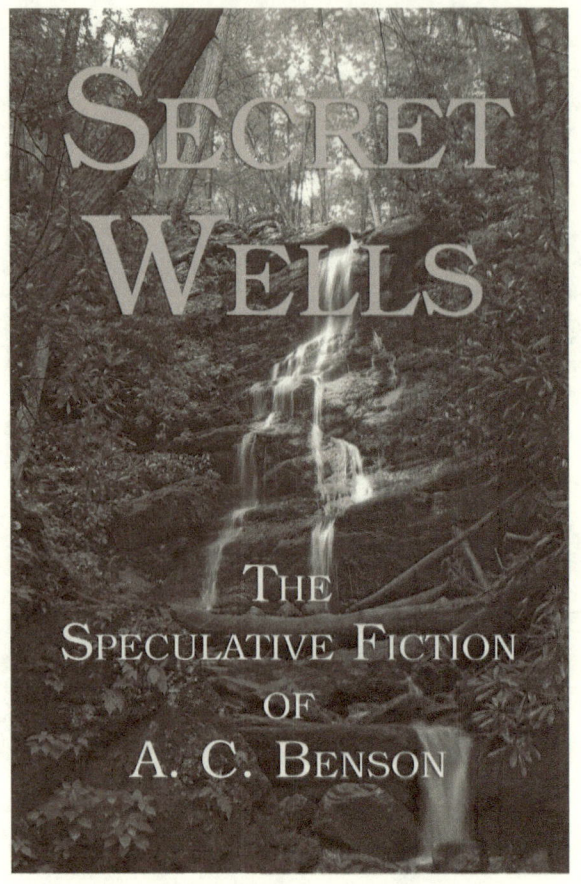

Secret Wells: The Speculative
Fiction of A. C. Benson
ISBN 1-61646-058-X

COACHWHIP PUBLICATIONS

ALSO AVAILABLE

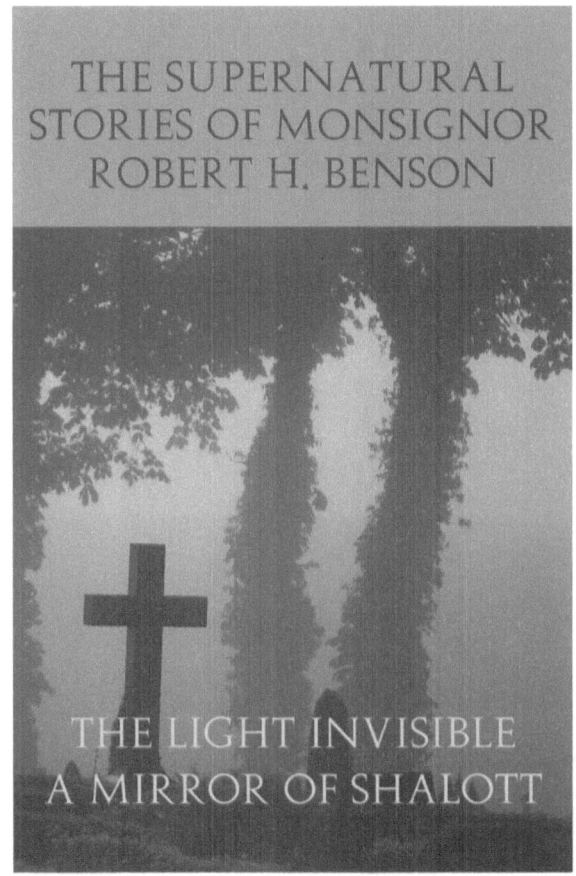

*The Supernatural Stories of
Monsignor Robert H. Benson*
ISBN 1-61646-004-0

Coachwhip Publications

Also Available

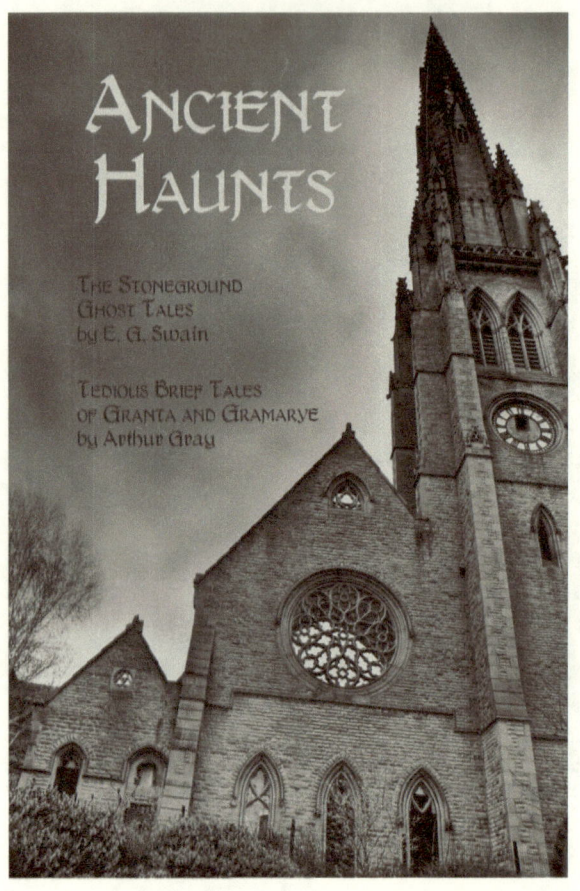

Ancient Haunts
ISBN 1-61646-005-9

COACHWHIP PUBLICATIONS

ALSO AVAILABLE

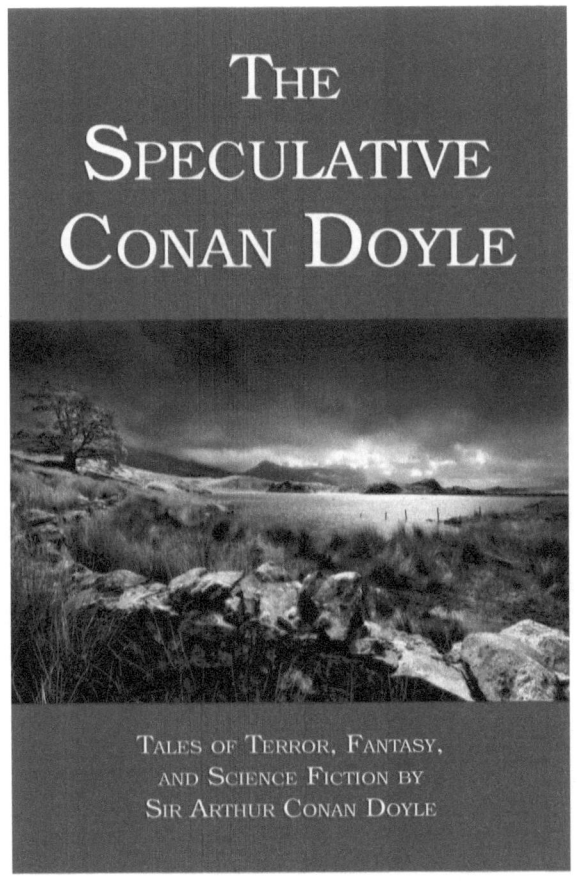

THE SPECULATIVE CONAN DOYLE

TALES OF TERROR, FANTASY, AND SCIENCE FICTION BY SIR ARTHUR CONAN DOYLE

The Speculative Conan Doyle
ISBN 1-61646-024-5

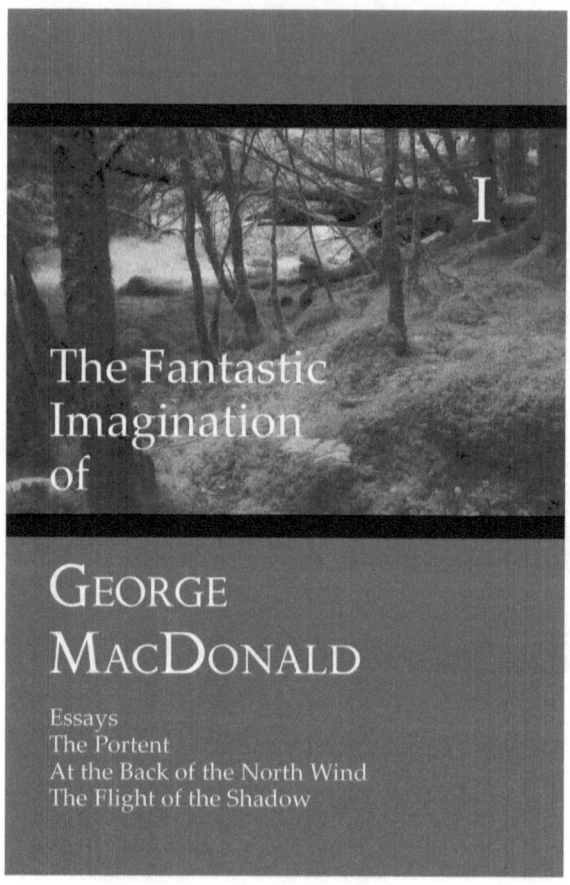

The Fantastic Imagination of George MacDonald

Essays
The Portent
At the Back of the North Wind
The Flight of the Shadow

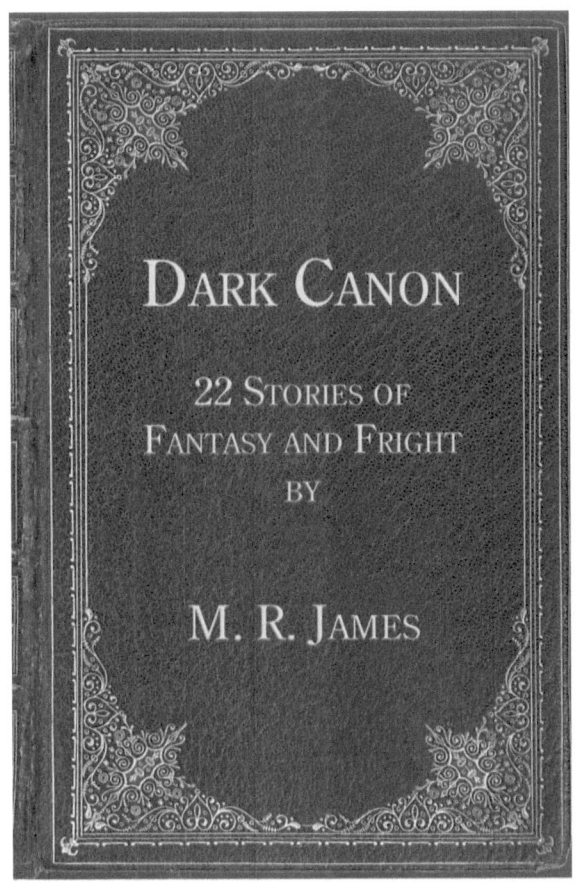

Dark Canon

ISBN 1-61646-020-2

www.ingramcontent.com/pod-product-compliance
Lightning Source LLC
Chambersburg PA
CBHW031416250626
47155CB00004B/1514